More praise f
The Monster and the

"*The Monster and the Mirror* utterly captivated me. With illuminating research, keen insight, and profound empathy, K.J. Aiello reminds us that people with mental health issues need and deserve to tell their own stories. Raw, heartfelt, blistering, and wise, *The Monster and the Mirror* is a stellar achievement."

— KATHY FRIEDMAN, author of *All the Shining People*

"Dear residents of the liminal and lonely space between reality and imagination: *The Monster and the Mirror* is a book that sees you, speaks to you, and reminds you that there is a rich, enchanted world around us, even if not everyone can see what we see. Cutting through the isolation and stigma of mental illness, Aiello shines light onto the landscape between story, psyche, reality, and imagination. This light is crucial for those of us who live with mental illness. What a gift."

— CARRIE MAC, author of *Last Winter*

"In *The Monster and the Mirror*, K.J. Aiello shows us that fantasy is a place of empowerment and enrichment and a place to find healing through agency and empathy. It's a profound, raw, and intimate story that explains what it's like to have mental illnesses while also offering vitally important reflections for those who live with them. Intricately researched, thoughtfully structured, generously and fearlessly told, this book is one I will cherish for a very long time."

— DAVID A. ROBERTSON, author of *Black Water*

"Equal parts journalist and memoirist, K.J. Aiello brings their deft skills to the page, creating a work that made me cry, rage, and ache, but also, at times, smile and even chuckle at the wry observations and pointed commentary. The author is both at the heart of this story and outside it, asking questions about not just their own life but of the culture in which she exists, and how it shapes all of us. *The Monster and the Mirror* took my breath away."

— CHRISTINA MYERS, author of *Halfway Home*

"The explorations and examinations of mental health woven through K.J. Aiello's *The Monster and the Mirror* are at once all too real and deeply affirming. The book — moving deftly between fantasy fiction, video games, and personal, honest recollections — asks us to identify the true villain among us: mental illness, or society's unwillingness to accept it as reality for so many. This is a gutting, beautiful, and insightful book."

— AGA WILMOT, author of *Withered* and *The Death Scene Artist*

THE
MONSTER
AND THE
MIRROR

MENTAL ILLNESS, MAGIC, AND
THE STORIES WE TELL

K. J. AIELLO

ECW

Published by ECW Press
665 Gerrard Street East
Toronto, Ontario, Canada M4M 1Y2
416-694-3348 / info@ecwpress.com

Editor for the Press: Jen Sookfong Lee
Copy editor: Rachel Ironstone
Cover design: Lisa Marie Pompilio
Author photo: Darius Bashar

LIBRARY AND ARCHIVES CANADA CATALOGUING
IN PUBLICATION

Title: The monster and the mirror : mental illness, magic, and the stories we tell / K.J. Aiello.

Names: Aiello, K. J., author.

Identifiers: Canadiana (print) 20240354680 | Canadiana (ebook) 20240354710

ISBN 978-1-77041-708-3 (softcover)
ISBN 978-1-77852-269-7 (PDF)
ISBN 978-1-77852-266-6 (ePub)

Subjects: LCSH: Aiello, K. J.—Mental health. | LCSH: Mentally ill—Canada—Biography. | LCSH: Mental illness—Social aspects. | LCSH: Literature and mental illness. | LCGFT: Autobiographies.

Classification: LCC RC464.A34 A3 2024 | DDC 616.890092—dc23

This book is funded in part by the Government of Canada. *Ce livre est financé en partie par le gouvernement du Canada.* We acknowledge the support of the Canada Council for the Arts. *Nous remercions le Conseil des arts du Canada de son soutien.* We acknowledge the funding support of the Ontario Arts Council (OAC), an agency of the Government of Ontario. We also acknowledge the support of the Government of Ontario through the Ontario Book Publishing Tax Credit, and through Ontario Creates.

ONTARIO ARTS COUNCIL
CONSEIL DES ARTS DE L'ONTARIO
an Ontario government agency
un organisme du gouvernement de l'Ontario

Canada Council   Conseil des arts
for the Arts   du Canada

Canada

PRINTED AND BOUND IN CANADA   PRINTING: MARQUIS   5 4 3 2 1

Get the ebook free!*
*proof of purchase required

Purchase the print edition and receive the ebook free.
For details, go to ecwpress.com/ebook.

For Uli . . . always.

For the Writerly Shenanigans . . . obviously.

And for all those who've walked these empty halls with me.

(And also for my cats.)

Contents

INTRODUCTION

T here is no one place where this book started—no single idea, no pinpoint of entry. No ah-ha moment.

In the summer of 2018, in a creative writing workshop hosted by a lovely little business here in Toronto, Firefly Creative Writing, the workshop facilitator asked us what we want to give permission to in our writing practice. My first thought was a single idea that flickered in my mind and that took me completely by surprise. In my notebook, I wrote: *to be okay being a child again.*

What I really meant by that was giving myself permission to return to magic. To love dragons and stories again, the things that had always given me comfort and, to a large extent, had saved me and helped me become who I am now. For many years leading up to that moment, I'd pushed away a big part of who I was—perhaps the most beautiful part, I've now come to believe—and that was my relentless pursuit of possibilities. As I started writing about that childlike permission, it led me to the words *what if*—which come together to form a question of possibility and permission combined, a question that I had held onto for so long during my toughest years. What if there are beautiful things in this world that can help me feel freer, more myself, give me hope and warmth? I could search it out. I could search out anything actually, even, perhaps, something magical.

"What if?" was a question I'd left behind a long time ago. It had been a dangerous question for me because it accompanied crushing rejection and, in all honesty, deep harm. Whenever I believed in possibilities, in possibilities for myself in particular, there was always something to dampen the magic that came with that question. Because "what if" pointed to the possibility of a better future, one that I believed wholeheartedly wasn't for me. My brain, my mental illness, and trauma had always proved that to be true. Every time I latched onto "what if," I inevitably convinced myself that magic, in any form, didn't exist, and somehow I was always left with a little less possibility . . . and subsequently a little less *me*.

Until, eventually, I lost that belief. I became empty.

Around the time I returned to that question in the writing workshop, I started to look critically at how fantasy in literature, films, and TV portrayed marginalization—mental illness particularly. I started to wonder why mentally ill characters were either alluded to but mostly invisible or slotted easily into the role of villain. In some narratives, mental illness itself was the villain as well as the punishment.

I thought back to my favourite childhood stories, and those that I'd also fallen in love with as an adult, and I began analyzing, wondering what they had helped me believe. Was it that someone like me, someone mentally ill, would always be cast as a villain? Or was it that someone like me could be the hero, not despite or because of my mental illness, but simply as I am?

What if the little kid I once was could be included in the magic, in the possibility?

What if these stories were rewritten?

What if these stories could include mental illness not as a punishment but rather as a simple reality because so many of us *are* mentally ill? Where would our place be in my favourite stories, the ones filled with magic and wizards, elves and dragons? Are we forever fated to be the mad scientist, the tyrant bent on maniacal domination? The murderous warlock who fractures himself into seven objects? The silver-haired Targaryen girl whose fate results in the slaughter of an entire city with only her vengeance and dragon as her weapons? Or something even worse.

Where were the stories that I needed as a kid, lost and afraid?

When I embarked on the journey of writing this book, I didn't think it would include so much *me*. I thought maybe it would be a collection of essays that leaned more towards an *academic* critique of literature and otherness. When I finished the first few drafts, before I sent the manuscript off to my editor, it was very much that. But with a few conversations with my editor, my partner, and some writer friends, I learned that there is power in the analytical, sure, but far more power in human experience—*in my own experience*. After all, haven't these stories predominantly been written *about* us but not *by* us? As it turns out, using my own story as a medium through which other fantastical stories can be told might be my magical superpower. Once I leaned into my own narrative, I learned just how much power I could wield, for myself, for others, and for the little kid I used to be who desperately needed to be her own hero.

Some of the themes and events I explore in this book were quite difficult to write, and there were a few occasions where I didn't think I could get through it. I suppose to some extent, this is par for the course. Like most memoirs, this is not a complete life retelling but moments in a life that feel most relevant to what I'm trying to say. Where I was able, I received permission from the individuals found herein, but in some cases, as I'm sure you'll understand, that wasn't possible. Having said that, in all cases except for that of my partner, I have left out identifying features in the memoir sections. I in no way wish to harm anyone. But life, as I know too well, always has a way of surfacing folks who are, themselves, harmful.

Given the subject matter of this book, some sections may be difficult for some readers. There are references to trauma, institutionalization, assault, abortion, and abuse. Take a breath. Read slowly. Be kind to yourself. These are lessons I've also learned along the way.

Throughout the memoir sections of this book, and as I take you through the most intimate parts of my life, there are some references using ableist language. This is intentional. Ableism is deeply embedded in our culture and how we, as disabled and mentally ill folks, are expected to view ourselves. Additionally, there are some references that are anti–sex work and some remarks made by other people which are painful. Including these is also intentional because women and nonbinary and trans folks have often been taught to feel shame about their bodies, sexuality, and sex.

As I worked through this book, in its many iterations, my own sense of self shifted. I began to look from an observer's perspective at a life that had been led (thus far) and started pulling the threads together so that the trajectory became clearer. I began to understand this person I was writing about, from the little kid she used to be, to the adult they became. And in many ways, I realized that I judged her too harshly. I treated her abusively, and I loathed her. She didn't deserve that. No one deserves that. We deserve to be free.

We deserve to set ourselves free.

I have forgiven her for the harm she caused herself. Please hold all this tenderly as you walk through the darkest parts of my life with me.

(I promise there will be dragons.)

"Whatever pain you can't get rid of,
turn that around and make it your offering."

—SUSAN CAIN

CHAPTER 1

The Monster and the Mirror

I'm a little girl. I'm standing, pressed against the cold chain-link fence of my public school. The children surround me, making a perfect half-moon. I'm looking at my scuffed white sneakers, my faded purple jogging pants. My jacket has a turquoise stripe. The children are laughing. I don't understand why. The sky is slate, the cold rushes up my nose and makes my ears ache. There is a little boy standing in the centre of the half-moon. He has floppy auburn hair and a cherubic face. Even as he laughs, his features sink into me and make me feel things I can't understand. My first crush, but I don't know that yet.

I burrow my chin deep into the collar of my jacket, pull up my shoulders. I look down, away from his dark brown eyes, his perfect and taunting smile. I am ashamed. I look at my shoes and imagine wings bursting from my back—great wings with glimmering feathers—and flying away. My fingers tingle, and I can no longer hear the children's voices. I can no longer feel their laughter. The sounds echo through the long, dark tunnel of my mind, but they don't reach me. I am far away now, flying on my great glimmering wings. I have split: my self and my psyche disjointed. I have dissociated.

Bolstered by the confidence of our classmates, the little boy finds that hyper-masculine bravado that scaffolds the actions of so many young men: he pulls down his pants and shakes his private parts at me. He laughs, thrusting his scrawny hips forward, and the children's voices crescendo.

I crash into myself, my wings broken. He has, like many boys before him and others who will continue after him, begun the insidious climb of power where his masculinity is a weapon to taunt and humiliate.

Something in my mind cracks. My chest burns, my hands numb. I feel a deep shadow inside me, and a coil curled up in my belly springs upwards, and rage erupts. I close the space between us, rip off his jacket, tear down his T-shirt, and score my nails down his chest. I can feel the texture as his skin shreds. His screams are muted. He turns and tries to pull out of my grasp, but I throw him to the ground and tear at him more. He twists as my nails claw down his back. Blood smears his skin, smears my hands.

In high school, years later, he will show me the scars and tell me how fucking crazy I am. I'll shrug and say he deserved it.

The memory cuts, and I'm standing outside the principal's office. I hear voices, hushed just enough to make it seem like they're keeping their conversation away from me. My behaviour is a concern for them. The level of violence that came out of me was an inappropriate reaction. Boys get away with a lot, for just being boys. But little girls aren't violent. Little girls don't butcher little boys.

My head throbs. I have been crying for so long that my lips hurt, my throat aches. I feel something shadowy slipping over me, wrapping a misty arm around me and smiling at my anger, my shame. The boy has been taken to the hospital. His parents want me expelled. My teacher wants me expelled. I hear the words *animal* and *monster*, and I know they're referring to me.

I close my eyes and recall the night I saw fireflies for the first time. It had been the in-between, twilight time, where all colours fade to muted grey and pale lavender. The tiny lights started from the ground, winking gently, and rose into the trees.

"Look, ducky," my mother had said. "Fairies."

I cry harder, gagging on my shame.

I hear my mother's voice rising, furious: "If you corner a puppy and kick it, what do you expect that puppy to do?"

She is quiet on the drive home. As we wind through the valley, I stare out the window watching the bare trees slide by in a blur of unforgiving steel broken only by the red clay hills. I have stopped crying, my hands are numb blocks in my lap, my chest has caved in. I want to no longer exist, so I make myself as small as possible by curling my shoulders inward, rounding my spine. I'm just a freak, just a monster. I don't know why I lashed out. I couldn't see right. I couldn't think right. I hear a whisper in my mind telling me that it's okay, that we don't need anyone. The smokey shadow clouds my vision, and anger feels just so good. The world has been thrown off its axis.

"Talk to me," my mother says. The grey trees continue, obscuring the cliffs in the distance. "Please, say something."

I remain silent.

"How can I help you if I don't know what's going on?"

I am a monster. This new something inside me is evil and corrupt. It's shadowy, and I can't quite see it. But I feel it there, curling around me, pressing against my mind. And I know that I'm different and shameful and all wrong.

I remain silent because that's the only way I can stop myself from screaming.

For a long time, I questioned the level of rage that came out of me. Not just that incident, but many more after that. When I felt threatened, something in me would break and all reason would evaporate. I've played those memories in my mind many times over the years—why?

Why was my reaction a violent one? What was this Shadow, this monster, that lived in the periphery of my life for decades until, one day, it simply took control?

I often thought that rage was just a part of me, embedded in me from the moment I was born. That deep down, I was a violent monster who needed just one trigger to release the caged evil—the Mr. Hyde to my Dr. Jekyll. I was ashamed of it, ashamed of myself and all the parts that made up the whole of me. But as I grew older and into my adult years, the question still lived, pressing just behind my lips: Why am I a monster?

Until a thought slowly slid into my consciousness, whispering at the edges—

Maybe, just maybe, something else was happening, and I was never a monster at all.

I. IN WHICH A MONSTER IS BORN

I found it easiest to understand my own mental illness as monstrous. I could only comprehend what was wrong with me in terms of good and bad, normal and abnormal. It isn't surprising, then, that I became fascinated by monsters. I'd told my therapist once that I felt like I was hiding a gremlin inside me; if anyone knew who I truly was, I'd be an outcast. But every now and then, whether I liked it or not, that gremlin came out. It ran wild under my skin, used my mouth to hurl words, and I had no energy to stop it.

The aftermath always took something from me—small slices from my skin, leaving me a little less *me* and a little more *monster*.

With years of distance, I now know that my outbursts were a response to not being allowed to explore my own seemingly monstrous emotions that I'm pretty sure were more volatile than what would be considered healthy. But for years, before I finally received an accurate diagnosis, the only way I felt real, felt *seen*, was through the narrative of monsters. Theirs were the stories that I simply understood, deep in my bones.

In grade eleven English class, we were assigned a variety of classic novels to write reports on. Out of all the choices, only one had a monster. So, naturally, that's the one I chose, although at the time I didn't know why.

Mary Shelley's *Frankenstein* might be one of the most famous Western stories about a monster. It's a story that also happens to be close to the truth.

Shelley's monster is created out of drive, ambition, and curiosity by Dr. Victor Frankenstein, a talented chemist and quite possibly the genesis of the mad scientist trope. Dr. Frankenstein wants to create life but is unable to do so himself (the irony that a woman wrote the novel isn't lost on me or generations of literary critics). So he sets about cobbling together body parts of deceased criminals to construct a living, breathing man. But when the monster opens his eyes, Dr. Frankenstein is horrified. What he has created is a twisted, gruesome being.

Anyone who's read Shelley's *Frankenstein*, if raised in Western and Euro-centric regions, most likely read it in school as I did and probably understands that it's not Dr. Frankenstein's creation that is the monster but Victor Frankenstein himself. Additionally, what is important to consider is whether, if Frankenstein's monster hadn't been so poorly treated, he would have been a monster at all. Is the idea of monster and monstrousness simply perspective? He wasn't created to be a monster specifically, but this monstrousness was forced on him, a label upon which perceptions of him are constructed. Frankenstein's monster is the epitome of speaking something into existence—*abracadabra, I create as I speak*.[1] Or, he is called monster as he exists.

---

1   Julian Sinclair, "Abracadabra," *The Jewish Chronicle*, July 5, 2018, www.thejc.com/judaism /jewish-words/abracadabra-1.466709.

Shelley writes the revenant as intelligent and articulate. He shows capacity for empathy, love, and kindness. When the creature is sent away by Dr. Frankenstein, he takes shelter near a cottage where a family lives. While he's there, he watches the family, learns to speak from listening to them, and even teaches himself to read from a satchel of books he finds. Eventually, he grows fond of the family and decides to approach them. It doesn't go well: the father, who is blind, is accepting of Frankenstein's creation, but the rest of the family are horrified by the sight of him and drive him off. "Who can describe the horror and consternation on beholding me?"[2] He is now angry (who wouldn't be?) and he gives up hope that he will ever be seen as anything but a monster. That's when he really takes on the monstrous identity and, soon after, brutally murders Victor's brother William. He also curses all of humanity, eventually vowing revenge against his maker. "Cursed, cursed creator! Why did I live? Why, in that instant, did I not extinguish the spark of existence which you had so wantonly bestowed?"[3]

However, the question remains: If he had never been rejected by the family he longed to be part of, and if he had never been labelled a monster, would he have become one?

In stories, and in real life, monsters don't always start as monsters. Criminals don't start their lives committing crimes. Everyone is a child at one point, innocent and incredibly malleable. In the course of their lives however, some who don't conform to traditional values or gendered expectations—what is perceived to be "good" and "respectable" or in some cases able-bodied and able-minded—can be considered monsters for that non-conformation. And then, after they have defied conventions enough times, like Frankenstein's monster,

---

2   Mary Wollstonecraft Shelley, *Frankenstein; or, The Modern Prometheus* (Durham, NC: Duke Classics, 1818), 126–127, e-book obtained from Libby through Toronto Public Library.

3   *Ibid.*

they are cast out. There, in the margins, is when they are forced to truly become monsters, nursing their spite and rage in isolation, roiling with emotions that are never spoken aloud.

An interesting and illuminating lens through which to view this kind of development is attachment theory, which is a theory in developmental psychology that was articulated by British psychoanalyst John Bowlby in the mid-twentieth century. It's held up pretty well over the decades as it proposes that behaviours in both childhood and adulthood are affected by the style of attachment a child had with their earliest caregivers. Ultimately, through observations of infants, Bowlby found that children who did not have secure attachment to any caregiver at all were likely to struggle with emotional regulation, self-conceptualization, and anger.[4]

Frankenstein's monster—with disrupted and absent attachments—became who he was forced to be and who people believed him to be, and, in the end, only *he* carried the blame.

If you corner a puppy and kick it, that puppy will become a monster. How can you then blame the monster for not being a puppy?

Which, of course, makes me wonder—was my own imaginary monster created, or was I born like this? I don't really remember a time when I didn't feel like I was abnormal, even now. But if I was born with these monstrous tendencies—rage particularly—what hope could I have had to live a life where my anger didn't destroy many people's perceptions of me? That's tough to swallow. Maybe if my teacher had been able to see through the rage and outbursts to the scared, confused, and angry little kid underneath, I wouldn't have been seen—or labelled—a bad person. And then maybe I wouldn't have believed myself a monster in the first place.

---

4   R. Chris Fraley, "Adult Attachment Theory and Research: A Brief Overview," Department of Psychology, University of Illinois at Urbana-Champagne, 2018, http://labs.psychology .illinois.edu/~rcfraley/attachment.htm.

Here's something that's even harder to swallow: if my mental illness and years of feeling like a monster are because of my early life experiences, including all those meetings and discussions where my behaviour was *treated* as monstrous, then that means the *real* me was never a monster at all. Instead, the real me became what everyone else was telling me I was when, really, I was just a little kid who never got the help she needed. And knowing that makes me both angry and sad because, even after all these years, I sometimes revert to those old beliefs and still feel like a monster.

(Despite this feeling, I'm pretty sure not many people think I'm a monster—or even a shitty person—now. And if they do, that's their opinion.)

Frankenstein's monster grieves for himself in his loneliness, for the loss of possible love and companionship, and for the certain impossibility of leading a normal life. Maybe he even grieves for a childhood he never had, for the friends he never made, for the lost possibility of enjoying long summer afternoons by a river. Frankenstein's monster never experienced any of these things, and he isn't given the space to grieve what was never his in the first place. His grief is never acknowledged, and he is simply cast away, assumed to be a monster and nothing more.

I feel this a lot. This same grief will probably sit with me for the rest of my life. It's a grief for what never was, for a stability that I didn't have in my childhood, youth, and well into my adult years. It's grieving what was lost while I was living with undiagnosed mental illness and treating myself abusively. I grieve for the possibilities that will never come to be: the sense of life accomplishment, of being able to look back on my youth with fondness, and not living with the shame of my past. I always feel like I'm trailing behind, a latecomer to adulthood, because I never experienced much of a childhood. But back when I was a little kid, before I could even acknowledge and comprehend what I was feeling, the only emotion I knew how to express was anger. And, over the years, that anger became my weapon. It became my monster. And everyone, including me, thought this monster and I were one and the same.

I am lying on my mother's bed. She is beside me. I turn my head and watch as her belly rises and falls with her breaths. Her dark curly hair is spread on the pillow, her hand perched on her wide hip as she lies on her side. She is looking at me. She has a mother's smile: soft and rosy. But that will change. Her pink lips are thin, her mouth small with one front tooth crossing over the other. It makes her upper lip look puffier than it really is. When she smiles, her brown eyes are warm, her cheeks turn the colour of blush roses. I love her smile. I hold on to it. I don't know when it will fall again.

There is a book resting between us. It has a black cover with gold and silver inlay. Its pages are onion paper, and I love the sound they make as she turns them. This book is a precious item, one of the most expensive in our tiny house. There is no title on the cover, just an image of a door bordered with dwarfish runes, something called the Evenstar in the centre. The spine says *The Lord of the Rings*, and I don't know who J.R.R. Tolkien is, but my mother seems to know him really well.

She is reading to me. This place is comforting, it's safe, even though I know in my small as-yet uncomplicated mind that she needs this more than I do.

The story is about small people called hobbits, a ring, and a wizard. The language is hard for me to understand, but her voice is soft, and she is so happy. I want to hold on to this. Maybe she will make a latticework of her fingers and keep us here forever. The outside world is scary—scarier than orcs or a black tower capped by an eye wreathed in flames. The monsters outside my house, the ones in the schoolyard, they look just like those who aren't monsters.

Those monsters have regular faces and they smile like I want to, but if I look closely, their smiles always make my skin cold. My mother tells me that they will be mean to me, and when they are, I know she's right.

"But you, my ducky, are a special little girl. That's why they try to hurt you."

"Be careful. The world is a cruel place."

"There is no one to protect you but me."

II. SET THE MONSTER FREE

I'm not sure I'll ever stop grieving when I think about that cocoon my mother and I created together. She told me stories about magic, but she also told me stories about evil men who leer at little girls. She told me stories about how her father once held her mother's head under water in the kitchen sink, and how her mother twisted away and gathered her up, and together they escaped. She told me about the darkness in the corners of her bedroom and a cousin or uncle, I don't recall, who rubbed his parts on her. I can't really remember friends coming to the house in those early years. I wonder if she feels bad about that, my not having friends. Perhaps she, too, was lonely. She had me, though. I was her friend. I didn't mind.

Grief doesn't necessarily mean someone has died. It can exist in the absence of anything tangible. Perhaps a longing for what was, or what could have been. Or holding that grief for a loved one when they are unable to grieve on their own.

It can, if left unattended, become something else. It can grow its own skin, create lungs and fingers, a heart with a beat that keeps rhythm with the ache in one's own chest. Grief can come alive and carry its own agency. And sometimes, just sometimes, that grief becomes a monster.

Patrick Ness's 2011 middle-grade fantasy novel, *A Monster Calls,* is about a thirteen-year-old boy, Conor O'Malley, his mother, grandmother, and a yew tree that Conor at first believes to be a monster. It's also one of my favourite stories about grief.

When the yew tree first visits Conor, the boy is afraid. The yew tree's "voice had a quality to it, a *monstrous* quality, wild and untamed."[5] It's not long before Conor becomes belligerent and demanding, angry at the yew tree's invasion of his world, both physically and in the psychological space he's holding for his feelings about his mother's terminal cancer. The yew tree tells Conor that when the yew tree comes back, he will tell the boy three stories. The yew tree then says that upon the fourth visit, it will be Conor who will tell the story—one of truth. "The truth?" Conor asks the yew tree. "Not just any truth," the monster replies. "*Your* truth."[6]

As Conor's mother's health continues to deteriorate, the yew tree returns to tell Conor his stories. As each unfolds, Conor becomes angrier. The stories don't make sense to him. They are contradictory, illustrating parallel truths that are difficult for a child to understand. When the yew tree tells Conor that good people can do bad things, and that bad things can happen to good people, he calls the yew tree a cheat. "Many things that are true feel like a cheat," the yew tree tells him.[7] What might seem, in a child's mind, clear and binary, isn't actually so. And grieving for a mother who isn't yet gone also confuses Conor. For him, grief only exists through death, and because he is feeling emotions of not just grief but also confusion and resentment, Conor becomes even angrier at the miasma inside him. He avoids talking to his mother because he is angry with her for being sick and he

5   Patrick Ness, *A Monster Calls* (Somerville, MA: Candlewick Press, 2013), 15.

6   Ness, *A Monster Calls,* 38.

7   Ness, *A Monster Calls,* 70.

knows that, sooner rather than later, she will leave him. These feelings erupt, and the yew tree invites Conor to become destructive. To smash and rage and ruin things.

Conor does. It's this moment that feels vulnerable to me, and it's one that also hits home because of the sense of fluidity to Conor's emotions and how they overwhelm him. Neither good nor bad, they simply are. But they are also consuming him, and, it appears, the yew tree is pushing the boy to destruction, to give in to these emotions, no matter how much he tries to bury them. Conor, believing that he is safe in this fictional world that the yew tree creates, thinks he is smashing a house in one of the yew tree's stories, but he is actually breaking everything in his grandmother's very real living room, motivated by his very real emotions.

In that moment, I think about Conor as the child I used to be, angry and confused and already grieving what I never had in the first place. I want to create a safe space for both kids—the real me and the fictional Conor—to rage. A space that could witness their emotions and reassure them that they're okay. I wish I could go back to my child self and tell her that every torn-up story, broken picture, clenched fist in class, I-hate-you, and seething, silent moment was *okay*.

The yew tree does this with Conor, allowing him to give in to his anger, saying to him that destruction is very satisfying. In the absence of adult words and coping skills that could help someone understand the complexities of thoughts and feelings, unchecked destruction can often feel like the only release.

I don't think my own mother understood these nuances, but Conor's mother does, which is probably another reason why I love this novel—it helps me visualize the possibilities of what it would be like to be mothered by someone else. Conor's mother lost her own father when she was a child and knows the grief Conor is experiencing. This shared experience and earned sensitivity allows her to see the yew tree and recognize the monster for what it truly is: a guardian of emotions, a protector during what is possibly the hardest time of Conor's life.

In the hospital, as Conor sits in furious silence beside his mom, unable to express how angry he is with her for being sick, she tells him:

> "You be as angry as you need to be. And if you need to break things, then by God, you break them good and hard." . . . "And if, one day," she said, really crying now, "you look back and you feel bad for being so angry, if you feel bad for being *so* angry at me that you couldn't even speak to me, then you have to know, Conor, you have to know that it was *okay*. That I *knew*."[8]

A few years ago, there was a video that made the rounds online of a dad and his toddler.[9] The video is sped up, parts edited for brevity, but it's just a video of a little girl having a complete meltdown. Her emotions are so unfiltered and overwhelming, her sobbing is a full-bodied effort. Her little limbs are flailing, and she is inconsolable.

In the video, her dad is sitting on the floor with her, saying nothing. He sits with his legs and arms creating a circle, a physical and psychological safe space for her while she has her meltdown. Occasionally, he will block her when a rogue limb darts out to smash the wall (or him when that rogue limb threatens to knock him in the face).

After a few hours (in video-time it's only a few minutes), the little girl's emotions are spent, and she's completely worn out (as I'm sure her dad is as well). She crawls towards him and wraps her arms and legs around him. When he realizes this is what she needs now, he folds

---

8   Ness, *A Monster Calls*, 187.

9   Heather Friend, "Dad Holding Space for His Daughter's Big Feelings," YouTube, November 24, 2021, https://www.youtube.com/watch?v=fbuvaOsqP-4.

his arms around her, draws his legs inward so she can curl up in the circle made of his body, and they sit there. He rocks her. Occasionally, she will shudder with a little sob. Then the video cuts. And of course, every time I watch it, I cry.

That's it. The little girl—who is also Conor as well as the kid I used to be—needs to set the monster free. It's not hard to imagine that she is struggling with her own monstrosity, not understanding why she's feeling these overwhelming emotions when the only way she can articulate them is through having a meltdown. But there is no slaying the monster here because there is no monster. What she is learning is that these emotions—*monstrous* emotions—aren't bad or fearsome. They simply . . . are.

III. THE MONSTER IS TRUTH

There is a fourth and final story in *A Monster Calls*. Of course, it's the most important story because it's the one that Conor must tell. It's the story of truth, and it's one of the hardest truths that Conor—or any-one—will have to face. "'You will tell me a fourth [story],' the monster repeated, 'and it will be the truth . . . not just any truth, *your* truth.'"[10] In a fit of rage, Conor screams at the monster that he doesn't know what the story is supposed to be. As he tantrums, Conor's emotions are raw, they are destructive, and filled with hurt. They are visceral. They are relatable.

Finally, overwhelmed with exhaustion, Conor admits that he does know the truth, but he thinks that to admit it would kill him. His truth: he wants to let his mother go because the pain of holding onto her is too much. And for this, he is ashamed.

After speaking these words, Conor lies down under the yew tree. As he appears to shrink, giving into the truth of the emotions he holds

---

10   Ness, *A Monster Calls*, 38.

for his mother, the yew tree grows. Its limbs curl around the boy—just like the father curls his limbs around his little girl in that video— cupping Conor as he closes his eyes and rests. The yew tree is no longer a monster in Conor's eyes, but a protector who has made a safe space for him to realize the truth.

As an adult with distance from my early years, this scene hits home for me. It's how I still feel about my mother. For years, the very idea of letting her go was *terrifying*, and yet it was what I secretly needed. I felt ashamed of this, like thinking this was doing something terribly wrong. How could someone not want their mother, not *fight* for their mother?

But even a story of a little thirteen-year-old boy can teach grown-ups something: It's okay to want to let go. Grief and release can live together, and once you let go, once you let the grief in, you will survive.

We live in a tiny house. My mother calls it a postage stamp. Its black shingle roof is crumbling, its white vinyl siding is cracked, rusting where the nails are struggling to hold it in place. My father tries to repair what he can, but they barely have enough money. Inside, though, my mother has made the house a home. There is a small kitchen that can hardly fit an even smaller counter and our table with its four chipped, mismatched chairs.

She cooks a lot when my father works long hours in the city. Sometimes I sit at the table and swing my little legs while I watch her bum jiggle back and forth as she whips up batter or kneads bread dough. She likes the colour green, so she's hung green curtains over the window that looks out over the gravel drive. She sweats as she kneads, her dark hair sticking to her temples like kiss curls.

My mother is chopping the tomatoes–*chop, chop, chop*–and she swipes them into a bowl filled with bright basil. She is talking to me, and I am watching her move through the kitchen, reaching for a drawer without looking, knowing where the knives are, the plates, the little jar of oregano. The kitchen smells like a witch's house. She glances at me, her cheeks flushed with summer heat, points the knife in my direction.

"You know, ducky," she says, "I had a hard time labouring with you." She likes to tell me about how I came into the world and how I almost killed her doing so. "Ripped me from stem to stern. Almost died."

She turns back to the tomatoes—*chop, chop, swipe.* "You were such a good, quiet baby. Always looking around. Hardly cried." She wipes the back of her hand across her brow. "You were beautiful. But your brother, he was a complete nightmare."

My brother is two years older than I am. There's a wildness to him, a desire to tempt fate. He drags huge fallen branches through the yard, dangles from the trees hanging over the rushing river, talks back to my father. He tried to run away once, with six apples and a change of clothes in a laundry basket.

My mother stops chopping and is silent. I wonder if she's forgotten what she wanted to say.

Her voice lowers to a whisper. "He was just a baby. He was screaming and screaming, and I pretended I couldn't hear him." She inhales a shuddering breath. I realize my legs have stopped swinging. "I'd done everything I possibly could to help him. I'd fed him, changed him, rocked him, sang to him. But he just kept screaming."

I have an image in my mind of my brother's face turning all red and twisted. A tiny shrieking monster. A very bad little boy.

"I couldn't take it," she says. "Your father was at work all the time, and I was so alone." The clock chimes. "I did something terrible. I picked him up, and I shook him, just a little. I yelled at him to be quiet. I couldn't take it."

I hear crickets outside, singing their shrill song.

"I realized what I'd done and put him back in his crib. I don't really remember much after that." Her hand slides along the counter, fingers in the tomato juice. "Your father came home to find me curled up in the closet."

She looks over her shoulder at me. Her thin dark brows are creased. "I love you kids so much. You know that, right?" I can see it on her face: my mother's grief is growing.

When she is not cooking or doing laundry or sleeping, my mother likes to write fantasy stories. She has a tiny desk that rests under the window at the far end of the house. It holds a Selectric typewriter my father bought for her, a manuscript growing beside it. Each day, pages are added as the sound of her typing fills the house. My brother and I aren't allowed to disturb her when we hear that *thunk thunk thunk, ding!* She loves magic and creatures and the possibility of no limits. She tunnels into worlds she creates, both on the page and in her reality.

Along with the manuscripts, she also types letters to agents and editors, carefully stacking them with sample pages of her magical stories and slipping them into envelopes. The silence she is met with is harder than the rejection letters she receives, and she gets a lot of those.

Sometimes she sleeps a lot. She'll stay in her pyjamas, and I can see her sleeping form on the rumpled bed through the crack of the partially open door to their bedroom. Her face is pale, her cheeks are no longer blooming mother's cheeks.

"What's wrong with Mom?" I ask. My dad says that she's just tired and to not disturb her.

I wonder why my mother is so tired all the time. I wonder why she doesn't want to play with me or why she's pale and sad. I wonder if there's a monster that's taking my mother's life, bit by bit. But I tell myself I don't believe in monsters. I tell myself they aren't real and that my mom is okay.

I tell myself stories, but as I watch my mother start to fade away, I am beginning to wonder if maybe the monsters are real.

IV. THE MONSTER IS THE AUTHOR

Monsters, for the most part, don't have much agency over their identities. Some monsters, like Medusa of Greek mythology, are created as a lesson. Medusa's story teaches us that a woman's virginity and innocence can be taken, sure, but in the end, she's the one to blame.

In early iterations, Medusa was one of the three Gorgon sisters, children of the ancient marine deities Phorcys and his sister Ceto. The sisters were monstrous to behold, with snakes for hair. However, Medusa's physicality changed in the mythology over the years, and the Roman poet Ovid characterized her as a beautiful maiden. Of course, virginity was (and still is in some places) a hot commodity as marriages were business transactions in which women were traded for goods, money, power, and alliances. But only a virtuous, untouched, and therefore, undamaged—read: virginal—woman was worthy of marriage. Thousands of years later, this really hasn't changed all that much. The traditional white wedding dress is still a popular symbol of purity and virginity.

In Ovid's tale, the maiden Medusa is raped by Neptune on the floor of Minerva's temple. While Medusa is being violated, she begs Minerva for help, but Minerva turns away in disgust and lets the god of the sea do what he wants. To add salt to the wound, Minerva casts Medusa out of humanity as punishment for being raped and thus defiling her precious temple. Minerva curses her with snakes for hair and with the power to turn men to stone with one look. (But only men, not women. I sometimes think some men should be turned to stone, at least for a little while, and have a good, long think about what they've done.)

Enter the hero, Perseus, barrelling into Medusa's lair, brandishing a sword and mirrored shield. He swings before he speaks, aiming to chop off her monstrous head and whatever thoughts are contained inside. He just wants to kill her before he even stops to question why she does what she does, why she is destined to live alone with her vengeful thoughts and resentments, why she is so filled with rage. Perhaps she's more angry about Minerva's betrayal than Neptune's.

I'd like to imagine how that story could change.

"Why do you men always come into my home and try to slay me?" she might hiss at him, her voice snake-like and filled with venom. "What have I ever done to deserve this?"

"This is all I know," says Perseus. "This is what I'm told to do. I'm told you're a monster who wants to kill men and we are to be afraid of you."

Medusa laughs and, for a moment, Perseus hears the laughter of a woman, not a monster. "What makes you think you know me?" she says calmly, in the same way she's been asking every single so-called hero who has tried to slaughter her, her snake-like hair writhing around in her peripheral vision, hissing reminders of how different she is. "Do you know who I am, or my name, or my voice, or how angry and frightened and confused I am? Do you know what it's like to live in my head, to live alone with my own thoughts that I'm told are monstrous? Do you know, bright, shining Perseus? Do you know what it's like in my head?"

Slowly, Perseus will lower his mirrored shield and step out from behind the stone pillar. He will take a step towards her, raise his gaze, and look at her.

"Will you hear me," she asks, "and not conclude that I'm a monster? Will you listen to my words and not be afraid of the dreadful horror that you think is my mind?" She pauses, hesitant, a woman who has never had bodily autonomy or the power to author her own story. "Will you think I'm crazy if I tell you how scared I am?"

Perseus puts down his sword and shield. He says, "I will listen, Medusa. And I'll stay with you until you are ready."

I want this to be Medusa's story because monstrous anger, fear, and grief are made even more monstrous if they remain unacknowledged, consequently becoming the scary and unknown Other. Medusa lives with trauma that no one is willing to hear. Instead of receiving empathy and care, she is made into a monster. But if Medusa's story could have been rewritten, would that have changed all the subsequent monstrous stories going forward?

I want this alternative narrative to be Medusa's story because it gives me hope that my story, now that I'm in my adult years, can continue to be one of safety and acknowledgement, too, and that mental illness, *monstrous* mental illness, is only monstrous because it's been externally categorized that way. And maybe the cycle of mental illness villainization can be stopped with one real conversation between a so-called hero and someone who has lived alone in their own rage-soaked and terrified mind.

I want this to be Medusa's story because I want it to be my story. I want it to be my mother's story, and my grandmother's story. I want all the so-called monsters to feel safe enough to tell their own stories.

The school has agreed to allow me back if I'm examined by a psychiatrist. I don't know what a psychiatrist is, but I know there's something wrong with me. My mom is angry, and I'm pretty sure it's me she's angry with. I know I'm different, and different is bad.

I am placed at the back of the classroom, where I can't be disruptive. I'm given special assignments that are "for the stupid kids," so the girl in front of me says. There are only two other kids who do the stupid-kid assignments. The rest of the kids are normal. I know I'm stupid, and I know that my anger is bad because I'm a terrible kid. A terrible kid with a shadowy monster living inside her.

The results from the psychiatrist's assessment are normal. My teacher and the boy's parents still want me removed from school, though, so a compromise is struck, and I am moved to another class. But even here, my legacy of violence and weirdo-hood follows me. I can't help the bubbling anger laced with shame and fear that I feel, and I don't know the right words to tell anyone. There is a wire cage over my mouth. I am immobile and chaotic in tandem.

There is another kid in my new class who likes to call me names. One day, she tells me I should kill myself. She ends up with the sharp end of my pencil embedded in her arm. My Shadow and I laugh, and I am sent to the principal's office again. Another silent ride home, and my mother slides into worry. She is trying to balance her unbalanced daughter and the creature that is coming in the night to take her own life. She doesn't have the tools to manage me or the Shadow growing deep in my bones. I wonder if she wants me dead, too, so I ask her. She gathers me in her arms, whispering softly. I can smell her, slightly sweaty mixed with fresh laundry. Her skin feels soft and hot.

"My ducky, my girl all bathed in pink and sunshine," she whispers into my seashell ears. I cry quietly and beg her not to send me back to school. She cups my face in her hands. "You can stay here with me."

I spend the next few days in the comfort of my own solitude. While my brother is at school and my mother sleeps, the land around my house, the forests of bare silvery branches, the slumbering farmers' fields, all become my realm. Magical creatures live among the deadfall by the river, a mermaid dwells in the water, sprites dance in the forest. My mother tells me about dryads and wood pixies, and I wonder if I'm a monster. I wonder why I was born like this. I murmur my worries into the forest and receive no response.

This world isn't to last. In the hopes that my outbursts have blown over, I am sent back to school. On the bus, I feel myself change. My shoulders curl in, my back hunches, and I refuse to look up. I tell myself I don't need friends. I imagine lying on the shag carpet in my small living room, leafing through the National Geographic atlas my father bought for us, discovering countries I can't even wrap my mind around. I had asked my mother where Egypt is, and she told me thousands of miles, and I can't even picture that, but I know there are pyramids there and old tombs, and I wonder if I will ever get to see them.

It's not long before it happens again. I am angry that I have to do the stupid-kid assignments, and I am angry that everyone thinks I'm a stupid and bad kid. I am sitting at my desk with my hands clenched around crayons as the teacher tells me to do the assignment or go to the principal's office. I feel all the kids looking at me, and the monster inside me starts to rumble. My face is numb, and I am breathing heavily, and the teacher says if there is one more outburst I won't be allowed back in class. The little girl in front of me giggles. I cross my arms and refuse to look at the papers with shapes and colours on them. The teacher reminds me of the consequences of my bad behaviour. I hear whispers and muffled laughter. My chest tightens, my fingers claw at the crayons. My anger hurts. There is a hissing whisper in my mind and dark mist in the corners of my vision. My Shadow has arrived.

I peer up at my teacher who is looking down at me. Her eyebrow is arched, her hands planted on her hips. I look at her corduroy skirt, the colour of rust.

"You're being a very disruptive little girl."

I burst up from my desk, open my mouth and scream a monstrous scream. My fists clench harder around the crayons, and I rake them down the desk, leaving a multicolour smear as I hear her telling me to "stop that right now." I scream again, and this time I know I'm in huge trouble. I'm in the worst trouble I've ever been in in my life, and I don't care, and I'm laughing, but it's not my voice. It's the voice of a monster, of a shadow. Of *my* Shadow. And now I don't care about anything. I don't care about the kids laughing or taunting or that boy's little pecker flopping in the cold air. I don't care about the teacher or school. I gulp in the air and scream louder, my hands swirling the crayons over my desk, creating a matted sludge. I am sweating. I feel the teacher's hands firm on my arms, and my Shadow, and I look at her and then I scream more because I am a rageful, venomous monster. She yells at me again: "Stop that! Stop that right now!"

I release the crayons, grip the edge of my desk, and heave. The desk tips over towards the kid in front of me. She shoots up out of her seat and backs away from the monster.

I don't care about anything anymore. All I think about is fireflies and dryads and the fields around my house and a dragon named Smaug. I want to be an elf like the witch of the silver forests of Lothlórien. But I am a bad little girl. I am a terrible little girl. I am a monster of a little girl.

My world tunnels, my vision tunnels, my body freezes. The Shadow billows out of me and I'm now empty. Crayons drop from my numb hands as the teacher's fingers pinch into my arm. She is tugging me, but I feel nothing.

I am sitting in the principal's office again. Tears running down my face as I look at the carpet. There is crayon under my grubby fingernails.

"Sweetheart," I hear a gentle voice. I look up to see the principal's secretary. She is a soft woman in a puffy white blouse and glasses that swallow her face. She is holding a little cup, and I see steam rising. I take the cup and the scent reminds me of playing along the borders of my gravel driveway where the little yellow and white flowers grow. I want to go home and stay there forever. I want to fall asleep and never take a step into a space where other people exist. I want to be invisible. I want to die.

"Hey, kiddo," the principal's voice breaks my thoughts. "Come on in."

I hand the steaming cup back to the secretary, and she gives me a smile that feels real. I step into the principal's office and see my mother sitting in a chair facing his desk. Behind him is a credenza filled with papers and books and photographs. On the desk beside him is a typewriter. He gestures to the empty chair beside my mother, and he lowers into his own seat. I watch his meaty fingers as he laces them together, resting them on the desk. My gaze slides to his steel hair. I look anywhere but his stern face as he peers at me over his half-moon glasses. There's silence, and I know I should feel bad about what I've done, but I don't feel anything anymore.

"I hear you don't like yogurt," he says.

I look at him, then to my mother. She nods in his direction—*hear him out.*

"I like yogurt," he continues, and I look at him again. I see a smile pulling at the corners of his wrinkled mouth. "Tell you what. My wife packs me chocolate pudding. I don't like chocolate pudding. And I hear your mom packs you yogurt." He leans forward, cupping his hand over the side of his mouth and whispers, "Wanna trade?"

I remain silent as they tell me that I'll be doing most of my assignments in these offices. The nice secretary who gave me chamomile tea will keep me company, and I'll spend recess and lunchtime with this nice man who sort of looks like Santa Claus but without the beard.

"Whaddya think?" he asks me.

I don't think about magical forests or dragons or monsters. I think about a castle, high up in the mountains, its walls protecting me, and my mother and the principal and his nice secretary will be my friends.

I nod—yes, I would like some chocolate pudding.

As my mother sleeps, my brother and I play. His room is filled with the most magical items any little sister could set her eyes on. When we move further into town, our yard shrinks to a fenced-in box. I will switch schools, but I'm not afraid. The Shadow seems to have shrunk, but I still feel something smokey in the corner of my mind. I pretend it's not there though. I'm hopeful that I will make friends and am curious what my classroom will look like. Our new house—one my parents are able to purchase from my father's surge in income—has given my mother an injection of hope. She fusses over paint colours and wallpaper with flowers that bloom so big they consume the rooms. She sews green drapes and orders custom blinds and tells us that this will be our forever home. We are happy. My father has left his job and becomes something called an independent contractor, making eighteen dollars an hour. I'm a little fuzzy on what that means, but I know my dad is happy, and he calls his own shots. He leases a van that he can use for work, and it rests beside my mother's new beige Toyota Tercel that has replaced our powder blue Caprice Classic. She calls it her Little Tank. Her cheeks are pink again. She dresses in nice clothes. I love her swirly skirts and colourful shoes with heels that clack on the floors. Sometimes, when she is downstairs and I hear the typewriter *thunk*ing away, I'll sneak into her closet and slide my small feet into a pair of peach-coloured heels that look so delicious.

My brother gets a paper route, delivering the *Toronto Star* around our neighbourhood. With his money, he buys paperback novels and a video game system. The video game system is set up in the living room because he has no television of his own, and he says this is a violation of his human rights.

Come Christmas, the tree is almost devoured by boxes of colourfully wrapped gifts. There are four stockings over our fireplace, and they are bursting. In the winter, my father plants tiny seeds in pots and lines them up on the dining room table where the sunlight streams in from the patio door. In the spring, he digs up dirt in the backyard, borders three gardens with railway ties, and plants the seedlings. My mother watches him from the back window, and I can see her smiling.

I excel in school, but I know there is still something wrong with me because these kids—kids I never knew before—call me names. One day, I come home and ask my mother what a "slut" is and what does "queen anus" mean. My mother purses her lips and makes a phone call. I spend more of my school days at home, in the quiet afternoons while my mother types on her typewriter. It's not long until her old Selectric is replaced by one of those new computers with a colourful apple embossed on the ugly box. The screen is black and tiny, and I see green words sprawling across the darkness as she types. Most times, she doesn't hear me when I tip-toe to the doorway, wondering what she is thinking, what she is typing so importantly.

In those afternoons, I discover my brother's room and the books contained on the small shelf beside his bed. The paperback spines are colourful, and they all have the same word across them—*Dragonlance*. I'm curious and pull one from the shelf. The colours are beautiful, the people on the front—elves and humans and dragons—are magical, dressed in their armour and gazing out at me. When they look at me, I know they want me to sneak the book into my room and open the pages. I know my brother will be angry if he finds out I've taken his books into my room, but if I'm careful enough, if I turn the pages just so, he'll never know I've been reading them.

I close my door. The sound as it shuts is soothing, a quiet *snick*, and I am alone with this book called *Dragons of Autumn Twilight*. I have never really been interested in reading before, but there is a half-elf and a dwarf and an insatiable kender named Tasslehoff Burrfoot, who is of a childlike race of humanoids that are just like me.

As I read, the words disappear, and worlds open up. There is a war, long-forgotten gods, and dragons are only legend. I want to be there. I want to be transported out of my life filled with words like *slut* and *stupid* and *bitch* and be adventuring with these companions under a starless sky. I want to watch the first silver dragon's wings unfurl, I want to feel the magic, I want to hear the bards singing in the seaside village. I am consumed with grief that I can't, that my life is in this world that is grey and lonely and devoid of magic.

The sun slides across the sky, sets, and repeats its journey. Each afternoon before my brother comes home from school, I return the book to his shelf. I consume the next one, and the next, and I know the real world isn't the world I'm supposed to be in anymore. The kids who look at me with disgust don't matter anymore. Monsters don't exist. There is no Shadow curling around my shoulders.

When I'm not reading the books, I am writing stories about them. I imagine other adventures the companions have, and I write myself into them. But caught in a shame that I don't understand, I rip up those pages and soak them in the bathroom sink. I watch as the blue ink bleeds out and the pages dissolve into mush, and I stuff it all down the drain, piece by piece, word by word. And then I tell myself that I'm stupid.

One day my father doesn't go to work. He tells my brother and me that he's just home for the day, and the next day he goes back. But the day after that, he's home again. And then again. And again. My mother says he is trying to find work, but that no one really has any money anymore. My brother and I hear them whispering in their bedroom at night. We know something is wrong. The garden in the back has gone fallow. There's a leak in the roof, and the bathroom window is rotting, mushrooms sprouting from the crumbling wood casement, and I watch them as I shower.

One afternoon, while my brother and I are quiet in our rooms, our parents come home from the bank. My mother is wailing—"What are we going to do?" Between words, she is gasping. I hear her thud up the stairs and see her disappear into their bedroom. My brother and I look at each other, eyes wide. My mother's sobs are loud and frightening. "We'll lose the house," she cries. My father ascends the stairs slowly, his broad shoulders slumped.

"Dad?" my brother says. "What's wrong with Mom?"

My father stops at their bedroom door. He turns and looks down at us. "Don't worry. Your mom is just upset."

I peer around him to see the rounded curve of my mother's back as she sits sobbing on their bed. Her hands are planted beside her as she heaves in an agony that I didn't know adults could feel. "Mom?" I whisper.

Slowly, she turns to face me. Her eyes are red and puffy, her face mottled. Her hand rises, and her thumb slides between her pink lips. "Who are you?" she says, and there is something scary about her voice. It's small, a broken bell. "I'm not your mommy. I'm too little," she says.

We look at our father. His face is grey, and he blinks at us. "It's okay," he says again. "She's just not feeling well." He disappears into the room, quietly closing the door behind him.

Darkness falls over our house. The green drapes my mother carefully sewed and hung are now collecting dust and fading. The wallpaper curls, the freezer and cupboards empty. My mother makes lentil soup, and I get so tired of lentil soup. They try as hard as they can, but it's just not good enough. My mother will rise to wake us for school, feed us breakfast, and go back to bed. Sometimes she's sleeping when we come home. She is becoming pale again, a wraith of the brightness that had once surrounded her. The computer with its funny little apple is quiet.

My mother is disappearing again, and in the place she once held for me there is now a yawning chasm.

And in that emptiness, something else is waiting to enter.

CHAPTER 2

The Druid and His Daughter

There's a box that rests on the top shelf of the bookcase. Under it, the yellow glow of the small lights illuminates the antique books, a jade giggling Buddha, a Japanese dish, the *Encyclopaedia Britannica*. The box could be mistaken for a shoebox: same size, same shape. It's made of dark brown plastic, strong enough to contain a lifetime, now containing the ashes of my granddad. The lid is sealed. On the side of the box is a small inscription—*G.J.S.*

I've only ever seen photographs of my father's father. There's one that is in sepia tones, creased at the edges. In it, G.J.S. is standing in front of an armoured bridge-layer balanced upon a military tank—a machine that could flatten a man like a pancake. My mother said he'd told her a story once of a comrade who got stuck in the backfire while inside one of those machines and was pulled through the tank's two-metre-long barrel like a piece of spaghetti. Maybe that's why G.J.S. drank a forty a day. My mother said the photograph was taken in North Africa before he served in the French Foreign Legion. She said G.J.S. had served in four armies, enlisting in each with a different identity, at a different age, an almost entirely different man reliving the same life, over and over again. Running from being a husband, from the possibility of fatherhood, from the nightmares that haunted him.

Quiet ripples of G.J.S.'s secret less-than-honourable discharge floats under the surface of my father's face. My mother says drinking and driving a tank is frowned upon in the army. Maybe he'd seen too many body parts fluttering, a confetti of flesh. My mother says he liked to tell stories when he was a third into the Jack, his soft sing-song Welsh voice telling how his mate shit himself when they'd backed their angry juggernauts into the ditches outside Hong Kong. He'd told her the inside of the tank smelled like sweat and vomit.

In the photograph, he is shirtless and squinting in the harsh desert sun. His body is small, lithe, and toned. His features are sharp, and even through time and muted earthen tones, I can see that his eyes are haunting, haunted. He's wearing cargo shorts, army-issue boots that are scuffed and worn, boots that had walked across fields of blood and rage. Thick wool socks slouch just under his knees.

I think he's handsome in a sweet, gentle way, and I can see my father in him. His looks contrast with the furious machine behind him. My mother says I have his mouth—"A mouth you could watch forever," she says. "But he didn't talk much."

His mouth is silent now, and I've never heard his voice. I wonder if it's the same gentle tenor as my father's. A voice that can capture a room or hum a Welsh lullaby with the same soft ease. His son—my father—inherited his need for silence, for observing. Both painfully shy with the iciest blue eyes that come from the deep northern wilderness of the Black Mountains. I know we are the same—grandfather, father, and daughter. The same retreating voice, the same mouth.

G.J.S. died in his sleep while my mother was pregnant with me. My father was twenty-six years old. His ashes now rest on the bookcase, and sometimes, when I'm alone in the living room, I look up at him and whisper, "Hi Granddad. Mom says we wouldn't have liked each other." She says I am as stubborn as he was, and, because of that, we'd be at each other's throats. I still like to believe that maybe we'd be thick as thieves. A wish.

The box and G.J.S. straddle the world between the living and the dead. He is both present and forgotten. His name hasn't been uttered in years.

I wonder if my father is searching for him when he takes me into the forest, looking for the fox's den, or the hawk's nest. Or when he teaches me how to string a bow or roof a house or gently whisper seedlings into soft green life. I wonder if he thinks of his father when he is tipping the developing tray back and forth in his dark room, red light casting a blanketing glow around us as the salty, acrid scented developing chemicals begin to reveal a photograph of a stag, antlers that same sepia in the sunlight.

I wonder if I make my dad happy like he tried to make his dad. I wonder if we will be best friends forever.

I. A TRUTH THAT IS ONLY TRUE BY ONE'S OWN DEFINED LOGIC

My father's ancestors believed in worlds we cannot see. Worlds only accessible to those gifted with magical powers: druids, seers, and bards. They believed these druids, seers, and bards lived in a liminal space, hovering between the thin veil that separated the world of mortals from the world of the fae, the mystical, the spiritual, the immortal. It's easy to take our twenty-first-century science and scoff at the ancient beliefs of the Celts, but I can't help but wonder if they hold some truth. What if we can't see everything that is around us? After all, we can't perceive most wavelengths; we can't see all colours or hear all pitches. And even within our own species we have different perception capabilities. Some feel colours while others taste shapes through a diagnosable condition called synesthesia, where neurons from one sensory area of the brain cross over into another sensory area, creating a mishmash of perceptions. A friend of mine once told me she can hear the colour yellow.

But still, I wonder if there is more to this. That maybe our reality is only what our brains and sensory organs are physiologically capable of perceiving. And maybe reality is far more subjective than we think.

Perception and memory are funny things. What we remember is only what we pay attention to, and what we pay attention to requires our perception. How one person experiences an event could be entirely different from how another person experiences that same event. This can be explained by neuropsychology and gives us a far deeper understanding of trauma and how traumatic events are processed in our brains. I have often doubted many of my memories, now scrubbed over with years of pushing them away. Colours fade, voices become muted. But there are moments, a particular feeling, a flash of an image that will trigger me, and I won't know exactly where to place it in the chronology of my life as I understand it. It will happen when I least expect it, when I think I've finally gotten past it all.

There's a theory on sensation and perception in cognitive psychology called empiricism, which states that all knowledge comes through our senses: touch, smell, taste, sight, hearing.[1] But if we think of ours as a species in relation to others—say, mantis shrimps—our sensory perception is entirely different. The mantis shrimp is a colourful little critter that lives among the coral reefs in the Indian and Pacific Oceans and has one of the most advanced colour-perception systems that we know of. Where we have only three colour sensory cells in our eyes, called photoreceptors, a mantis shrimp actually has *twelve* different photoreceptors.[2]

---

1   *APA Dictionary of Psychology*, s.v. "empiricism," https://dictionary.apa.org/empiricism.

2   Olivia Congdon, "All Eyes on the Reef," Australian Academy of Science, https://www.science.org.au/curious/earth-environment/all-eyes-reef.

That's a lot of colour resulting in a vastly different *experience* of colour. Can you imagine a sensory experience if our wavelength perception was blown wide like that? What would our relationship to our surroundings be like? Our behaviour would be dramatically altered and, because of that, so would our understanding. Our knowledge and belief systems would change.

While obviously we aren't mantis shrimp, these creatures illustrate how limiting our sensory experience is, and this therefore limits our reality to something that is far more subjective than what most people feel comfortable believing (outside of neuroscientists, that is; having studied neuroscience in university, I can honestly say those folks live for this stuff). There are considerable gaps in our perception and memory that our brains will fill in, but only what we need for survival. These very subjective details that we pay attention to—either subconsciously or consciously—will be sorted in our short-term memory. Based on our previous experience of what we *believe* to be true, our brain will decide what's important, and that important information then gets stored in our long-term memory. All of this classification creates the framework of our reality—our belief systems, what we understand, how we learn, and our behaviours. It scaffolds our interactions and how we believe we are perceived by others. It creates the architecture of our subjective world, and from this structure we make all our decisions. This is also where *cognitive bias* comes from, which is the subconscious affirmation of what we already believe to be true—meaning that whatever we pay attention to will affirm only that and exclude anything contradictory. You might see how this can be damaging or dangerous.

Dr. Dirk Bernhardt-Walther is a psychologist at the University of Toronto, and his lab studies just this: how we perceive our world and what we do with that information. Our biology, he says, instructs us to pay attention to whatever supports our goals. The information that is thrown at us as we go about our day incites a cascade of events in our sensory organs and then in our brains. From there, we create the concept of our personal reality.

How we perceive our reality can also be a result of differences in our brains and neurophysiology: psychosis, schizophrenia, bipolar disorder, or in the case of individuals who process differently, autism or ADHD. If both a neurotypical person and an autistic person were to attend the same party and experience the same stimuli, Dr. Bernhardt-Walther said to me, "their reality is getting constructed from [that sensory information] and ends up being quite different. It becomes a complex puzzle of baffling social interactions for the [autistic] person." Even among individuals without mental illness, there are differences in constructed realities, only, "they're getting smoothed over in society and expectations."[3] This also speaks to why many mentally ill folks work really hard to hide their symptoms, trying their best to conform to what is believed to be normal. When they simply can't conform to whatever "normal" is, this adds to their own sense of self-perception. Those societal expectations end up giving way to stigma. This has very much been my experience: calling in "sick" to work, hiding my rage, feeling crushing shame at the thought of my own traumatic past. When, really, none of it was my fault nor was any of it a testament to my character. Having *survived* is the real testament.

There's a large degree of mostly non-voluntary interpretation at multiple levels in our sensory processing. But just because the interpretation of an experience is only in one's mind, does that make it untrue? Does that mean it's impossible? A person who lives with hallucinations—which can be a feature of schizophrenia and bipolar disorder—and perceives there to be a leprechaun on their shoulder is without a doubt having an experience of witnessing a leprechaun.

---

3   Dirk Bernhardt-Walther, Zoom call with the author, September 29, 2021.

Their sensory organs and neurophysiology are telling them that there is a leprechaun. It's their truth. Simply because someone does not live with psychotic episodes that result in hallucinating a leprechaun doesn't mean the leprechaun doesn't exist for the one who *is* witnessing it. To only remain with one's staunch belief means to believe in a tautological truth: a truth that is only true by one's own defined logic. It is fundamentally flawed and narrow-minded. It's also dismissive.

Don't get me wrong, I'm not saying we should all believe that the leprechaun is there. But perhaps we shouldn't dismiss another's experience of that leprechaun.

Our diverse biology really is beautiful, but if used as a weapon, it can be harmful. My reality is entirely different than yours. Does that make my reality or your reality wrong or right? What is truth? There is something fundamental to examine here; a concept that has troubled philosophers since Socrates started his dialogue, and even earlier. That realities are as varied as, say, hair or eye colour is one of the phenomenal things about being human. There is so much to learn from the realities of one another. But this is also where a disconnect can lie and where belief systems can force others with different or so-called abnormal realities into a marginalized and liminal space. As Ailsa Bristow, a good writer friend of mine, said to me, "This initial formation of a liminal space is a form of violence."[4] This marginalization can take the form of cultural biases, behavioural misunderstandings, prejudiced beliefs about gender or race. It can also push those with mental illnesses who exhibit symptoms that are often too uncomfortable to witness into an isolated and dark place. Seeing a leprechaun and having to keep it a secret because you're afraid of what people will think is a terrifying, lonely place to be.

---

4   Ailsa Bristow, Zoom call with the author, September 9, 2021.

Fantasy, for me, has been a place where I can construct alternate realities, particularly around my own experiences. When I learned about liminal fantasy, something in me fell into place. I'd found a missing piece of the puzzle.

Liminal fantasy is a fantasy narrative where the fantastical is interwoven with reality in a way that isolates the protagonist, who is of both worlds.[5] They exist alone in the tunnel between portal and portal, between world and world. It's in this space, among the veil between worlds, that anything can happen, but the only rule that exists is the one that forces the protagonist to remain in the liminal space, isolated and alone. The interrogation of this reality (why am I here, what does it mean, how can I leave, is this even real) only places the character in even deeper isolation, left doubting their own senses while the reader is also wondering why no one else is as concerned about the magical happenings. Fantasy like Yann Martel's *Life of Pi* and almost everything Neil Gaiman has written dive into the liminal, and it's easy to see the isolating, fantastical element in these works.

It's also, for me, easy to see how this can be relevant to someone living with serious mental illness, who feels like they straddle worlds—so-called reality and their own. The idea that the protagonist is usually alone and isolated, doubting their own experiences, is the liminality that resonates with unique and subjective experiences of mental illness. This has certainly been my own experience, existing somewhere in the margins, feeling dense fog around me, doubting my own thoughts and, sometimes, even my own existence. It's also, I think, similar to how my father felt when he was no longer able to wander in the forests, when the recession hit us so hard that he had to sell everything. I wonder if he felt that same dense fog but, having

---

5   Farah Mendlesohn, *Rhetorics of Fantasy* (Middletown, CT: Wesleyan University Press, 2013).

been raised with the harmful belief that strong men are in control of their emotions, was unable to articulate it.

One of the amazing things about this type of liminal fantasy, in my opinion, is that while the character might be isolated and questioning their own experiences—a lot of which is underscored by gaslighting from other characters or even themselves—there is the rich possibility that the character can use this liminal space, where the rules are different or non-existent, to be anything they want to be. They can transform.

As she writes about the power and social impact of fairy tales, disabled author Amanda Leduc rightfully argues that "we have used this storytelling form to illustrate that which is different; whether that difference is disfigurement or social exclusion, fairy tales often centre in some way around protagonists who are set apart from the rest of the world."[6] This liminal space in fantasy can be isolating, yes, but it can also be taken back, reclaimed by the marginalized, thereby showing the power of liminal fantasy to help everyone start to understand what difference is. It can use the familiar—settings, beliefs, rules—and place them in a fantasy space where other possibilities can also exist. Bringing both readers and characters into an in-between world allows them to keep what they know to be regular and true while also challenging those beliefs. Without knowing what I was doing, I used the fantasy fan fiction (fiction that retells popular stories and is written by reader fans) I was writing when I was a kid as a similar liminal place in order to help me cope. I took those stories of magic and dragons and *able-bodied* and *able-minded male* heroes and added my own female characters who were overlooked and bullied. Those characters were my heroes. They were the golden generals who commanded legions

---

6   Amanda Leduc, *Disfigured: On Fairy Tales, Disability, and Making Space* (Toronto: Coach House Books, 2020), 20.

of dragons, wielded powerful magic, and destroyed evil (usually violently; women are allowed to be rageful and messy too). Sometimes I even went so far as to write myself into those stories. Hey, I was a kid.

There is something enduring about dipping into that type of magic. *This* is the possibility that liminal fantasy can give—at least for me. It was a place I slipped into when the real world was simply too much for me, when the only time I felt seen and heard was when I was being bullied. I had no idea what I was doing then, but decades of distance and reflection has helped me see how fundamental a liminal place was for me. I'm sure I'm not alone.

My mother says my father talks to trees. Part of me believes this, but my preteen self knows it simply can't be true. Still, when he takes me deep into the woods, I wonder. I watch his broad back as I trail behind him, the forest cupping us with deep green and mist. I can taste the rich moisture. I can hear a bird. My father's footsteps are light, his hips sway in a confidently unaware way. His tan vest pulls at his shoulders, heavy with the weight of film cases, lenses, and light readers. I can see the black straps of two cameras pulling at the tissue of his neck. His hair is starting to turn silver. Not grey. Not steel. Silver, like the wings of a silver dragon chasing the sun into the horizon.

My father doesn't talk about his father, but my mother says he's always looking for my granddad when he walks into the forest, and that he learned everything he knows about the wilderness from him. She also says that his father was tough on him. I don't think my dad is tough on me. I just want to make sure I'm the kid he wants me to be. I like being his little helper as he tells his stories through the camera lens, and I wonder if he felt the same way with his dad. I want to be part of this sacred space that my granddad occupies in my father's mind. My dad never really seems to be in this world, always somewhere else. He doesn't like people; he doesn't like being around them or listening to them talk. He says people are silly and he has no patience for that. I know that he would rather be wandering the forest, sharp gaze scanning the maidenhair ferns, travelling up the cliffs and inspecting the crevices for a black widow spider, or hunting the forest floor for a calypso orchid. He says the best time of day is when the sun is just beyond the horizon at dawn, or lazily dropping at dusk. That's when the forest will tell you a story. That's when the veil is thinnest and the magical creatures come to life. He says the greens are vibrant after the rain. I've spent days soaked and miserable all for the perfect photograph. When he develops them, he tells me which ones I can claim as my own.

"C'mon kid, hurry up," he says over his shoulder. I am lagging because I'm tired. He woke me just before dawn, in that time when the air breaks into birdsong and the dusty light of the sun that has not yet arrived. When we leave the house, the sky is starting to lighten, colours shifting to more jewel-like tones.

We get on the road, and I know my responsibility is to keep us from getting lost. I am the map reader, and he has taught me the cardinal directions, the difference between miles and kilometres, which roads are highways and which ones are county roads. I tell him we have to head north on the highway until we reach a small town with a donut shop that makes the biggest donuts I've ever seen. He nods. He already knows this, but he is testing me. I have passed.

"How many kilometres until we reach Tobermory," he asks, his voice firm.

I look at the map, count out the squares, and look at the legend. I hesitate. I don't want to get it wrong. I look up at him. "Two hundred?"

"Are you sure?"

I look back to the map. I don't know. I count again. Nod.

"No. Try again."

"But, Dad—"

I'm embarrassed. I don't want to get it wrong. I want him to say, "You got it, kid," and then smile at me. I count again.

"Two hundred and . . . fifteen?"

He nods, just a dip of his head.

We stop at a Tim Hortons on the side of the road, and he buys a Boston cream donut for me and an apple fritter for himself. I like being with him. I don't have to talk. He doesn't have to talk. My mom says we are so much alike, and sometimes her voice is a little sad when she says that.

"How far now, navigator?" he asks me. I stuff the rest of the donut in my mouth and glance at the map.

"About one hundred kilometres," I respond.

"And if we travel at one hundred kilometres per hour, how long will it take us to get there?" I think hard, the numbers tumbling around in my head. He must see my face twisting with the effort, and he huffs. "Come on, it's so simple. You know the answer."

The numbers are evaporating, the answer doesn't exist, and I know he will be disappointed in me. I know I should know this because it's so easy and now I want to curl in on myself and I can see the impatience on his face.

"Think. If we go at a speed of one hundred kilometres in one hour, and it takes one hundred kilometres for us to get there, it will take us how long?"

I don't want to screw up. My voice is small. "An hour?"

"Yes." He shakes his head, slides into the car, and starts the engine. I'm quiet, and he turns on the radio. We listen to CBC as we pass through small towns and farmers' fields until we reach Tobermory. We are heading to something called a glass bottom boat that will take us into Georgian Bay and towards Flowerpot Island. I have no idea why the island is called that, except that I assume there's loads of flowers and maybe the people living there like to garden.

My mother says my father talks to the trees, and I'm starting to believe this might be true. My father only talks about his father when he starts his evenings with two glasses of wine followed by a gin martini. The liquor lets him travel between worlds, where his body can't feel the discomfort of the truth of his own father: that G.J.S. was an alcoholic war veteran whom my father tried to please but perhaps never really succeeded in doing so. Despite my granddad being long gone, I wonder if my father searches for him in those in-between quiet spaces among the trees, near waterfalls, as we watch an industrious beaver build its dam, the fox's den filled with her tiny kits. The stag we saw as we were wandering through a meadow near dusk. There is an eerie quality to my father as he walks through the fields, one hand bracing the camera around his neck.

I wonder if he is walking into different worlds when he's in the forest, walking the footsteps of his father. Maybe the claws that inflicted the wounds his father had while he served in the war also stretched through time to my father. Maybe through the generations, my father's fathers lost what was once theirs: magic.

I want to follow my father. I want to be there, in his magical place. I want to step through into a land where possibility exists and magic is threaded through every vein. And it's starting to hurt my heart that I can't be there, that *there* doesn't really exist. That my life is here and now in a world that is grey and untrustworthy and filled with shadows that live in my periphery. That magic is power, and I am powerless. And maybe, just maybe, my father is a child of the druids.

II. A MAKE-BELIEVE WORLD WHERE ANYTHING IS POSSIBLE

I used to play Dungeons & Dragons with my brother and his friends, but those memories are now faded and quiet. I have turned down the volume on the sounds and how small I felt when playing with all those boys. When my mother joined in on our Saturday night adventures, she took up so much space. Everyone thought she was the coolest person, and I fell into her long, long shadow. I just remember feeling cold and annoyed and masking it over with high-pitched, slightly manic laughter. No one noticed the venom in my voice.

Then, in the summer of 2021, I started playing D&D again. It had been nearly thirty years since I'd stepped into that space, spending a few hours biweekly living in a different world, role-playing a different character of a different species. My friend, the game master (GM), walked me through the rules again, helping me choose which species I wanted to play and what alignment, which would dictate my character's behaviours and decision-making, and what skills and class. I decided to play a half-demon who could wield magic and was slightly scrupulous and entirely surly with zero loyalties. I was a bit shocked at how fun that was.

So, every other Thursday night, six of us spread between Toronto and Mexico City would hop online and be whomever (or whatever) we wanted to be, wandering around magical lands and getting into all sorts of shenanigans. With these people, I found a strange virtual companionship: biweekly, shoot-the-shit nights that often lasted until the small hours of the morning. We nerded out, ribbing one another and laughing until we couldn't breathe. It wasn't that I'd forgotten what that felt like. Rather, I was experiencing this camaraderie for the first time. I wasn't accused of stealing anyone's space. Nobody talked over me (except when we were all yelling at each other at the same time). And I was playing with another woman on the team who was just as delightful and sharp-tongued as I'd imagined non-masculine gamers to be.

During that time, all of us were giving over to make-believe, suspending our disbelief and stepping into the Otherworld of our own making (well, the GM's making). It was also in those nights that I started thinking about my dad and how he walked in a liminal space while he was in his forests, allowing himself to be someone else entirely, someone who maybe felt truer to himself than the blue-collar father of two who'd lost his own father and felt a choking shame about struggling to make ends meet while his wife was living with depression and worsening mental health that looked an awful lot like dissociative identity disorder. Perhaps it was the only way he could cope. Existing in the forest meant that none of that real-life stuff mattered . . . at least for a while.

This idea of an Otherworld can do a lot for us, particularly those of us who have lived in the margins: it can be a field in which other identities or aspects of the self can be explored in a safe way. When I was a kid, this Otherworld was my fan fiction, my sketches of dragons and wizards, and, in some ways, playing D&D, although the latter really only started helping me in my forties. But still, the fictional aspect of the Otherworld was where possibilities lived. And now, through these Otherworlds, I can see how those whose minds have taken them through psychosis, delusions, hallucinations, mania, or depression could find understanding through storytelling. Perhaps, even, this was making it easier to understand myself.

My father's Otherworld was the forest, and although I didn't know this at the time, I now understand that this helped him tap into and release an aspect of himself that didn't fit with the rest of society. It was his liminal space, a place between the real world and one of imagination where it was okay for him to both be himself and believe in something more. For my father, the forest was somewhere we could chase the perfect, shifting light, where anything was possible. Maybe he really missed his own father and this was the only way to hold on to him, even if it was only in his memories. Similarly, for me, writing and role-playing fantasy scenarios is my own liminal land where I can explore the possibility that someone like me—someone who lives with trauma and mental illness—can be a hero.

It's cold. A deep cold that makes the snow squeak. The air is muffled, my nose prickles every time I take a breath. My snow pants keep my legs warm, my jacket is thick and heavy. My dad is ahead of me, his boots softly whispering in the powdery snow. I hear his breath over my own. We are surrounded by thick cedars, their needles dark green, almost black. The sky is nearly as white as the snow. Shadows deepen as we walk farther into the forest. No one is here but us. Somewhere to my left, snow tumbles from a tree, *thump*ing on the ground. Something scurries.

I don't know where we are going, but I trust my dad. He seems to know the way, even though I can't see any trail and the trees are close and there's not much sunlight despite it being daytime. The snow is thick and hard to walk through, but for some reason it excites me. I love being in this forest because it doesn't feel like I'm here, like I'm real, like this place is real. Mom says there's magic between trees, and I believe it. Dad knows this, too, although he rolls his eyes when Mom says that. But in this forest, nothing else exists but the woodland critters and the powdery snow and the magical creatures roaming deep between the trees, watching us as we carve a path through to wherever it is my dad is trying to get to. Or maybe he's not trying to get anywhere. Maybe he's just letting the forest take us wherever it wants us to go.

I feel good here. I feel safe. And even though I know I'll never be normal, there isn't any anger here or lips curling in sneers or harsh words or shadows following me around. I feel like an empty vessel waiting for my dad to tell me what to do, and that will help me become a better daughter, a better helper.

We step out into a clearing. The snow is a white blanket only marked by one trail. My dad points. "Deer," he whispers without looking at me. He smiles. "Cool, huh?"

I believe anything can happen in this forest. I believe we've been transported into another world that exists somewhere between a magical realm and the ugly real world we left behind.

Not long ago, my dad gave me a bow. He said it was his before I was born. It's black and velvety brown, curved at the ends, and it's difficult to draw, but I make my muscles work hard, and when the arrow releases, it's like a breath has been pulled from my body and flown with it. When it hits the hay bale yards away, I hear a satisfying *thunk*. I'm close to the bullseye, and my dad just nods, a faint smile flickering across his mouth. "You're plucking the string when you release," is all he says.

We don't shoot animals in the woods. He only wants to capture them on his film. Watch them as they move, unaware that we're burrowed into the snow and foliage. I can't picture my dad hurting anything. His hair is nearly the colour of the snow now, his beard deep reddish-brown. His eyes a sharp blue, and, when he glances at me, I know he's thinking something. My dad doesn't do anything without thinking about it first, without having a reason. Otherwise, he doesn't look at me, and that makes me feel invisible in a way that makes me feel like maybe I can do anything because no one will notice.

"Just past that patch of trees." He points across the small clearing to more trees, thicker than the ones we just left behind. "The river." His breath puffs in a plume of white.

"Just a river?" I've seen more rivers than I can count.

Again, he doesn't look at me. "A river is never just a river." He plunges his foot into the undisturbed snow. I watch him walk out into the clearing, and for a moment I wonder, if I don't follow him, will he come back to get me? Can I stay here, rooted in this spot, quiet and undisturbed? Will I never have to go back home, back to being the wrong kind of invisible at school, back to being me?

I wonder, if I stay here in the forest forever, will I eventually become one of the magical creatures that I pretend live here? Will I become the Lady of the Forest?

Can I stay here, in this mystical place, just for a short while, and pretend I'm someone else?

The space that both my father and I escaped into during that time is similar to a space fantasy gaming fans will sink paycheque after paycheque into. D&D goes beyond saving throws and perception checks—it can provide a platform for exploration of other parts of the self that one might struggle with. Players have significant free will, dictating the direction of the narrative. The unpredictability is something that a good GM will respond to, creating and recreating scenarios in reaction to the players' decision-making. The world woven through D&D ends up becoming another plane of existence for a while.

While D&D might still be the most popular tabletop role-playing game, it provided the foundation for the growth of other RPGs and RPG-based literature and video games. RPGs like creator Miquel Tankard's SINS and White Wolf's Changeling: The Lost depart from the traditional D&D-type approach, anchoring their premises far more in character and behaviour, allowing players to purposefully explore other psychological aspects of themselves. These fantasy-based games provide a bridge into a mind-constructed world where many topics are explored, including madness, power, evil, and moral ambiguity. They allow players to safely step into a field outside cultural and social constructs and play with the possibility of what could be considered taboo, either for the individual or for society at large.

I wanted to learn more about the experiences that women, non-binary, and trans folks have with D&D. Part of me wanted to see if I was reflected in those stories, to see how deeply this ability to step into a reclaimed liminal space helps folks safely test other aspects of themselves.

Nathan Fréchette is a queer and disabled author, publisher, and parent. He has played D&D since the 1990s. Nathan is also trans, and for him RPGs helped him unpack trauma related to his gender. "[D&D] helped me explore masculine roles," Fréchette says,[7] his voice gentle, his words clear and sure. He is a man who, while soft-spoken, seems confident in himself, articulate. But in the '90s, Fréchette said he was met with resistance, seeming at the time to be a girl playing boys' roles and in a game that was (and still is in a lot of ways) a very masculine, white-dominated environment. But as he continued to play, he found a like-minded group, and his exploration of what it meant to be male was carried out in a place where safety was present, where mistakes could never be made because the game could always be reset. Whereas in reality, if he had explored masculinity that deeply, there could have been life-altering consequences, maybe even life-shattering. For many trans folks, exploring gender in any sort of external, real-life manner can be dangerous and traumatizing, as Fréchette experienced.

I ask Nathan if he would have ever realized he was a man if not for D&D. He hardly misses a beat when he shakes his head and says, "No. Not at all." D&D, he says, is a safe place where one can put their characters through the same trauma the player has experienced in their own lives—being denied gender affirmation—and thus explore how those characters live and move and continue on. Sometimes playing out different scenarios helped Fréchette move through traumatic moments, gaining a different, more authentic understanding of himself.

Artist and community organizer, Kitty Rodé echoes similar sentiments as Fréchette. For Rodé, who is Brown, queer, and agender, live action role-playing (LARP) was an integral component to understanding their own trauma and identity. A sense of alienation threaded through Rodé's childhood, and leaning on fantasy helped them reconceptualize identity, family, and community.

---

7   Nathan Fréchette, Zoom call with the author, August 16, 2021.

In their teen years, Rodé created a character to roleplay, they told me, thinking to themself, "'this character is going to be totally different from me. I'm going to explore something totally outside myself.' And really, it's just another iteration of myself. Another facet of myself that I've neglected . . . just emerging in a different form."[8]

Not all LARP and RPG spaces have become safer for racialized and marginalized folks, however. That racism can exist in a fantasy space is a very real thing, Rodé explains. "Things are getting better," they say, adding that conversations around inclusivity and safety are starting to trickle into LARP and RPG spaces. "But there is so much resistance. There is a lot of racism. It is still a male-, cis-, white-dominated world." For folks like Rodé who are already racialized and marginalized, using these platforms as testing grounds for exploration of identity and processing trauma could become retraumatizing.

Today, Rodé is a community organizer and is working on a project called the Golden Feather Initiative which works towards creating and maintaining safer community practices, focusing on LARP and geek/nerd communities. In doing so, Rodé found these worlds beneficial and rewarding enough to want to change them, a testament to both their own power and the power that fantasy can provide for marginalized and racialized folks. Of course, I am wondering if this is also the case for mentally ill people.

It was through Rodé that I learned about Changeling: The Lost, a tabletop RPG similar to D&D that plays with Celtic lore. It premises a world where players are the "Lost"—people stolen from the mortal world by the Fae, taken through the Hedge to live subserviently in Faerie (also known as Arcadia), the land of the Fae. When

---

8   Kitty Rodé, Zoom call with the author, July 12, 2021.

they are stolen, the Lost are replaced by a Fae changeling who adopts the stolen one's life, right down to their physical appearance. Meanwhile in Faerie, the Lost forget themselves, their previous lives, and even start to take on Fae characteristics that closely resemble insanity. When players play the role of the Lost, they are assumed to have "awakened" to their reality and must escape Faerie or become truly insane.

Regardless of outcome, there is a permanent difference between the Lost and humans in that "their emotions are more powerful, and the emotions of others are almost like nourishment to them; the Lost feel joy and sorrow, love and hate with maddening intensity."[9]

The tragic part of the Losts' struggles is the realization that since there is a changeling in their place and living their life, they have never been missed by their loved ones. Once the Lost return to the mortal world—if they even can—all that awaits them is more isolation, loneliness, and confusion as they try to reconstruct a life that was lived by someone else. Meanwhile, the secret knowledge of Faerie lives with them, further isolating the Lost from the mortal world. If one were to utter any of the truths they experienced, they would be rebuffed by humans and even considered insane. For some, a life behind the locked doors of an asylum awaits them.

I think about my first car ride home from the psychiatric hospital, how grey the sky was, how muted the world. How was I to integrate back into it? This memory is like the Losts' struggles when returning to the mortal realm. Nothing will ever be the same. "Changed in form and feature, scarred by their durance . . ."[10] The scars are permanent. The mist will always shroud. They live forever in a liminal space. This feels incredibly relatable to me.

---

9   Justin Achilli, et al., *Changeling the Lost: A Storytelling Game of Beautiful Madness* (Stone Mountain, GA: White Wolf Pub, 2007), 25.

10   Achilli, et al., *Changeling the Lost*, 12.

Insanity is an interesting concept. It has no definition in the fifth edition of the *Diagnostic and Statistical Manual* (*DSM-5*) and is, for all intents and purposes, a colloquial term that is often used derogatorily and even as a weaponized label. First used in the mid-sixteenth century, it is a Latin derivative of sanus which means "health." Insane, therefore, means "not healthy."[11] One who has the perceived unhealthy characteristics of abnormality, is separated from reality, and has a constructed belief system that departs vastly from the here and now and what is generally accepted to be known fact. The insane are thusly pushed into a liminal "unhealthy" space. They live physically in the real world while their minds travel the world of non-reality—hallucinations or delusions or depression so deep that intrusive thoughts become commands. Similarly, if the players of Changeling: The Lost fail to escape Faerie, they become more Fae (read: insane) than human. Changeling: The Lost is truly a game where insanity is for the losing party, a punishment for failure.

Forgetting aspects of oneself and one's place in a constructed reality is like stepping through the Hedge of Changeling: The Lost, wandering into the mists of the moors and disappearing. But when the player is no longer lost in the land of the Fae, they still always remain the Lost, no matter where their body resides. There is no life to return to. What they knew before—if they even knew anything— has been eradicated. This derealization and sense of floundering upon a return to a previous existence is just as real as the fantastical beliefs, hallucinations, and delusions people experience while ill. The fact that the Lost of Changeling: The Lost sometimes develop emotional and mental disorders when they return to the mortal world is unsurprising, and some even wander back into Faerie, intentionally or not, just as many who have experienced an episode of mania or psychosis will

---

11   *Online Etymology Dictionary*, s.v. "insane (adj.)," www.etymonline.com/search?q=insane.

often unknowingly wander back into the realm of a different reality during their life, a condition of relapse.

But what if those who are relegated (or in the case of the Lost, stolen) to the Hedge figure out that they can claim this liminal space for their own? What if one of the Lost comes to full consciousness, aware of being Lost, a stolen person, but decides they want to claim the liminal for themself claiming a Mad identity? Through gaming, we can explore other ways of being ourselves, fully and without punishment. This might mean that for some, like Rodé and Fréchette, gaming can be used to process identity. While in our real world, liminal margins have often been constructed as a punishment for those who are different, perhaps with gaming we can reclaim this space in a way that gives *us* the power. Again, my friend Ailsa said something about this that I simply couldn't ignore:

"You pushed me here. Now you get to play by *my* rules."[12]

My dad is selling all but one of his cameras. He has one lens left, one light reader. Film is expensive, my mom says, and we don't have money anymore. He stops waking me in the morning, stops taking me into the forest to watch the fox and her kits, to find the doe wide-eyed and blinking in the evening haze. He stops calling me his little helper. I don't see him very much anymore. The house is no longer one entity but a collection of rooms that exist on their own, and we each spend time in our own worlds.

Meanwhile, the phone rings a lot and every time it does, my mother gets upset. She says they are people demanding money we don't have. Whenever the phone rings, I can hear my mom hissing into the receiver, can see her as she sinks her head into her hands. I can tell when she's crying because she makes this scary moan that

12   Bristow, Zoom call.

sounds like she's begging. Our washing machine breaks, followed by the refrigerator. One night, someone takes my dad's work van out of our driveway, and my mom says something about repossession and how can he possibly pay his bills if he can't work and that he needs the van to work.

My mom tries to feed us with what she has, but sometimes the food grosses me out. One afternoon, I come home for lunch, and she has a sandwich for me made from something called headcheese, which she tells me is all we can afford. I don't want to eat it. The texture makes me gag. "Can I have some cereal?" I ask, and she gets angry. I take a bite, try to chew, but I can't make myself swallow it. I spit it back onto my plate. I feel bad because I don't want to be a picky eater. I don't want to be difficult. My mom is angry with me, yelling at me to "eat the fucking sandwich."

"I can't," I tell her. "I can't, it's gross."

She rises from the table, presses her hand on the back of my head, and pushes my face hard into the plate. I'm scared and shocked and ashamed. She is yelling and I am trying not to breathe in the sandwich.

Her hand releases me, and I sit silent, motionless. Tears are making hot tracks down my face. There's headcheese on my mouth, my nose.

My mom stops yelling, stops moving. She looks at me, her face frozen, her hand hovering in the air as though she isn't quite sure it belongs to her. Then she exhales, sinks into the chair, puts her elbows on the table, and drops her head into her hands. I don't move. I don't want her to be upset anymore. I want her to smile at me, her cheeks soft and rosy and warm. I want her to call me her ducky with seashell ears. I want to be in the forest with my dad.

"I'll make you something when you get home," she whispers. "Go back to school."

I do, hoping no one can see that I've been crying.

I make my room a world of my own. When I close the door, I walk into a space of my creation, a field in which I can explore. I walk out of this world and into a magical one, a liminal one, a place where I can be free. Where I can be me. In that space, I am discovering the power of stories. When my mom is okay, she makes sure that I have enough lined paper and pencils. She knows I write, but I don't let her see any of my writing. I close my bedroom door, slide my Beethoven cassette into my boombox, and lie on my tummy on the floor. I write for hours, humming Symphony No. 7. I write stories with the characters of my favourite fantasy novels—Dragonlance—but I weave myself into every story. I make my own character strong and brave. I make her cool and with lots of friends. She is someone everyone turns to for advice and to save the day. Time passes, and I don't notice. The sun arcs through the sky, and it doesn't matter. I am crafting tales.

I start to move to sketchbooks. I stare at the covers of those Dragonlance novels for hours, looking at the drape of the red robes of my favourite wizard, the colour shattering off the knight's armour, the flow of the honey hair of the Golden General, an elf named Laurana. I put pencil to paper and feel my hand sweep, creating the outer curve of a giant wing. Another sweep and the robust body of a dragon forms. Then I write about that dragon.

My parents find enough money to buy me paints. "The best," my mom tells me, handing me the small tubes of primary colours made by a company called Winsor & Newton. She hands me a sable brush, and I know they don't have the money for this, so I hold it reverently and listen as my mother sternly gives me instructions on how to care for it.

I explore with colours I can only picture in my mind, and I love the smell of the paints. The glossiness of the linseed oil makes my mouth water. The acrid scent of the turpentine reminds me of tipping the developing tray back and forth in my dad's now-unused dark room. I make a mess, and I don't care.

But something else is happening, someone coming into my room in the darkness of night, and I don't understand. So I make a story of it. The only way I know how to explain it is to imagine.

I imagine a dark place, a tower in a swamp. The tower rises into the sickly green sky. There are clouds in the distance that look like jewels, and there's lightning but no thunder. When I look at the tower, it is clear and crumbling. But then when I look away, it fades into a distant memory, almost as though it never existed in the first place.

There's a sorcerer who is trapped in the tower. The Sorcerer feels unloved and has built the swampy rotting marsh around the knife-like tower. The Sorcerer believes that he belongs there, in the darkness and decay, surrounded by an echo of the rot that he thinks is inside him. I walk closer to the tower, and suddenly I am in it, and I don't know how I got there. The tower is filled with books, shimmering magical books, stories I can't even fathom. The Sorcerer is crying, but when he cries, he looks at me like I am the only one in the world who can make him feel better.

"You have a lot of books," I say. "They look so magical."

The Sorcerer nods, wipes his glittering tears, and says, "You can have one, if you like."

I am happy with this because I love books, and I can see the magic coiling around these ones, wrapping through the spines, bleeding into the paper. I stretch out my hand, hoping I can choose one myself.

"But," the Sorcerer says, "you need to do something for me."

I feel cold down my back. I don't hear my voice responding.

"You must love me in a way no one else will love me," the Sorcerer says. "And I'll love you in return." He presses his long thin finger to his lips, and I know to be quiet.

"Then can I have a magical book? Then will you feel better? Then will everything be okay?"

The Sorcerer nods and his edges are blurry. His velvet robes ripple deep red to black, and I can't really see his eyes. His skin is bone white. He speaks without moving his mouth, and I feel his hand on me in places that make me feel weird, and I am a little afraid but he tells me it's okay, that this is right, that I make him feel safe, and wouldn't I like a book? Wouldn't I like a magical story? A place where I can let my imagination run free? Wouldn't that be fair?

I don't fight. I don't say anything. I don't know what I'm even supposed to say or think or how to feel or act or move. I see the Shadow in the corner, watching, waiting, biding its time. It smiles at me, and I want to reach out and let it envelop me, and I don't know why. I don't know why I want to give in to that Shadow and its rage, but I feel like this twisted creature is now who *I* should be.

When the daylight comes and I am not in the tower, I become good at sliding away, at not being here, not being now. I used to slide away only when the kids at school were teasing me. But I am starting to do it all the time now. I do it at school. I do it walking home from school. I do it at home, alone in my room. I don't really remember the tower or the words the Sorcerer says to me. I can't quite make out the exact quality of his tears. His voice is elusive, and that elusiveness is comforting. Maybe nothing he says is really real. Maybe it was all just my twisted imagination.

When I'm alone in my room, I imagine flying away, and it feels good. I sit in the middle of my bedroom and look at nothing. But in my mind, the world expands and I imagine I'm a dragon, my wings so huge they span city blocks. I can destroy with one sweep of my great wings. I can carry armies on my back, and my silver scales shine so bright it hurts to look at me. My dragonfire can ignite stars. My dragonfear can topple empires. There are no dark and rotting towers. There are no foul swamps and feathering edges and whispers that fade as soon as they are uttered. There is no Shadow slung across my back, threading its misty fingers through my mind.

When I am a dragon, I am invincible.

One evening, as I am lying on my tummy painting a red dragon, I feel something strange. A twinge in my belly, an ache in my lower back. I go to the washroom and discover I've started my period for the first time. I ask my mom if that is indeed what it is, and she smiles in a sad way and tells me I'm growing up. I feel nothing as I change my underwear and apply a pad. I return to my bedroom, press play on my Beethoven cassette, and continue imagining and writing stories about dragons and elves and wizards.

Only this time, in that brilliant place in my imagination, in my writing and drawing and the world that is in my head, I let my magic destroy the world.

CHAPTER 3

What Is Evil?
And Other Othering *Questions*

It's my first day of high school. I have my binders and papers and pens in my new backpack, and I am following my brother and his friend as they tell me which halls to stay away from, which teachers are cool, and where the smokers gather. I already know I don't want to be with the smokers. They wear weird clothes: black velvet, black hair, black lipstick, and tall black boots. They listen to music that is angry and sort of sounds like someone is screaming, but my brother seems to like it.

"There's the jocks," my brother says. "They're all troglodytes." His friend nods. I make a mental note. "There's the goths," he adds. I ask what a goth is and his friend rolls his eyes. I don't receive a response. "There's the geeks and losers and you want to stay away from them."

I wonder if I'll be a geek or a loser.

My brother and his friend continue to impart their wisdom on me, and I know they are so smart and wise. I trust them. They will look after me.

I walk beside the sister of my brother's friend. She is nice and I like her. Her hair is the colour of cornsilk, and she says words like "rather" and "grand" and "rubbish."

I want high school to be my fresh start. I want to reinvent myself. There is this boy who is a year older than my brother and he is the cutest in school, with wavy blond hair, soft blue eyes, and dimples in both cheeks when he smiles. He doesn't really know who I am so I know I will never get a chance to talk to him. As if he would want to talk to me anyways. Boys think I'm gross. One boy told me, "You need a nose job. Your nose is disgusting," and I know he's right because when I look at my nose now, I know it's gross. I told my mom and she said, "That boy is an asshole."

My assigned locker is near my friend's so I don't have to be alone. I don't want to tell her that I'm jealous because her parents are rich, and she always has the nicest, newest clothes. She's really tall and skinny so I could never borrow her stuff. My mom tells me I'm short and built like a boxer. My friend gives me her old sneakers and I feel like a million bucks in them despite them being too big. "Her father is just a crook and her mother isn't that bright," my mom says when I tell her about my friend with cornsilk hair, and I wonder how she knows them. But my friend is always nice to me, and her mother has the softest voice and says my name so elegantly with her accent. She says a lady will always carry tissue and lipstick in her purse, and she shows my friend and me how to put it on.

"My mum is my best friend." My friend says "mum" the proper way, and I like how that sounds and I believe her.

"My mom is my best friend too," I say and something funny settles in my chest when I say it.

When I get to my class, I see the kids and their faces are fresh and they are cool, and I know I'm not cool like them and I'm scared they will find out. They will find out about my mother who doesn't leave the house, who sleeps all the time, who tells me the world is bad. They will find out my father can't find work and we're poor. They will find out about the stories I write, or about the Sorcerer and what he makes me do. He whispers to me, telling me he will give me magical books if I do what he wants me to do. I hate him. I can't get rid of him. The only thing that makes me happy is the books he gives me and the stories I write about them. My existence is divided into the shades of grey that live between the tower in the swamp, and the silver and sunlight that is my imagination.

And the Shadow growing in me, threading through my spine, wrapping into my brain, making me angry and resentful and feeling slightly . . . *strange*, like I've stepped just to the side of my body and nothing is quite real.

When the bell rings and school is let out, my friend and I meet at our lockers and walk home together. We notice the cute boy with the brightest eyes and sweetest dimples walking behind us. He lives in our neighbourhood and has a twin sister who is so beautiful I'm afraid to talk to her. I want to be beautiful. The only part of me that I like is my long hair that my mother says turns to gold in the sunlight, and she tells me she used to have beautiful long hair when she was young too, but that life is cruel. I love the drawings I create of dragons and wizards. I'm getting really good at drawing dragons and wizards, but I don't want to show anyone because dragons and wizards are for losers. I still read my magical books. I still write about them. My bookshelf is now filled with Dragonlance novels, and my brother and his friends play Dungeons & Dragons and they seem to have so much fun and I want that too.

The school year continues, and my marks aren't very good. I don't know why I'm not trying. I feel numb most days. I don't like classrooms. I don't like the kids when they look at me. I only like my friend and my stories. I am failing math, and I always used to be good at math. My art assignments are late, and my art teacher is really nice and tells me, "If you work hard and try to hand in your assignments, I won't dock you marks." She says I'm a good artist, but I still can't get my assignments in on time. I feel tired a lot. All I want to do is write my stories and draw my dragons and make my mom and dad happy. I want to save them from being poor and sad. I want to be a good girl.

One day, while I'm walking the hallways of my high school, a beautiful girl passes me. She is petite and elegant. I glance at her as I pass and she opens her petal-like mouth, soft eyebrow arched, and says, "Whore." Then she's gone. I continue my way to class, afraid. Does she even know my name? What made her think that, say that? Do I dress wrong? Do I walk wrong? I'm not even sure there's an answer to that because I have done nothing to her.

Then I wonder, as I slide into my desk, how could she know that I am not innocent and haven't been for years? How could she know what I've seen, what I've done? How could she know about the tower and what happens there?

Does she see my Shadow? Does she know?

Does she know that there's evil brewing in me?

I. THE DRAGON AS A PROTECTOR

To define *evil* feels vague and nebulous. Dr. Julia Shaw attempted to do this in her bestseller *Evil: The Science Behind Humanity's Dark Side*. In it, she lays out what she considers to be the science behind evil, although categorizing a rather subjective cultural construct as "science" is pushing it, in my opinion. While her research is presented methodically and with thoughtfulness, she relies on questionable claims and builds to a crescendo: that we all are capable of the worst evil, including pedophilia, murder, and torture.

Considering such evil in ourselves is difficult, and being able to scientifically verify that *all* people are capable of such evil, collectively and individually, is a rather grand sweep. However, the subject matter—evil—is one that has hung around for thousands of years in various iterations across cultures. It's a foundation in religious texts; it's what anchors many laws (that and ownership); and it's also deeply embedded in entertainment and pop culture. An entire genre of films,

TV, games, and literature is dedicated solely to the exploration of evil, whether it's a chainsaw-wielding "madman" or a deeper, more thoughtful critique like Jordan Peele's 2017 horror film *Get Out*, which cast evil as racism and fetishization.

The problem with Shaw's framework of "evil" is that it takes the subjective and claims it's actually objective. We can all pretty much agree that torture and other crimes against humanity are horrific acts committed by pretty shitty people. But it's nearly impossible to create a definition of "evil" to work within, pedagogically and empirically, because it's culturally, socially, and moralistically constructed. It's a part of a zeitgeist.

However, that doesn't mean we can't examine how evil is perceived and executed in the stories we tell and who we tell them about. Who, in these stories, is the evil villain? And what, exactly, makes them villainous? By examining how we perceive evil and how we define it within a given time and culture—a perspective that changes—we might be able to understand what we also see as *different*. Mental illness is often cast as something that causes evil; therefore, the mentally ill become the embodiment, or container, of evil.

In fantasy, this theme is used a lot. In high fantasy, the villain has lived in a castle up in the mountains and is inaccessible. In fairy tales, evil needs to be conquered in order to deliver a fully formed moralistic lesson. In sprawling, epic, and immersive fantasy, worlds pivot around the concept of good versus evil, hero versus villain. Right versus wrong. These stories have been told primarily from the perspective of the hero (who is usually a straight white cis male, able-bodied with no mental illness or neurodiversity), therefore creating a blueprint for the reader of what it is to be good and heroic.

(Look at Marvel's Captain America, who literally underwent a scientific experiment to change his body from small and thin to beefy and tall; or the human and elf heroes of my early-teen favourite Dragonlance novels, who are tall, white, and mostly pretty buff; and in anything that Sarah J. Maas writes, where the fae princes are absolute Adonises.)

Evil often exists so that the hero can have something to be heroic about. This is particularly poignant in Marvel's Phase Four television series *Loki*. From the very first episode, the titular character, who is also the same god of mischief from Norse mythology, brother of Thor and adopted son of Odin, learns that the purpose of his entire existence is to be something the heroic Avengers can avenge. They're heroes because Loki is a villain.[1]

What good is a strapping man in his prime brandishing a sword without a dragon to slay? Or a Perseus without Medusa? Or Harry Potter without Lord Voldemort?

In some narratives, characters who are at first heroic end up becoming villains through "madness," as in HBO's *Game of Thrones*, based on the series of novels by George R.R. Martin. Daenerys Targaryen is one of my favourite characters from the show (second to Tyrion Lannister). Not just because she's a girl who fights back against patriarchal and tyrannical bullshit, or because she claims her agency, or because she rides on the back of a massive fire-breathing dragon (this might be the main reason why I love her—because dragons). It's actually because she tries *so damn hard*. She wants to do the right thing, despite the odds. She knows her family has been "cursed" with madness. She knows the hurdles she'll have to overcome, being a woman in leadership. And yet she frees thousands of enslaved people (yes, there's a very real white saviour narrative here, which in itself is a problem for a whole other book), she dispenses justice, and she single-handedly saves Jon Snow and his companions from the army of the dead, losing one of her dragon "children" in the process. She bears her grief solemnly and appears to learn

---

1   *Loki*, season 1, episode 1, "Glorious Purpose," directed by Kate Herron, featuring Tom Hiddleston, aired June 9, 2021, on Disney Plus, https://www.disneyplus.com/series/loki/6pARMvILBGzF.

from her mistakes. She's basically the small-screen version of the hero I wanted to be as a kid, the same hero role I wrote for myself.

Little do we know that the loss of one of her dragons is the first in a series of rapid-fire events that vastly changes the trajectory of Daenerys's character arc. Throughout the series, she is defiled, assaulted, hunted, and generally treated like a brood mare. But the most reckless and unjust treatment she receives is from the show's writers. In the penultimate episode of the final season, "The Bells," Daenerys has finally achieved what she set out to do eight seasons ago: march her armies to the gates of King's Landing to take back the Iron Throne, thus becoming the true Queen of the Seven Kingdoms, a position that was held by the Targaryens for three centuries before Robert Baratheon overthrew the Mad King, Aerys, Daenerys's father, forcing her and her brother (the last Targaryens) into hiding.

For context, her family name, Targaryen, is synonymous with madness and therefore violence. Her father was a deeply paranoid man who delighted in watching people literally burn. This points to not just the seemingly everlasting and tiresome belief that mental illness equals violence, but also the belief that a brutal childhood begets a murderous villain. The entire set of circumstances around Daenerys's early years results in tyrannical adult behaviour, no matter what she might do to subvert her prewritten destiny (leaving aside that this is her prewritten destiny in the first place). That evil is either created at childhood or inherited from an insane parent is threaded throughout storytelling, and the mad villain is just as pervasive in fantasy, made larger and more mythic with magic and dragons and no real-world limits. Evil is not ascribed to an action but rather to the entirety of a person.

To assume that a shitty childhood riddled with trauma means that a person will grow up to become a dangerous adult is doing a disservice both to the child and the adult they will grow up to be. It delegitimizes how someone experiences and processes trauma. It also irritates me every time I see this trope played out as it simply has not been my (or many others') experience. It's actually the complete opposite of the truth, where folks with mental illness are far more likely to be *victims* of violence than to perpetrate it themselves.

It's important to examine childhood trauma, the psychological effects and tools children use to cope and how those experiences help shape the adults they will one day become. In her seminal work *Trauma and Recovery: The Aftermath of Violence—From Domestic Abuse to Political Terror*, Dr. Judith Herman unpacks the previously misunderstood nuances of trauma and behaviour. Herman writes about the psychology of child abuse, where it's the act of surviving abuse that scaffolds the architecture of future coping mechanisms. While she doesn't write specifically about neuroplasticity, what she describes is exactly what happens to the brain. In a theory commonly referred to as Hebb's Law, the brain wires and rewires itself in reaction to external stimuli. It is also influenced by genetic factors, but it's the environment that holds the reins.

Trauma is often misunderstood as only being an event or series of events. This isn't entirely true. While these events usually need to happen for trauma to occur, trauma is actually the *experience* of those events and subsequent processing. How one person experiences a traumatic event can be entirely different from how someone else might. And children are particularly vulnerable given how formative those years are, psychologically and neurophysiologically. Herman states, "The pathological environment of childhood abuse forces the development of extraordinary capacities, both creative and destructive. It fosters the *development of abnormal states of consciousness in which the ordinary relations of body and mind, reality and imagination, knowledge and memory, no longer hold.*"[2]

---

2   Judith Herman, *Trauma and Recovery: The Aftermath of Violence—From Domestic Abuse to Political Terror* (New York: Basic Books, 2015), 96. Italics added.

In Herman's research, survivors of childhood abuse tell how their child-self would adopt dissociative techniques, some even sliding into full dissociative fugues (where a person becomes so separated from reality that they don't remember what occurred during the episode—like a blackout). I think this was how my mother processed her trauma. She was able to slide outside of herself during times of extreme stress when I was a kid, and she became someone else. The trauma that I experienced witnessing my mother transform like that wasn't necessarily in the actual witnessing, but the silence that came crashing down after. It wasn't acknowledged in my house. We didn't speak of those things. Life carried on as usual, however "usual" may have looked. And a big part of me now wonders if that silence also further entrenched my own mother's trauma. I wonder what would have happened if we had talked about it, if it hadn't been so secret.

Based on my own life experience, I think about the splitting of consciousness in order to protect the psyche and sense of self a lot, and I wonder about how a protector might form in the mind, perhaps one that might also fit the criteria of "evil." If the self splits, would one of those splits be a protector or a Shadow? Or maybe, in a maladaptive way, the self would become both? What would that look like? Does the protector have a gender, a voice, an elusive presence? And how much influence would this shadowy protector have over the individual? How violent would they become if they felt threatened? Maybe they appear as a black dragon, a leviathan born in flame from a stone egg to become the protector of a young silver-haired girl.

Let's return to Daenerys. Having been born just after the overthrow of her father, King Aerys, and the slaughter of almost her entire family, Daenerys was immediately whisked away into the night along with her older brother, Viserys. Daenerys and Viserys are the last living descendants of House Targaryen, and their existence is a threat to the new king, Robert Baratheon.

Daenerys has a rough start. Living in hiding in the Free Cities of the east, across the Narrow Sea from Westeros, she becomes Viserys's ward. During their time in exile, Daenerys and Viserys are always running, dodging King Robert's assassins, living off the trust and honour of others. Meanwhile, Viserys is plotting his revenge and solidifying his plans to sail back to Westeros to retake the Iron Throne in his family's name.

Viserys abuses Daenerys, threatens her life, assaults her, and uses her as a tool in his plans for domination. To him, she is nothing but a pretty girl to be sold to the highest bidder, which he does when she is barely a teenager. She is to become the wife of the khal of the Dothraki, Drogo. When Daenerys protests, Viserys says he would let every single one of Drogo's khalasar rape her to get what Viserys wants: the Dothraki army to sail with him in his invasion of King's Landing.

Like many survivors of childhood trauma, a large part of Daenerys's self-conceptualization is formed through these experiences. Her sense of threat is not unfounded, having lived in fearful exile her entire life and having suffered abuse at the hands of her brother. The violation of both body and trust she experiences from Viserys mirrors that of many childhood abuse survivors. It leaves an indelible mark on one's psyche.

The abuse and harm Daenerys experiences culminates when she loses her first child. This moment, combined with the loss of her love, Khal Drogo (who starts out as her captor and repeatedly assaults her), changes Daenerys. She transforms from a scared little girl into someone who has simply *had enough*. She is at her breaking point. For many survivors, this breaking point can birth a simmering rage. Daenerys's rage is accompanied by an unquenchable thirst for revenge and the realization that she is the one to take back the Seven Kingdoms of Westeros.

Let's take a tangential path here. An *inciting event* in psychological terms refers to a traumatic event or series of events which can introduce mental illness in someone with a genetic risk factor (that's the theory *really* simplified). In the theory known as the *gene-environment interaction*, an individual with a genetic heritability of mental illness may experience the onset of mental unwellness if exposed to environmental stressors. This is also the hypothetical answer to the debate of nature versus nurture: it's both. But again, this is all theory.

Theories can also make for rich storytelling. It could be said that this is Daenerys's inciting event, both narratively and psychologically, even if this story is a bit reductive. It's what drives her to the brink, and in the final episode of season one, Daenerys takes the witch who murdered her son and her husband and burns the woman alive. As she watches, Daenerys's face is impassive, neither pleased nor remorseful. She is simply doing what she believes she must. Then she steps into the fire with the burning, screaming woman, accompanied by her three petrified dragon eggs—her unborn rage and protectors.

When dawn comes and the fire has reduced to ash, Daenerys is crouching among the rubble, untouched by the flames. Around her ankle, her arm, and draped over her shoulder, are three tiny dragons.

It's inspiring to watch, cinematically: the swell of music, the barren landscape, and the girl now naked, cleansed, and witnessed by fierce warriors who kneel before her. The sound of a dragon screeching into the dawn echoes as the screen sharply drops to black. It's chilling, awe inspiring, and there's something about it that sinks into me every time I watch it. This small girl, once shrinking and fragile, becoming something so powerful and otherworldly is what I'd written about when I was young. It's more than just the reemergence of dragons in a fantasy world or a girl who has now harnessed what will become near-unprecedented power in these three dragons. It's something else, something deeper: Daenerys has split. Her self and psyche are now separated into young girl and three soon-to-be massive dragons. Daenerys's traumatized self has been gifted with the power to transform her psyche—and what will soon be her protectors—into three mythical but still very real creatures.

The question remains, though: If Daenerys hadn't been subjected to such abuse, would she have been the one with the power to birth these dragons? And would she have been written as a slaughtering tyrant at the end of eight seasons, having succumbed to the Targaryen curse of mental illness (read: violence)?

It's a tired narrative, one where female characters are written as the outcomes of men's actions towards them (remember Medusa?) and where a woman's destiny can only be shaped by trauma. But I suppose if one were to fit this trope, what better destiny than to become the Mother of Dragons?

As the story progresses and as Daenerys grows in power, so do her dragons. Her favourite, Drogon, is the largest of the three siblings— the contrasting opposite of Daenerys's small stature and silver hair. It seems like Daenerys and Drogon share a telepathic connection. During the coup of Meereen, the city she has conquered, Daenerys and her guards are surrounded by assassins. The camera focuses on a terrified Daenerys who, with a deep breath, closes her eyes and calls to Drogon telepathically. He responds, his shrill dragon cry cutting through the screams of the battle, and he emerges from his own flames to save his mother. This is the first time Daenerys climbs onto Drogon's back as he flies above the violence and carries her to safety.

Wrapped in dragons and magic and fantasy, it's a pretty cool scene. Daenerys, dressed in fine silk, climbing onto the back of a terrifying dragon and flying away gives me goosebumps, and I secretly (okay, maybe not so secretly) wish that dragons were real. It's awesome in every sense, and my childlike self still wishes I'd had a dragon of my own to take me out of the prison-like tower in my imagination. In a way, I also see the growing presence of my Shadow to be similar to Drogon: a massive beast that is dangerous, nearly untameable, and altogether alluring (although not a real dragon, obviously . . . but that would be pretty cool).

After I'd watched that scene the first time, I couldn't stop thinking about it. As I did so, a thought began to percolate, and I rewatched the scene, again and again, and others similar to it—most of which involved Daenerys destroying fleets of ships or conquering cities on the back of her dragon.

In the end, all the pieces that make up the mosaic that is Daenerys Targaryen, from her fraught birth to her arrival at King's Landing, culminate in the slaughter of an entire city, single-handedly and with one fully grown dragon. That it's Daenerys Targaryen who eventually becomes the villain of the series and not the Night King (a literal magical humanoid who was created to be a weapon and the end of the "world of men," but low hanging fruit must be left alone, I guess) is a form of violence. It's a continual misrepresentation of what it means to be degraded and defiled, and what it also means to be mentally ill. It's archaic that these events that Daenerys experiences throughout her life could only have one trajectory: evil. Again, mental illness is written as synonymous with evil and violence. Fantasy just provides a magnification, amplified by magic and dragons.

I return to the same question: Would we accept Daenerys and her three gargantuan slaughtering beasts if her story wasn't wrapped in fantasy? Would we be okay with this tired "childhood trauma begets murderous adult" narrative? Of all people, I'm down for a story about dragons, but if we look at it this way, it sounds like something out of a cheap psychological thriller, and that just doesn't cut it anymore.

Summer is coming and we can feel it in the classroom. Kids are starting to get antsy for the end of the school year, and there's excitement in the classrooms. Voices are louder, colours brighter, classes feel longer. I can see the field through the open double doors of the art room from where I'm sitting. I can smell the art supplies—the pastels, the oil paints, the paper. I can also smell the freshly mown grass.

My friend with cornsilk hair has made friends with a few other kids who are a year older than us. There are two girls who seem really nice and smart. I like them because they're sort of the in-between cool. Not too cool that they'd be ashamed to hang out with me, but not too geeky either. They seem confident and live outside of town, and one of them is dating my friend's older brother.

The cute boy starts hanging out with us, and every time he turns his cerulean gaze my way, full lips pulling in a smile, I want to crawl into my own ribcage. But I also want him to keep looking at me. I don't want him to turn his bright gaze away.

One day, when we are all outside, he slides closer to me and says hello. He makes a joke and it's funny and I feel warm inside. I wonder why he's talking to me. "I like your hair," he says. We talk. I'm floating. My fingertips are numb, and it's the most exquisite numb I've ever felt. It's vibrant being beside him, and he stays near me after my friend has left to go home. I'm lost in his sweet dimples and sense of humour. He asks if he can walk me home. I nod, trying to keep my smile from breaking my face apart.

We talk about nothing really important. He makes jokes, and I think they're funny. He talks about his beautiful twin sister and how they sometimes have terrible arguments, and I picture screaming and then wonder if they are disappointed in each other after they fight. Will they be in trouble? Will things have changed after the yelling stops? I wonder if each fight chips away at them, reducing them to less and less with each word hurled. But then I wonder if that's just all I know.

We stop in front of my house and turn to one another. He looks down at me, and he's so close I can smell his cologne and it's wonderful. I can't believe someone like him would want to spend time with someone like me. He reaches out and brushes a lock of my hair.

"Can I walk you to school tomorrow?" he asks. I realize he's afraid I might say no. My mouth hurts from trying not to grin like an idiot. I nod. He nods.

My tummy is still flopping as I walk in the house. I head to my bedroom, close the door, and drop my backpack. I look around at the Dragonlance books, the drawings of dragons and wizards, the collection of paper with scrawling across every page—my private stories.

A boy, a real boy, likes me. And for a little while, his smile is still fresh in my mind, his bright eyes driving away memories of the swamp, the tower, the Sorcerer and his glittering shard-like tears. The Shadow. For just a moment, I think maybe I'm not bad. Maybe there's another part to me that is good and whole. Maybe evil doesn't really exist.

I continue to play D&D with my brother and his friends. I'm excited because I get to imagine a whole other person, a different life, magical adventures. I think it's sort of like the stories that I write, and I'm not sure what my character should be. I want to be useful, but I can't imagine being useful in real life, let alone in a magical one. My brother's friends are all interesting and smart, and when they talk, the other boys look at them and listen and respond. My voice is small. My thoughts are small. I'm small. So I decide to play a small character, maybe a thief, someone who is childlike because I can't imagine growing up even though I know I am.

I decide on a kender—an innocent race from my favourite books, Dragonlance. The kender are small, bright-spirited, plucky people who completely lack boundaries around personal belongings. They're often misunderstood as thieves when, really, they're just curious and cheerful with no cultural understanding of ownership. I want to be curious and cheerful, but also if I wanted to play a powerful wizard or a valiant paladin knight, my brother's friends wouldn't like that. I would be stealing their space, their heroism, their masculinity. So my character is purposefully annoying, the quintessential little sister, and for hours every Saturday night, I irritate my brother and his friends because I exist and because I can. I try to talk to them, and sometimes they respond, but when they do, they don't look at me. I try not to get irritated, so I play the role I'm supposed to, meanwhile envisioning blasting them all with a fireball spell.

When I'm alone, I write my stories and sketch my dragons. I write a story about a woman general, an elf who leads an army of paladin warriors and rides a silver dragon. I use words like "burst" and "sunlight" and "flames." My mom has stopped writing, so one evening I read her my story about the elven general and her silver dragon and legions of shining warriors. I want her to see that I'm doing what she does, and I know she'll understand how much I love magic and dragons and writing stories and that I want to be just like her. I clutch the papers in my hands as I sit on the floor and read to her. Occasionally, I'll look up and see her face, and she's looking at the wall. I see dark smudges around her eyes. Her lips are pale. When I finish, I hold my story and ask her what she thinks. She tilts her head, raises her eyebrows, and says, "It's a little boring."

I lower my head, press the papers to my chest, and take my story to my room. I close the door quietly. My movements are slow and my hands shake, and my papers are blurring in my tear-filled vision as I pull at them, hearing the ripping sound and feeling satisfied that I'm destroying my story. It's stupid anyways. I'm stupid and boring and a failure. I hate myself. I rip and rip and rip until I have confetti of stupid stories. I quietly move to the washroom, run the water, and soak the stupid pieces of my stupidity. I stuff them down the drain. I have to rip them into the tiniest pieces and run them under the water for a long time, but I'm patient, and when I'm done, I go back to my bedroom and look at a picture of a blue dragon I drew, the colours so rich and delicious and it smells like Prismacolor pencil crayons, and I rip that up too. Dragons are stupid. It's all boring and stupid. I will never draw another dragon again, I tell myself. I will never write another stupid, boring story.

"What have you done?" my mother says when she sees the mess of my blue dragon and anger. I bury my rage, tuck my chin to my chest, and remain quiet. My mother says I've been childish and that she's aghast and has no idea where this behaviour is coming from. I don't really know either. All I know is I feel angry all the time. I live a partial existence between the real world, my fantasy world, and the dark, rippling tower of the Sorcerer and how he makes me feel.

The Sorcerer is pulling me into his tower more often now, and his secret is too heavy for me to hold. My bones are breaking under the weight of it. I'm glad no one sees, least of all my parents. They don't see because I make sure they don't see. I behave because I'm really good at that. My mother still sleeps a lot. My dad is working a little more, and we don't eat lentil soup as much, but things are different in my house. My mom isn't like she used to be. My dad never returned to the forest, and I know we exist just because there's nothing else to do. Time has stopped in this place.

As I play D&D, I notice something that I've never seen before. Two of my brother's friends like to sit beside me, and I'm not sure how I feel about it, but there's something inside me that is telling me to fall down that rabbit hole of attention because maybe it will make me feel better, even just for a little while.

When we play, my brother's friends all sleep over, sprawled out on the basement floor with their sleeping bags and pillows. My mom lets me stay down there, too, because she thinks my brother will protect me, but sometimes, after everyone seems to have fallen asleep, I feel a hand snaking out to cup my bud of a breast, which isn't even a breast because it doesn't feel like it's attached to my body. I lay very still because I know if I don't, I won't be allowed to play anymore. And I love playing so much. I love walking into another world. I get to be as irritating as they all expect me to be.

I get to be angry, and I get to steal things. I make my voice louder, and it feels good when my brother rolls his eyes at me. It feels so damn good to excel at what they all expect me to be. It feels good to make them suffer the consequences of what they are forcing me to be. What they truly deserve.

II. THE SELF SPLITS

It was in between my first and second hospitalizations—a few years after high school—that I was riding a public bus on my way back from university to my tiny, shared apartment, when I decided to stop at the bookstore. I didn't want to go home. My apartment wasn't even a home for me; it was a space where I kept a few things and that reminded me of how deeply I was spiralling.

But in the bookstore, I wandered. I didn't really have any money, but still I browsed the shelves, inhaled the scent, ran my fingers along spines and covers. I've never been great at *not* buying books, and I had twenty dollars burning a hole in my pocket—twenty dollars that I should probably have saved for groceries, but a particular book on a front table caught my attention. It was a middle grade hardcover book that everyone had been talking about and that I thought sounded absolutely ridiculous. It was about an orphan boy who, at eleven years old, learns he's a wizard and goes to a wizarding school. I was *way* too grown up to read silly nonsense like this. Magic was stupid. Magic was for kids.

But still, the red cover with the steam train and awkward-looking kid with a lightning scar on his forehead drew me in. What was it about this novel that had everyone so excited? I decided to spend most of my last twenty dollars to find out.

Over the next few years, as each volume of the Harry Potter series trickled out, I waited to get my hands on a copy. I inhaled those books, feeling a sense of being seen. A kid who was neglected, bullied, felt as though there was no hope, who actually got a chance to realize his own magic, this is what I'd wanted when I was a kid. That was something I could cling to. And I wasn't the only one. Those books have earned J.K. Rowling a *killing*, making her one of the wealthiest people in the world.

Then in June 2020, Rowling penned a tweet that questioned the use of the phrase "people who menstruate": "I'm sure there used to be a word for those people. Someone help me out. Wumben? Wimpond? Woomud?"[3] It was at this time that I also learned what TERF meant— trans-exclusionary radical feminist—and it appeared that Rowling fell neatly into that category. Someone who considered herself a feminist, but only insofar as extends to women who identify with their assigned female gender at birth . . . therefore excluding trans women. While doubling down on her "support of trans people" who she "knows and loves," she continued to state that removing "sex" does harm to cis women and feminism.

While I don't identify as trans, I am well aware of the harm language such as Rowling's causes. I have often questioned my own gender. I've never really felt male or female. I struggle to use they/them pronouns. I also struggle to use she/her pronouns. I have, for many years, withheld my own complex feelings about my gender. It wasn't until a friend introduced me to the concept of genderfluidity, and helped me see that gender is a spectrum on which most people fluctuate, that I felt something fall into place. Sometimes I think of myself as a woman, sometimes I think of myself as not having a gender. And sometimes I *feel* masculine, but

---

3   J.K. Rowling (@jk_rowling), X (formerly Twitter), June 6, 2020, 5:35 p.m., https://twitter .com/jk_rowling/status/1269382518362509313?ref_src=twsrc%5Etfw%7Ctwcamp%5 Etweetembed%7Ctwterm%5E1269382518362509313%7Ctwgr%5E2a4716bb7092b03foc1f 484d9eeaoe6d15a3c050%7Ctwcon%5Es1_&ref_url=https%3A%2F%2Fwww.glamour.com %2Fstory%2Fa-complete-breakdown- of-the-jk-rowling-transgender-comments-controversy.

not a man. But how is all of this performed? Does this mean that one day I'll wear floaty dresses and lipstick and the next I'll wear cargo pants and boots? (The answer to which is neither; I'd much rather wear pyjamas all day.)

The belief that only women menstruate makes me deeply uncomfortable. As someone who struggles with identifying as a woman, and as someone who has had a very complex and often violent relationship with my female body, Rowling's doubling down on her claims has given me a visceral reaction. I want to hide my body, bind my breasts, turn away from the fact that I do menstruate, because all of those aspects of my physical self feel like a violation. They aren't who I am. They aren't even a part of my identity.

It took me some time to realize what Rowling was saying and the harm that her words have caused a lot of folks. I am probably one of the last to also realize that the pen name she chose for her psychological thrillers—Robert Galbraith—also happens to be the same name of American psychiatrist, Robert Galbraith Heath, who was a proponent of conversion therapy and the belief that mental illness was a result of biological defects and could therefore be fixed. Granted, Rowling denies any relationship between her chosen pen name and the real-life psychiatrist, but the two facts—Rowling's pen name and the psychiatrist's—live in tandem in many people's minds now, and it's not a good look for her.

This is a betrayal for her fans, like me, who felt kinship with Harry precisely because they also felt different, unseen, othered, bothered because of class, race, or, most importantly for this conversation, gender.

This betrayal saddens me. But once the floodgates were open with this information, there was no going back for me. I started to look critically at those books—particularly the two central characters, Harry Potter and Lord Voldemort.

Rowling did a great disservice to Tom Riddle, the child Voldemort used to be. Just as the HBO writers of *Game of Thrones* did, Rowling writes Voldemort with an implied assumption that evil is both a product of upbringing and a family trait of "instability and violence."[4]

As someone who grew up with both mental illness and trauma, I have a hard time with that.

Tom, like Daenerys, had it rough. But unlike Daenerys, Tom's hardship didn't continue in near perpetuity—it's made clear to the reader that Dumbledore is there to save Tom, whether that's from a life as an orphan (which has its own problems, the othering of orphans and adoptees being just one of them) or from the path of evil, a direction that Tom is clearly already barrelling towards.

As a child, Tom experienced no love or kindness, and he subsequently created a hard exterior that formed a large part of his behaviour and personality. It is theoretically true that a child who is abandoned, neglected, or experiences abuse then carries a risk for this type of psychological protective system. But is evil a foregone conclusion? Can't we find a better way to tell these stories?

There's a lot about Voldemort that is problematic in my opinion, but what stands out to me the most—and what I feel so acutely—is his Horcruxes. In the Potterverse, a wizard can fracture their soul and embed it into an object, making it a Horcrux. Thus, the wizard cannot be killed unless the Horcrux is destroyed first. It's a way to achieve immortality, but it is also more than that: it is a "violation of nature"[5] to fracture one's soul, for, in order to do so, one needs to take a life. In the sixth book of the series, *Harry Potter and the Half-Blood Prince*, Harry learns that Tom most likely had already created a Horcrux during his time at Hogwarts. This would have made him

---

4   J.K. Rowling, *Harry Potter and the Half-Blood Prince* (Vancouver: Raincoast Books, 2005), 178.

5   Rowling, *Harry Potter and the Half-Blood Prince*, 413.

still just a child when he first killed, reinforcing the belief that evil like Tom is born, not created, that one has no agency over their own destiny. They simply must be who they were born to be. One cannot explore other possibilities.

Let's look even deeper.

A Horcrux is a container in which one puts a part of their soul and therefore embodies the essence of who they are. But it's not the *entirety* of their being, simply a part they need to keep safe. By the time Harry and Voldemort hash it out in the final book, Voldemort already has seven Horcruxes. He has therefore contained eight distinct and different aspects of himself. If one were to put this in diagnostic terms, it appears similar to dissociative identity disorder (DID).

Part of the criteria of DID includes "disruption of identity characterized by two or more distinct personality states, which may be described in some cultures as an experience of possession."[6] This experience of possession resembles the splitting of a soul, but rather than more than one split living in one body, the person—Voldemort in this case—places those splits into objects. *He* possesses *them*.

Regardless of the actual experience of folks living with the disorder, as I believe my mother did, DID is often used as a mechanism through which a villain's story arc is crafted, particularly in speculative fiction. This also makes me wonder if my mother never sought help because she felt shame from mainstream culture's treatment of her condition as villainous and irredeemable. The only thing my mother knew about mental illness growing up was that it was *bad*.

I find DID fascinating. The possibility of more than one personality inhabiting the same mind and body is . . . well, it's mind-blowing. That our brains can work in such a way as to split into different identities in

---

6   *Diagnostic and Statistical Manual of Mental Disorders: DSM-5* (Arlington, VA: American Psychiatric Association), 2017, 292.

order to protect the self once again reminds me of Dr. Judith Herman's work with trauma survivors and the fantasy stories and worlds those children created for themselves in order to survive. It's what I witnessed as a kid with my own mother. When I saw the little girl come out, I wondered how that could happen to someone. It didn't make sense to me that more than one person could live in one body. It sounded like stories I'd heard about demonic possession or pure evil instead.

Knowing what I know now, I also see how the story of DID was already framed to me as something that was malignant and evil. And that's simply not fair to my mother.

When I consider how dissociative identity disorder is characterized in fantasy—particularly the Harry Potter series—or in films like M. Night Shyamalan's psychological thriller *Split* (2016)—I wonder why evil is one of the first places to go when faced with the unknown. Why is the one who is split usually the evil one? It must have been scary for my parents that day when they came home from the bank, failing to renegotiate their mortgage. I think about how terrifying and also shameful that must have been for them: the weight of the responsibility of two children, two lives completely dependent on them, two mouths to feed, two small bodies to clothe, two people to love and guide and finally set out into the world to make a life of their own. And then to be told that, as parents and caregivers, they'd failed. Each time the phone rang, debt collectors on the other end, the doom my parents felt that our home would either crumble around us or be taken, must have been . . . *terrifying*.

I remember my mother desperately trying to curl into herself, back rounding, as she sat on the bed. I remember her sobs, the moans that she simply couldn't hold back. And then I remember when that changed. When her voice pitched just a little higher, her eyes becoming softer and wider, and it wasn't my mother looking at me anymore but someone else. A little girl.

And then I remember the silence after. It was as though it never happened.

Years later, I finally plucked up the courage and asked my mother if she knew she had another identity living inside her. "Yeah," she'd said. "I know I have multiple personalities. And I know it must have scared you kids."

But then when I asked her again later, she claimed she didn't remember saying that.

When I'm not dragged into the rot of the tower by the Sorcerer, or when the anger isn't brewing at the corners of my vision, slowly forming a Shadow, my time is filled with the dimpled boy; when he smiles at me, it feels like I'm resting in a bed of feathers. Sometimes, when we are standing at my locker at school, I will watch his hands and his fingers and they look like they could weave magic. His forearms feel like they could lift me out of the dark tower and finally show me what summer looks like. Even when he's talking to someone else, his blue eyes will always slide towards me. He feels like a lighthouse.

He asks to walk me home again, and I nod. When school lets out, he meets me at my locker, and we weave our way through the other kids in the halls and out towards the back of the school. He tells me he's glad he gets to spend time with me. I can see him blush. He says he likes my long, long hair and that I make him nervous. We've stopped walking, and I have no idea what he's just said to me because it doesn't make sense. I'm not that girl. I'm not the one who can turn the heads of sweet, cute boys with sweeps of blond hair and crystal blue eyes. I'm not the girl that a boy would want to spend his time with. I'm not the girl who makes a boy's palms sweat. I'm all wrong. I'm all tainted. I'm all broken.

But when he turns and I watch him looking down at me, the corner of his mouth pulled up in a smile, I think maybe I *could* be that girl. He asks, "Can I kiss you?" I nod and he steps closer, cups my cheek, and kisses me. It's not like anything I've ever experienced. It's sweet and tastes wonderful and my tummy is hurtling around my abdomen in a very excited and slightly uncomfortable way. I can hardly feel my fingertips, can hardly register my face. All I am is a receptor for the sensation of his mouth, and it doesn't feel wrong in any way.

He pulls away and continues looking down at me. "I wanted to do that a long time ago," he says shyly.

When I get home, my parents aren't there. The house is cloaked in grey and a voice snakes outwards, pulling me towards the tower and all the rot that lives in there: "What if I tell him how sick and disgusting you are? Do you think he'd want you then?"

The Sorcerer. I stop breathing. My mouth, tasting sweet gentleness just moments ago, twists. My nerves are flayed, on fire. "Fuck you," I spit. "Fuck you fuck you fuck you."

I drop my backpack, grip a knife that appears beside me, and launch myself towards him. I chase him as he screams and runs from me. He is afraid and runs into his library and slams the door shut. The tower is shaking with my fury. The swamp is bubbling. The stone is crumbling. I see nothing but rage, and I want to kill him. I want to slice him to shreds and watch as I raze his world to the ground. I bang at the door, hard and fast and loud. I scream and scream and scream and I can't stop. I don't want to stop. My voice is massive, and I remember raking my fingernails down that boy's small body all those years ago. I remember flipping my desk at school. I remember shrieking at my teacher. I remember the claw snaking out to cup my barely formed breast, and I become all rage. The Shadow is behind me now, fully formed and real and gripping my shoulders. It mirrors my violence, and I turn and kick backwards, my heel colliding with the shuddering door. I've dropped the knife because I don't need it. I will tear it all down with my bare hands.

My foot goes through the door. I hear wood splinter and feel it tearing at my sock. I stop, my body frozen, and look down at the knife on the floor. I breathe, one breath, two. I am numb. My consciousness has shifted a little outside myself, as though I am out of focus. I look at the Shadow, then the door and the hole the size of my heel, and I feel nothing.

"You're fucking crazy," the Sorcerer says.

"I hate you," I respond.

I turn, my Shadow and I, slow and shredded, walk out of the tower, and close the door behind me.

My mother doesn't really smile anymore. When she does, there's something different about it. She'll look out the window to the backyard now overgrown with weeds that have swallowed dreams that were never to come true, and her thin mouth curls up, her eyes empty. I think she might be angry, but I can't tell anger from bitterness anymore.

One day, my father tells me he has been meeting with people to help him with something called personal bankruptcy. I already know. I let him tell me, though, and I'm sure it's not easy for him to admit that he couldn't do what he thinks is expected of him. I watch my father as he admits a moment in his life that he considers a failure, and I wish we had the forest again. I wish my mother would read *The Lord of the Rings* to me again. I wish I could whisper into the trees and wait for the water sprites to visit me by the river. I try to be as good a daughter as possible because something is also happening to my brother and it's making my parents upset. He's in his bedroom all the time, and one day he demands to paint it black. My mother isn't okay with this, but he does it anyways. He's grown his hair long, and my mother calls it auburn and says he's handsome. My brother becomes good at smiling when he has an audience, but that smile is empty.

One day, my brother comes home past his curfew, and my mother is angry. He has dyed his hair black. It's a sheet of darkness that contrasts with his pale face. My father's mouth curls as he shakes his head and walks away from the gruesome sight of his son.

My brother resides in his cave of a bedroom, and I hear that angry music again that reminds me of zombies and screaming and pain, and that's what he reminds me of too. When my brother comes downstairs, ready to go out with friends, and is wearing tight black pants, a billowy shirt, fishnet stockings on his long fingers, and white face paint, my father says, "You look like a fucking faggot." I didn't know my dad could say things like that, but my brother tells him to go fuck himself, and I watch as he leaves the house, chasing the evil that he thinks he is.

I wonder if my brother has a Shadow too.

I try to fill the void that he is creating with his anger and bitterness by being as dutiful and good as possible, but it's becoming too big for me. I try to hide my Shadow, even as it constantly hovers behind me, holding my rage and loathing. But I can't let it out because our house is a sad cave and my mother sleeps a lot or argues with my brother, demanding to know why he's failing all his classes, and my father watches his World War II movies, and my brother continues to twist into something else. I can't add to that. I have to be the proper daughter, the one my mother says they never have to worry about. When she says that, she cups my cheek, whispering, "You're just what I wanted you to be." She doesn't see my clenched fists or the breath that I can't draw in.

I don't tell my parents that I'm failing my classes either. I'm not interested anymore and fall behind in my classwork. I wish I could sleep all the time. I don't want to make my mother frustrated. I want to make her proud and keep both my parents safe. I try to believe I can save them. I try to believe I can protect them and be who my mother wants me to be. Despite how angry I feel all the time. Despite how evil I know I am becoming.

My days are cut through by the bright light that is my new boyfriend. He likes to watch me sketch dragons and brags to his friends that his girlfriend is so talented. I struggle to keep my anger from him, but sometimes I'll sit in furious silence, the Shadow gathering in the corner of my bedroom, and I have no words to tell him how angry I am, so he will sit there, silent, too, wondering what he did wrong. This makes me even angrier until I tell him he has to go home now.

Sometimes, though, when I can't stop thoughts from flipping around in my head, we will curl up on my bed and he will whisper stories to me. I'll close my eyes and feel his arms around me and envision the stories he tells. But what I really want to do is tell him a story of a kid who, once upon a time, believed in dragons and magic but who is now corrupt and wrong and the dragons are fading away, consumed by the Shadow that is growing every day, consumed by their own brain that is starting to betray them.

I flunk calculus, and my mother is shocked. She doesn't get angry with me like she does with my brother, but one day someone from the guidance office comes into my class and pulls me out, saying I am going to spend the next few days with a psychologist to do some testing. I don't really think much about it. I've done testing like this before. Maybe the first test, all those years ago, was wrong. Maybe I am a screwed-up kid after all.

The psychologist is nice, and I complete a whole bunch of tasks like finishing sentences, finding concepts that match, shapes and numbers, puzzles and ideas and pictures. I try my best, but I think maybe I really am stupid because I stumble a lot. I don't want the other kids to see me in the guidance office with this psychologist because I don't want them to think I'm the stupid kid. I don't want to be the stupid kid again.

On my last day in the office, the psychologist asks me questions about my friends and feelings, my family and childhood. I tell her my parents are the best and we are so happy and "my brother is my best friend because he lets me hang out with his friends." I tell her about my golden boyfriend and that I don't have issues with trust. The lies come easy, silver rolling off my tongue. I am so good at lying now, and I know she believes me. I can see it on her face. The way she nods, the small smile when I tell her about walking in the forest with my dad or how my boyfriend likes my drawings and likes to tell his friends how talented I am. I don't tell her about my stories, though, or how, when I'm really angry with my mother, I'll rip them all up in front of her. I'll tear at my drawings, colourful and filled with life, and smile at her as she watches the pieces scatter on the floor, pain rippling across her face. I don't tell the psychologist that I relish in seeing that pain I cause my mother because I'm so angry with her.

No. I'm a good girl, I tell her. I'm happy, I tell her. Things are bright and wonderful and perfect, I tell her.

I'm really good at telling stories. Better than my mother knows.

I am sent back to class, and for a few weeks, nothing happens. I'm sure they forgot about me or maybe I'm not important enough for them to tell me about myself. But then I'm pulled out of class again and directed to the guidance office, where my mother and the psychologist and the guidance counsellor are waiting for me at a round table in the sunshine-bathed room. We sit down together, and the psychologist talks to my mom about me, and I sit and listen to the stories the psychologist weaves about my mother's daughter. My mother starts to smile, looking at me like I am the most beautiful creature in the world. Occasionally, her hand will flutter to her chest and she will say something like, "I knew she was bright, but I didn't know *that.*"

The psychologist explains to my mother what "percentile" means and how high her daughter is on that little chart with numbers that decides the complexities of my smartness. "There's nothing she can't do if she sets her mind to it," the psychologist tells my mother. "Life will be good, and with the continued support of a loving home, she will succeed."

My mother says, "We've always tried to encourage her at home. We know how important it is to guide our children the right way." She nods at her own statement, believing she's succeeding in her task.

I'm glad I'm smart. As I look at the graph of my smartness, I see how high I am and I want to be higher. I want to be so high on that chart that no one can touch me.

My marks skyrocket after that. I am top of my class, and I pay attention and I don't really have to try all that hard because I know I'm smart and that's the effort I need to put in: remembering that I'm smart. Remembering those numbers on the graph and that I sit near the top of the bar that towers over the others. I want to grow large like that, towering. I want to be the brightest tower in the world. I want to crush the earth with my light.

I wake up every morning, go to school, and do well in class. I've stopped eating, though, because I'm just not hungry. I don't bother with lunch; I simply don't think about it. My boyfriend has gradu-ated and is in college, and I'm starting to wonder why I'm with him. I want to cast everything aside and be the best because that feels like the only weapon I can wield to drive the encroaching Shadow away. I try to keep calm because my brother is always raging. I try to be good because my parents are already so hurt by life. But some-times I can't help it. Sometimes I just want to rage too. Sometimes I want to break out of my own skin and scream and scream and scream. I want to spin in circles and laugh so loud that everyone will see me. I want to smash and dominate, benevolent and terrifying.

The Sorcerer's swamp has seeped into my days, my mind. The tower pierces my thoughts. But then one day, the Sorcerer leaves his tower, enters my bedroom, the sunlight streaming through the window. It is the same as always, but this time, I hear a voice, "What are you doing?" and I see my mother standing there. She is frozen as she looks at me, and I hold my breath and look at the floor, wishing I weren't quite so naked and wanting to tell her that I never wanted this, that I don't know what to do. I want to beg her to please not be angry with me, please don't hate me, please, please, I don't know what to do.

"You're disgusting," she whispers. "Take a shower."

What my mother sees is never spoken of again. I know to speak it into life is wrong, but the silence is confirmation that *I'm* wrong, that *I'm* bad. We never speak of the weight that I am losing or that I'm not sleeping at night or that I now believe in the concept of evil and maybe I am that evil. I don't tell my mother that there is something about being evil that also excites me because I'm just so tired of being her golden girl with seashell ears all bathed in pink and sunshine. I'm tired because it's so hard to pretend. It's hard to remember that I was once my father's little helper. It's hard to remember that I am still just a girl because I'm starting to feel like something else.

My mother says my boyfriend isn't good enough for me and that he's not very smart. "His mother is trashy," she says, and I feel like I just don't want to hear any of this anymore. I hate when she talks about the people I love because her face arranges itself in such a way that I can't argue with her. I can't tell her that I think she's wrong because, in our house, she's right. She's always right. I hate that she's always right. Because of that, because of everything—the tower, the Sorcerer, the Shadow that I can see taking shape, hovering just over my shoulder, invisible to everyone else—I am going to explode. And I want to. So badly, I want to detonate.

One evening, after my boyfriend has left, I tell her about that hate. I tell her and my father that I'm tired of them. That I'm tired of everything. That I'm tired of this house that is crumbling, I'm tired of being poor, I'm tired of school. My voice is rising, and my anger is frothing over, and, before I know it, tears are falling and they make me so angry because I want to be terrifying, and terrifying is authoritative, and I'm so fucking tired of no one seeing me. I'm so fucking tired of my life not belonging to me, my body owned and judged and used. I'm tired of my parents not admitting what they already know: that something has been slowly destroying their golden sunshine of a girl. I let my voice rise because I simply can't help it. I yell at them that they've failed. I tell them that I hate them. I tell them that I want this whole fucking house to burn down. I tell them that they make me want to die.

And then I stop. I shut my mouth. *What have I done?*

"Sit down," my father says, and his voice is low and terrifying. His face is a sheet of white. My mother huffs. "Where on earth is this behaviour coming from?" as I sob on the couch, begging them to listen to me. Just listen. Hear me, hear my words.

"You will shut up," my mother says. "And you will behave."

I don't know what is happening. I feel out of control. "Please let me go to my room," I whisper, because I can't be here right now. I feel my anger expanding, and it's scaring me. I'm so scared.

But my father says, "You will keep your ass right there." I feel pressed down, crumpled, but still filled with rage. I want to leave. I want to run. I beg them to let me go. "I'm too angry. I can't control myself," I tell them through my tears, my body vibrating with hate. "I'm going to explode." I don't want to snap, but I'm too exhausted to hold back.

"Are you threatening us?" my mother says. "Is that some sort of threat?" I keep shaking my head over and over. No threat, Mom. Please, Mom. Please let me go. Please let me go. Please let me go.

I'm losing control.

My mother turns to my father, plants her hand on her hip, and says, "We need to have her committed."

With those words, my body slackens, my mind blanks. I hear her, but she's just a ringing in my ears now. Nothing they're saying makes any sense, but suddenly, none of it matters anymore. I slide out of myself, and I am no longer that girl. In my mind, that girl is gone, left rotting in the swamp. And I want to tear her up with my bare hands for her weakness, bury her so far down that no one will ever find her. I want to no longer be that weak, broken girl, so my lips curl, my brow arches, and I laugh a deep-throated laugh. I laugh at my parents. Because the most hilarious, intoxicating, eviscerating thing just happened: their daughter has died, and in her place there is nothing but the Shadow filled with evil.

And then, with a breath, the magic disappears, the elves sail into the west, the pantheon of gods fades to legend. The dragons lie down, wings slackening, and they close their eyes. Their fires burn low . . . low . . . low. Until they fade out.

I am gone.

CHAPTER 4

The Ghosts of These Empty Halls

I had abandoned my dragons. They curled up, tucked in their wings, and fell asleep in the deepest, darkest recesses of my rapidly crumbling mind. Once asleep, their scales—glowing and rippling, metallic—dulled to darkness. For a short while, I could still feel them breathing as they slept, the air billowing in their mighty lungs. I could still smell the smoke from their fire, could still feel the magic trickling through my skin, my veins, braiding itself with the alcohol, the drugs, the endless sleepless nights. And as the months slide by, I say two words to my golden boyfriend: it's over. I don't know why though. I don't know why it should be over except for the fact that I am no longer who he thought I was. Not that I ever was anyways, but now I'm not right, not normal. My mother says, "You're better off without him." I'm not sure why she says that, but maybe she's right. Maybe I'm better off alone. I have a few photos of him, and I ask her if she'll keep them for me, don't throw them away, but I don't want to see them. She nods quietly. "Of course," she murmurs.

I leave the house and begin my journey towards drowning in any illicit substance I can get my hands on. It feels like flying when I punch back shot after shot like gunfire. It pushes away the memory of the dark and rotting tower, the Sorcerer's hands and breath. I am with my Shadow now, wholly and completely. Now I discover the deliciousness of my body and what it can do to observing eyes as it beckons and fucks. What it can do to lips and mouths and skin while burying shame and anger and hate. I craft myself into a weapon, and it feels so good to cut.

And then, one day, I simply no longer believe. I no longer believe that those leviathan beasts ever existed. That the water sprites ever bathed in the river. That the fairies ever rose from the grass, twinkling in the hazy twilit air.

I no longer believe there was a swamp or a tower or a Sorcerer, who has now faded into the background of my memories, who made me do things to make him happy in exchange for books that could take me out of my grey life.

I've been accepted to every university I applied to. Some even want to give me money to attend, so I choose the one that will give me the most. The marks just swirl around me. I have aspirations of becoming amazing—whatever amazing is. I am climbing the mountain of my smartness, and I'll leave everyone behind. My mother prides herself in the daughter she has raised, knowing she, too, has succeeded in something.

I don't eat. I don't think about food. The pounds are sliding off me, and I like seeing my bones, watching my breasts shrink to almost nothing. It feels good to see my hips retreat to a time when I had none.

I move into university residence, and I feel a wall rising up. I'm not like the other students. They don't spend nights in heated sex with strangers. They have no nightmares. They aren't haunted. Their faces are bright and clean and fresh. And I realize I don't know how to make friends anymore. I tell my mother I can't make friends, and she says, "Well, people don't understand us. *I'm* just fine."

I return home for Thanksgiving weekend, and my parents are proud of me. My mother keeps calling me her bright girl in university. "If I had had the chance, I would have gone to university," she says. "But it's not that important anyways. People with degrees aren't really that smart." She waves it away, chin lifted, eyes narrowed. "It would have been a waste of my time. I had better things to do. Like raising you kids to be the amazing people you are and watching you go out into the world." She smiles at me.

I don't know what to say to that.

Then she says quietly, "If I could do it all over again, I'd never get married or be a mother."

I'm not allowed to be angry, so I ignore the rumbling in my chest.

My dad smiles at me like we could be friends. He offers to make gin martinis for us and shows me how. I memorize the exact volume of the ingredients, watch as he shakes the silver capsule. He smiles at me as he does so. The liquid pours out clear and bright. We drink, and I feel special. I go out that night alone with the intention of drinking more of these delicious gin martinis. I prepare my clothes, my face. I put on a mask of scent. I know how to dance, to move my body in just the right way. It's all I know anymore. I lean against the sticky bar, watch the light flashing across a dance floor, illuminating the throng of people like a movie reel of the silver screen. The music is a blanket. I drink. I drink some more. My body is filled with the silver liquor, filling veins that were once home for stories of dragons and magic.

A young woman walks up to me, chin held high, hooded eyes inspecting. Her chestnut hair is thick and curly. "Hi," she says. I nod. "You were in my physics class." I nod again. "Wanna dance?"

I smile at her. We join the music and flashing lights, and she throws her head back and laughs. Her drink spills over a hand that is so delicate. I can see her slim throat, and I'm sure mine isn't slim like that. She grins at me, and I wonder why she even wants to dance with me. We close the club, and she throws her arm over my shoulders and says, "We should get some food."

I come home from university on the weekends, and I spend my time with my new friend, going out every night if we can, stumbling back to her home in the small hours before dawn to make egg sandwiches. We wake up hungover and do it again. I spend more time with her than I do at home. One day my mother looks at me and says, "She's garbage. You can do better." My father's gaze doesn't meet mine.

My new friend starts an engineering program in university and tells me she's going to be doing a co-op placement. I won't see her much because she's moving to the city. I don't tell her I'm failing my classes. I don't tell her about the dirty things I do when she and I are not together or who I do them with. The early morning taxis, makeup smeared, smelling of someone else's cologne. Failing to remember names or faces. I stop going home on weekends, and snow falls. I'm scrambling. I'm spinning. I stop going to class.

One morning, I wake and there's no more colour. The vividness that was once my days has dulled to darkness and varying shades of grey. The air is thick and murky. My body is sludge. I can hardly breathe, but I wonder why I even bother breathing. What's the point of breathing? I slide out of bed, shower, and dress. I leave my dormitory and am confused as to why there are smiles on other students' faces. What are they smiling about? Why do they talk? Their voices are off-kilter. I can't understand what they're saying. I can't understand their bright, busy, and hopeful stress. I can't understand the concept of a future. I skip breakfast. I walk to class, and my footsteps make no mark in the freshly fallen snow. No one sees me pass. I am silent as I walk into the lecture hall. I sit at the back, a breeze of frigid air. I take no notes and decide there's no point in my being here. I leave and resolve not to return.

The following morning, I wake again. There's still no colour, but now the edges of my vision are blurs of objects. Lines aren't defined. I can't tell my desk from the window. My phone rings but it's not real. I can't remember when I last ate but then realize that it doesn't matter. I pull the covers over me and sleep some more.

The days smudge together, and the snow continues to fall. I don't hear from my new friend, and I know she's busy being smart and earning a future. I call her once, twice, but her voice is strained, and she says she needs to study. Exams come, and I don't take them. I fail every one of my classes. A letter arrives telling me my golden child scholarship, the gift for being all pink and bathed in sunshine, has been revoked. My tower is crashing.

I feel my Shadow pressing on me. It's a slight twinge, a tightening of my muscles. A dryness in my eyes, and I know I'm crumbling away. Like small bits of my body are flaking off, floating into nothing. One day, it's my fingernails. A few days later, the slough of skin is followed by chunks of hair on my pillow. My eyes begin to water, shrinking into a gelatinous mess until I can no longer see. Finally, I lose my mouth, my tongue, the flesh of my cheeks. I wake up a wraith. I float through the filmy days unnoticed. I feel a tightness around my neck. The haunting Shadow, lurking in the corners of my dormitory. It gnaws at my bones, demanding my attention.

I call my mom. She answers the phone, and I hear the fatigue in her voice. She asks me what's wrong. I say, "I don't know."

"How can you expect me to help you if you can't tell me what's wrong?" she says.

"I don't know."

There's silence.

"I'm sorry for bothering you," I whisper. She sighs and tells me to call her later. I place the receiver back in the cradle. The grip on my throat tightens, my shoulders curl in. I look to the mirror on the back of my dormitory door, and I can see it now, pulsating behind me. It's huge and misty and dark. Its claws squeeze my shoulders. It whispers in my ear. It weighs more than a black hole.

And I am a ghost.

I rise, walk to the door, and put my fist through the mirror.

I. THE HOUSE OF MENTAL ILLNESS

When I was really sick, I doubted my own mind. There were so many thoughts and elusive memories, and I could never be entirely sure what I was supposed to recognize, what was truth and what was my imagination. My memories were in tatters. My body was just a little bit not my own. My surroundings were just a little bit unreal. A deep, unending fog settled over me, and in that fog I fought and kicked, begging to be let out, to find some shore. I was trapped, looped into the fragments of time and memories fluttering around me. I was terrified to be alone in a house of my own mind. I'd open the rotting curtains, darkness and fog coating the leaded glass.

In the Netflix limited series *The Haunting of Hill House,* there is a Red Room, the room at Hill House where souls are trapped, a place that feeds on desperate needs. It's no surprise that gothic horror often explores the mind, removing the protagonist from anything that is safe and comforting, dropping them into a place—sometimes a deeply unsettling house—where they doubt their own experiences. It is just as I once was, in a house that existed in my mind.

Shirley Jackson's 1959 novel that the TV show is loosely based on, *The Haunting of Hill House*, is an acutely observant interpretation of psychology and trauma. It's a simple story that draws from themes that are similar to the ones in the works of Henry James and Edgar Allan Poe, in that Jackson not only isolates and disorients her protagonist, Eleanor Vance, but the reader as well. Neither Eleanor nor the reader is entirely sure what is truth and what is a manifestation of Eleanor's mind. Perhaps the truth *is* Eleanor's observations, whether they were generated from her mind or not.

New York Times bestselling gothic novelist Andrew Pyper told me that this fear "of losing one's mind in the gothic [is] really about encountering that which you least wish to encounter. In fact, that thing is often something a character has denied, or forgotten, or buried so deep that they aren't even consciously aware of it."[1] For me, that which I least wish to encounter is losing myself to mental illness. Feeling out of control is terrifying. Nell Crain, the central character in the TV show, describes this same fear to her siblings; she is afraid of those moments when time and memories "flutter around us, like confetti."[2] What she wishes to avoid is the sensation of never being really *here*, never being quite sane, and being completely separated from normalcy. Like Nell, I find this to be more frightening than ghostly jump scares, and that's something that *The Haunting of Hill House* digs into brilliantly.

If these ghost stories are taken as a metaphor for the psychological, the fear that I've experienced lies within myself, in the fear of losing my mind, in the things that I have kept buried but are still fundamental traumas that, for better or worse, define a big part of who I am. It's a fear of the ghosts that wander the halls of our own minds. Sometimes, in gothic horror, the viewers are asked to walk alongside the mentally ill, the ones who are afraid, who may very well know that they are fated to also become ghosts walking the empty halls alone.

In that vein, Jackson sets the stage for these themes with the introduction of Hill House itself:

> Hill House, not sane, stood by itself against its hills, holding darkness within; it had stood so for eighty years. Within, walls continued upright, bricks met neatly, floors were firm, and doors were sensibly shut;

---

1   Andrew Pyper, email message to author, October 26, 2021.

2   *The Haunting of Hill House*, episode 10, "Silence Lay Steadily," directed by Mike Flanagan, featuring Victoria Pedretti, Kate Siegel, and Henry Thomas, aired October 12, 2018, on Netflix, https://www.netflix.com/ca/title/80189221.

silence lay steadily against the wood and stone of Hill
House, and whatever walked there, walked alone.[3]

A house that lives of its own accord, trapping souls within its
walls. Perhaps a red door beyond, a room designed solely to keep its
occupants unaware that they are slowly being consumed.

Gothic horror does exactly this: it consumes, slowly and in a way
that gently, horrifically, eases the participant into an oleander-wreathed
trap. If looked at just slightly askew, through the filmy leaded glass window, gothic horror could be allegorical for the betrayal of one's brain:
the slow immersion into mood swings, like a long, seemingly endless
hall; departures from reality, the haunting thoughts and racing heart that
come from getting lost in a maze of corridors and darkened rooms. The
feeling of falling forever into an obscured and deceptive snare, unseen
and unheard. It takes the lonely, the sensitive, and the imaginative and
places them in an environment that borders the possibilities of reality.
It's about the feeling of becoming caught in mental illness, and, to be
honest, it still scares me. That maze-like mind of mental illness is one of
the most frightening places I've ever been.

While Jackson's main character, Eleanor Vance, is iconic in horror
literature, director Mike Flanagan's 2018 iteration has received critical
and mass acclaim, and not just because of its storytelling or how it steps
away from the usual ghostly scares, instead delivering a deeply unsettling haunting experience. It's because of how it tackles mental illness.
The series confronts mental illness with a disarming directness, compassion, and a deep, nuanced understanding. Flanagan departs from
the traditional trope of gothic horror that often uses mental illness as
a scare vehicle, diverging from films like *The Woman in Black* (2012)
and *Mama* (2013). *Mama* features the ghost of the deceased mentally ill

---

3   Shirley Jackson, *The Haunting of Hill House* (New York: Penguin Books, 1959), 1.

mother who was apprehended because her illness rendered her unable to parent. The story briefly features a near-crumbling and terrifying asylum in which Mama (whose name is actually Edith) had been institutionalized, abused, and neglected. Regardless of her treatment in the asylum, Mama is cast as "insane," capable of violence, underscoring the trope that a woman who struggles to mother her child is the ultimate wrong. When she finally dies by suicide, her insanity is both her punishment and the main threat in the movie. Simply put, her inability to mother is framed as evil, and madness is the vehicle with which that evil is delivered.

While Olivia, the Crain family matriarch, experiences madness and then, subsequently, because of that madness, struggles to be the parent her children need, the story makes it easy to sympathize with her. She's not the evil villain. Silence and neglect are.

The narrative of Flanagan's *The Haunting of Hill House* revolves intimately around the Crain family of seven and occurs over two timelines, with each character given their own story arc in both: the summer that the young Crain family lived in Hill House, and the present where each now-adult family member lives with the trauma of that summer—literal hauntings, psychological torture inflicted by ghosts, and, ultimately, the suicide of their mother. This past trauma is both a shared one and an individually isolating one. In both the past and present, the entire family orbits around one another without, it seems, ever really touching one another's worlds. The family includes patriarch, Hugh Crain; mother, Olivia Crain; eldest to youngest siblings, Steven, Shirley, Theo, and twins, Luke and Nell (full name Eleanor, named after the protagonist of the novel). Familiar sibling dynamics are reflected in the eldest, Steven Crain, and his incessant need for rationality, responsibility, and success. He rolls his eyes at Nell's ongoing challenges, scoffs at the idea of ghosts (and that their family has been traumatized by them), and harbours deep resentment towards their father for hiding the truth about what happened to Olivia. He's also really great at ignoring Nell's mental health crisis, oblivious that his father performed the same avoidance with their mother, mirroring the stigma that becomes a theme in the family.

In contrast, Nell is the epitome of the childlike innocence that Steven scoffs at: doe-eyed with wonder and fragility, she is the one who isn't seen, often overlooked by her four siblings. She is innocently relentless in her hope for their family to find harmonious balance together, and when her mental health crisis is at its most dangerous, she naively calls her oldest siblings with the belief that they will help, despite their history of silence around the same issues their mother faced. They ignore her calls.

My own trauma is also linked with intergenerational silence. It's both clear and difficult for me to see these dynamics between Hugh and Olivia, and Steven and Nell. Hugh and Olivia feel similar to my own parents, my father minimizing my mother's mental health challenges, hoping that simply not talking about it at all will fix it. It's so very easy for that mentality to slide down a generation. All it might have taken is one additional missed call combined with years of dismissal, and I could have been Nell, destined to walk with the ghosts of my own haunted mind.

When the family is young and living in Hill House, Nell is mostly unseen by her father and, during the events of her mother's mental health crisis, she is pushed to the background. Even when little Nell tearfully tells her father that she is haunted by a ghost, the Bent-Neck Lady, Hugh Crain brushes Nell's fears away.

Despite there being seven family members, there are eight characters. The first character, and the one that spins the entire Crain family into motion, is the house itself—the embodiment of mental illness. Both

Jackson and Flanagan introduce Hill House as an entity with a psyche, almost living and breathing. In both the novel and the show, Hill House is described as having a consciousness, one that is "not sane." Olivia Crain even says the structure of Hill House is "schizophrenic."[4] In episode ten, "Silence Lay Steadily," Nell says the house is a living creature, one that has organs, eyes, bones, a heart, and a stomach that consumes and digests (as stomachs do). It's the stomach that is the infamous Red Room, the one that lures in its victims, offering them a place of peace and solace curated especially for each individual family member. But once inside, the Red Room slowly consumes them.

Despite the show being labelled horror, there really isn't a traditional antagonist of *The Haunting of Hill House*, but rather a set of circumstances that creates the perfect storm for one family's fate. If Hill House is a stand-in for mental illness, can it even be considered an antagonist in the classic, unrepentantly evil sense? Maybe mental illness only becomes an antagonist when ignored, when unseen, as happens to Olivia. Maybe the perceptions of mental illness, and, by extension, the mentally ill, have been perpetually narrativized as an unknown and therefore scary Other. In Flanagan's interpretation of mental illness and trauma, he doesn't speak around this uncomfortable topic, but rather addresses perceptions of mental illness through use of metaphor and, on occasion, even head-on storytelling, particularly with how Steven Crain views his mother and youngest sister. As an adult, Steven often reiterates his belief that it's been mental illness that's haunted the family all those years. And he's not wrong in that, despite there being ghosts as well. The ghosts *are* mental illness.

These are the main themes of *The Haunting of Hill House*: silence, neglect, denial, and misunderstanding. These are familiar themes for

4 Flanagan, "Silence Lay Steadily."

those who live with mental illness, including me. These are what take the lives of Olivia and Nell Crain.

These are also what nearly took my own life all those years ago.

I watch the watery light pool on the linoleum floor, cut into perfect squares from the mesh on the window. It slides across the floor with the ticking of time. I'm cold, lying on this strange bed, draped in these strange blankets, in this strange place. There's no warmth here.

The room is rectangular. There is no furniture but the bed that I'm lying on and a chair in the corner. The doorless doorway is at my feet, and I see a man in a bathrobe shuffle by, glancing my way. He stops, looks at me, continues on. Comes back, stops. A voice sternly tells him to keep moving. He tells the voice to fuck off. The voice tells him they don't want to have to remove his privileges.

I remain quiet. I don't want to have my privileges removed. Although I don't know what my privileges are or why privileges are necessary. But I know why I'm here, and nothing is the same anymore. I'm not the same anymore. The exact colour of the sunlight filtering through the mist outside isn't the same anymore. The idea of me isn't the same anymore. I don't even know what that idea is, or if I exist, or if this is real.

A petite dark-haired woman appears at the doorless doorway. She has a cart with her that is filled with trays of empty vials, packaged medical tools. "Morning, honey. I need to take some blood," she says.

I unearth my arm from the blankets and glance down. I am now aware of the dull throb from the tiny holes that have been punched in it. I look at the purple bruising in the crux of my elbow, the tender flesh of my wrist. A spot of blood is crusted there. "From where?" I mumble.

She enters, dragging the cart behind her. "Oh, honey, I'm really good at this." I want to believe her, but her attempt at sincerity feels too saccharine. She slaps on some gloves and swabs the aching flesh of my arm. I don't want any more blood taken. I don't want any more medications pumped into me. I don't want to be looked at like I'm a selfish, spoiled girl. I run my tongue over my dry lips and taste the remnants of charcoal. I'd barfed up so much charcoal. After each bedpan I filled, another was thrust under my nose.

Do you want me to shove a tube down your throat?

The nurse fills a vial with my thick dark blood. She clips on another vial. And another. I think about asking her why she needs so much of my blood, but I really don't care.

She pulls out the needle, removes her gloves with a snap, smiles at me again, and leaves. I look back to the floor and the slices of light. I glance up to the window covered with a cage of perfect squares. The green outside is deep and rich, the water running rivers down the window. It reminds me of the forests with my father. There's an ache in my chest that has been growing. I want it to stop, but I'm too tired to fight it. Nothing is right. I'm not right. My brain is broken, and my body isn't mine. It belongs to the Shadow now. All of me belongs to the Shadow.

I see the man shuffle into my view again. He wiggles his fingers at me in a coy wave. I don't wave back. "It's my fourth time here," he tells me. "I got a VIP pass."

I wonder if I'll get a VIP pass. I hear the voice again telling the man to keep moving or he'll have to go to his room. I turn over, a taste in my mouth like metal shards, and look at the concrete wall beside me.

I'm not a girl anymore. I'm not human anymore. I know I almost died. I could see it on the doctor's face—the way his brows stitched together, the set of his mouth. My mom was angry that the police brought me into the hospital instead of an ambulance. She was angry that I waited so long in the emergency room. She was angry with all the pills I'd swallowed, one after the other, like little soldiers marching off to war. I have sticky spots on my chest where the monitors kept track of my fluttering, dying heart. My wrist hurts where the doctor pulled my acidic blood from my arteries, my pH dropping from all those little soldiers, one by one, fighting to free me.

I hear raised voices, a shriek. A woman is upset. She's moaning. Moaning like my mother did that day when they came home from the bank. I wonder if she is a ghost as well. I wonder if anyone can see her. I wonder if she will fade too.

The man shuffles past my doorless doorway again, and I hear the voice tell him to go to his room. I reach out and trace my finger along the seam between the concrete blocks and wonder how many empty ghosts have walked these empty halls. I wonder if I will remain here forever.

II. MENTAL ILLNESS AS A METAPHORICAL GHOST

There's comfort in the illusion that we have full control over our decisions and behaviours; that these behaviours, thoughts, and actions belong to us and therefore, we are solely responsible for and in control of ourselves. This makes sense, and it is an assumption around which we have created everything, from understanding relationships both with each other and with our belief systems—our psychological world schema. How we view ourselves in relation to others is based on this schema, as are fundamental beliefs such as our individual values, perceptions of others, and sense of self. So, any irregularity in these expected behaviours and beliefs contradict what we know to what we know to be normal. Despite living with mental illness for over two decades, I still have a hard time wrapping my head around the fact that sometimes my own mind is out of my control. I have to remember that there is nothing wrong with who I am, but rather my mental illness has created a set of circumstances that make normalcy impossible (whatever normalcy actually is). Is that my fault? No, but still, in my own mind, there's room for blame. I stigmatize myself. As my mental illness took root, wrapped up as I was in self-blame, who I was became unseen and unheard, and I walked through my life as though I were a ghost in the mist, filled with shame and self-loathing.

When I watch Nell Crain try to explain how she feels to her father and siblings, before she returns to Hill House and is consumed by mental illness, her description is alarmingly on-point, and it's a bit difficult to watch simply because it hits a little too close to home. "Everything's twisted,"[5] she tells Steven in a voicemail—a call not received—in the middle of the night as she sits in a motel room on her way back to Hill House where it all began. By the time Nell speaks with her father, Hugh can hear in her voice the danger she's in. Even though his daughter says it's okay and to go back to bed, that she's sorry for waking him, he knows that the house is coming to claim her, just like it did Olivia two decades ago when she lost her life. Hugh finally hears Nell and launches into action.

This is a father-daughter dynamic that I wish I'd had, but my own father found my mental health crisis confusing. He had no access to tools that could help me, but neither, I think, did he want to acknowledge what was happening to me. To him, the decisions I made or didn't make were baffling and nonsensical. I can't blame people for not being able to understand the lack of choice that mental illness presents, in the same way that I can't blame my father for not realizing that I had no agency in what was happening to me. But still, it makes forgiveness difficult, both in forgiving myself and my father.

In his book *On Monsters: An Unnatural History of Our Worst Fears*, Stephen T. Asma argues that we have "used magical means to resolve

5   *The Haunting of Hill House*, episode 1, "Steven Sees a Ghost," directed by Mike Flanagan, featuring Victoria Pedretti, Kate Siegel, and Henry Thomas, aired October 12, 2018, on Netflix, https://www.netflix.com/ca/title/80189221.

the contradictions of life."[6] It makes sense then that something as contradictory as abnormal behaviours that are difficult to understand would be met with a "magical means," whether that's magic as we know it in fantasy or in a ghost story like *The Haunting of Hill House*. To reconcile this, the Crains and the viewers are offered an explanation— ghosts and a haunted house—for something as seemingly inexplicable as Olivia's serious mental illness and suicide and, later, the ripple effects it has on the entire family.

Nell, the most tragic character of the show, is never truly seen. As a child, she is relentlessly haunted by a ghost, the Bent-Neck Lady. But when she tries to explain it to her father, it seems like Hugh chalks it up to childish fantasy, giving her a well-meaning yet patronizing smile. His denial of what happens that particular summer in Hill House is as much a persistent haunting as the ghosts that haunt them. Nell is a metaphorical ghost among her family. Until, inevitably, she literally becomes one.

III. THE NIGHTMARE

I don't remember when the night terrors started, I just remember how they made me feel. Sometimes I'd dream of asteroids hitting the earth; the last thing I'd see was the fiery rock plummeting towards me just as I'd wake. Other times, my dreams would be filled with dried up oceans, whale bones scattered among cliffs of grey reefs. Empty dust of what was once life. I'd wake gasping, trying to unblock my mouth so I could finally, finally scream.

When I was *really* sick, the night terrors became something else entirely. They coalesced into one thing, one entity, a smokey darkness

---

6   Stephen T. Asma, *On Monsters: An Unnatural History of Our Worst Fears* (Oxford: Oxford University Press, 2009), 197.

that would fill the shadows of my room. I'd hear the whisper as it slowly ascended the stairs, feel the heavy air as it turned the corner, and I'd watch, paralyzed, as it would appear to shrink under my doorframe, slide into my room, and expand again. Slowly, it would grow, reaching out a vaporous arm towards me as it slid closer to my bed where I lay, unable to move, my voice caught in my throat. My Shadow.

When I finally would be able to move, I'd be too terrified to reach to turn on the light. But I would, eventually, the darkness retreating, the asteroids halting, the oceans filling, once again, with salty water.

The last time this night terror happened, I wondered what exactly it was that I was afraid of. Was I afraid that this thing would kill me? Afraid it would take my soul, dragging me into another dimension— the Upside Down, as described in the sci-fi Netflix series *Stranger Things*? Or would it drag me to hell—a trope that has been entrenched in paranormal horror for decades. I can understand why these narratives can be so popular; being controlled and rendered immobile, with no ability to make your own choices, is far more terrifying than death.

Nell Crain's sleep paralysis begins when she is just six years old. After just having moved into Hill House, Nell wakes to find the dark form of a woman standing at the end of her bed, neck bent unnaturally. This apparition terrifies Nell, and her screaming wakes her parents. Her father, Hugh, tells her about dream spillage: that sometimes night terrors are so strong that they appear to spill into our real world for just a moment. This is a chilling and loaded statement, a double-edged sword, both explaining and dismissing Nell's fear. But what Hugh doesn't know is that this first visitation foreshadows Nell's fate. This apparition is a ghost of the future, the ghost of Nell's inevitable mental illness coming to claim her.

The Bent-Neck Lady returns to Nell that same night, hovering over a paralyzed and terrified Nell. This is the first time Nell experiences sleep paralysis: a not-so-uncommon condition where an individual is temporarily unable to move right as they're falling asleep or waking up. The person is always aware during the process, which often involves hallucinations, the sensation of suffocating, and, for some, a deeply disturbing terror.

For millennia, the only explanation for sleep paralysis and nightmares in general was a supernatural one, usually involving a malevolent force: a demon or evil spirit. One look at Swiss artist Henry Fuseli's 1781 oil painting *The Nightmare*, and the possibility of nocturnal supernatural forces becomes horrifyingly real and relatable. *The Nightmare* depicts a sleeping woman draped in pale cloth. A demon is sitting on her chest while a dark horse—the night*mare*—peers at her from behind an ochre-coloured curtain. Some interpretations of this piece include the incubus: a male demonic presence that saps sexual energy. Other interpretations, however, include a state of sleep paralysis, nightmares, and night terrors. It's this interpretation that I find most fascinating.

Author Christina Myers experienced her first episode of sleep paralysis in her late teens while she was backpacking through Europe with her friend. They had been staying in a house on an island that she described as dark and cold, when, in the middle of the night, she awoke feeling frozen and "like there was a weight on me." She speculates that the stressors of an unfamiliar and slightly unnerving environment might have been the catalyst for her first sleep paralysis episode.

Since then, she experienced episodes of sleep paralysis between two and three times a year, often accompanied by what she describes as lucid dreams. Sometimes during these lucid dreams, she sees a giant spider, sometimes a shadow in the corner of her room. In those moments, she is sure that whatever it is she's seeing is real. That there's "somebody in the room, in the shadows."

> That part is more terrifying than not being able to move
> or not being able to speak . . . And yet, I'm also aware
> that I'm not asleep. Sometimes you have really wild,
> scary dreams, but there's some little part of you that is
> like, "Oh, I'm having a dream." But in these instances,
> it's so real, and it's in the space that I'm in . . . I'm aware
> in my room and there is something there.[7]

It's hard not to believe that *something* isn't something *else.* Something malevolent. And it's not surprising that, for many, a paranormal explanation is the most reasonable one. I can't blame those who lean on that explanation at all.

One woman I spoke with—she asked me to keep her name private, so I'll call her Rachel—experienced her first episode of sleep paralysis when she was a preteen. "I would mentally wake up, but my body would be completely frozen." During these episodes of hovering between sleeping and waking, Rachel also experienced auditory and tactile hallucinations. At one time, it was a cat hissing in her ear and raking its claws down her back. At other times, she said, "it felt like something was trying to get in my body."[8]

Sleep disturbances aren't unusual in Rachel's family. While he doesn't experience sleep paralysis, Rachel's brother has night terrors so extreme that sometimes he will injure himself. I wondered if there was something there, this commonality between Rachel and her brother. They both grew up in a violent home where they often experienced fear. When she and I spoke, she contemplated that maybe the feeling of being trapped, of not being in control of her own body was a manifestation of how trapped and vulnerable she felt growing up.

---

7   Christina Myers, phone call with the author, October 27, 2021.

8   Rachel, phone call with the author, October 27, 2021.

While there is no certainty there, it does give pause. Maybe Nell Crain shares that commonality. Maybe I do too.

IV. HORROR GIVES US A VOCABULARY

In an essay for *This Magazine*, Dr. Adam Pottle makes a compelling argument for the values of horror and how they assist in processing themes and events that are nearly impossible to unpack: "Horror has always been a marginalized genre, a misunderstood, even reviled vehicle dismissed as a disgusting, juvenile playpen for amateur talents." He's right; quite often it is. And there is some horror out there that truly should be reviled, just like exists in any other genre. But when deconstructing our fascination with horror, Pottle says we need to ask ourselves what it is we are afraid of in the first place. Horror films "not only frighten us; they enlighten us by giving us vocabulary that allows us to articulate—and therefore confront—our fears."[9]

This is what narratives like those told within the walls of Hill House give us: a way to confront that which is terrifying—in this case, isolation and the inability to trust our own minds, as personified by Nell in particular. These stories give us a safe way to interrogate our own beliefs, particularly those about mental illness. But why do so many people find these stories of mental illness twinned with the paranormal so *terrifying*? Why is mental illness the haunting *and* the haunted Other? Why are the allegorical narratives we create ones of haunting and ghosts and shadowy demons lurking in the corners of our rooms, and why are they so ubiquitous? In particular, folklore that features both sleep and mental illness spans through both time and geography.

---

9   Adam Pottle, "How Horror Helps Us Overcome Our Fears," *This Magazine*, February 26, 2020, https://this.org/2020/02/26/how-horror-helps-us-overcome-our-fears/.

I can't say that ghosts don't technically exist. Maybe belief makes them exist. But they are also manifestations of something we weren't able to explain for a long, long time. Some believe that ghosts truly exist on their own as the cause of these experiences, whether the experiences are psychological or physical. For others, they are representative of something else, something harder to explain, lurking underneath. Nell Crain is perhaps doubly haunted, both by the real Bent-Neck Lady and the mental illness that the ghost foretells.

When the tattered Crain family finally abandons Hill House in the middle of the night, Nell's Bent-Neck Lady still appears to her in other locations, reminding her that she can never truly be rid of her ghosts. When Nell meets the love of her life, Arthur Vance, the Bent-Neck Lady and the accompanying sleep paralysis seem to disappear. Nell is happy. She's safe and loved and sure of her future. Her husband also hears and sees and believes her. To him, Nell is not a ghost.

When I watch the scenes with Nell and her love, Arthur, I understand her feeling of safety and acknowledgement. When she is with him, I also see her confidence. It took me a long time to lean into that feeling in my own life, to allow someone else to help me carry the weight I always feel. A partner, loving and respectful, helped me keep my own Bent-Neck Lady away.

But unlike my story, it's already been made clear that Nell's is a tragic one. Just months after Nell and Arthur's wedding, Nell's new husband dies suddenly of an aneurysm, and the Bent-Neck Lady returns. Nell's fate is thrust once again into motion.

In episode five, "The Bent-Neck Lady," the identity of this apparition that has haunted Nell for two decades is finally revealed. Nell, now a grieving widow and having slipped into a full mental health crisis, returns to Hill House to face her past. The house pulls her in, luring her with visions of hope and happiness and the ability to be seen by her (ghostly) family. She dances alone in the crumbling, empty halls of Hill House, a look of calm on her innocent face. The statues watch her twirl by. When she is drawn to the uppermost floor, she unknowingly wraps a noose around her neck, still believing in the bliss that is possibility. She only becomes afraid when she realizes she's stepped over the ledge, her slippered feet desperate to keep her from falling as they scramble at the ledge. Behind her, the ghost of her mother watches. The house watches. Her *fate* watches.

Nell slips. She hangs. She continues to fall through time and memories, witnessing moments in her life, neck broken and passing into death as time breaks apart around her. She drops in front of her past self, just hours ago, screaming as she witnesses her own terror reflected back at her. She falls again and sees a broken and traumatized Nell trying to help her twin brother enter rehab. She falls again, this time hovering over her dead husband while her past self is frozen in bed, witnessing the horror. Again, she falls, floating over a six-year-old Nell. Again and again and again she falls, scattered through the schizophrenic time that is Hill House. She sees no loving memories, no moments filled with sunshine. Only pain. Mental illness does that, and sometimes I hate it for that.

The scene cuts as the Bent-Neck Lady screams. It becomes clear that the Bent-Neck Lady is Nell herself, her neck snapped, the ghost of her future that has now become her present. Like her mother, Nell Crain never stood a chance. She now walks the ghostly halls of Hill House, bound forever in her own shattered mind, trying to pull shards of time and consciousness together.

And there, in the abandoned halls of Hill House, she walks alone.

I take a meal in my room, brought in on a brown plastic tray. There are scrambled eggs, two pieces of toast, a tiny square of butter, orange juice, and coffee. The nurse tells me I can only eat in my room this one time. After that, I have to eat with the rest of them. I wonder who the "rest of them" are, and I'm not sure I want to eat with anyone or why I can't eat here on the bed. From their enclosed station, I know the nurses can see me, but I never see them look my way.

I glance at the tray and before the nurse gets to the doorless doorway, I say, "Can I have a fork, please?" She looks at me over her shoulder and shakes her head. "No forks."

"I won't stab my eyes out," I mutter.

The eggs taste a little too yellow. The toast doesn't taste like bread. The orange juice hurts my throat. I can't get the metallic taste out of my mouth. I eat anyways. When I'm done, I push the tray to the foot of my bed and fist the covers under my chin. I need to pee, but I don't want to leave this room. I wait. For what, I don't know. But still, I wait. Time collapses, and I begin to wonder why I'm here. I see the shuffling man again; I hear the television from the far room where I'm supposed to eat and be friendly and social and invisible.

I want a shower. I can't remember when my last shower was. I run my fingers through my hair. They come back grainy. Quietly, I slide out of bed. The floor is cold on my bare feet. The sun is hiding behind the mist. I look at the caged window again and wonder why there is even green grass outside. Why do they keep perfectly healthy trees? It's a lovely Band-Aid, a coat of living paint to hide the ghosts inside.

I leave my room, stand outside the doorless doorway, and look at the enclosed nurses' station. I see one of them look up from a magazine, glance at me, then look back down again. I walk to the locked door of the nurses' station and wait. I'm sure they know I'm here. I don't want to be a nuisance. I want to get out of here, so I have to be sweet and gentle and docile and not at all myself.

There are two nurses seated inside the glass-enclosed room. Three of its walls are covered with the same wire squares as the window in my room. I wonder when they decided metal nets were necessary.

I wait. My feet are cold. I lift my hand, give a small wave. One of them looks up at me, then back down again, saying something to the other nurse. I wait another moment and wonder if maybe I'm not supposed to be here. Maybe this isn't how things are done. Or maybe I'm just see-through. They continue talking. I look back to my doorless doorway. *My* doorless doorway. I've already settled my sense of self within these concrete walls.

The gate opens, the nurse looks at me, says nothing, brows arched. I say, "I have to pee." She nods, closes the gate again, and I wait. She says something one last time to the other nurse, plucks keys from a desk, and leads me to a room with a door across from my own. She unlocks it and ushers me inside. The bathroom is all white. White tiles checker the walls and floor. There are no hard edges. Everything is rounded and set into the wall. The mirror over the sink is brushed steel, and my reflection is pale, wobbly, and worn-down. There is no curtain over the shower. There are no towel racks. Nothing I can hang myself with or smash my head on. I look at the drain in the middle of the floor as I pee. The world outside has dissolved into a memory.

I finish my business, and when I open the door, the nurse is standing outside. I feel the need to tell her that I'm done as though I'm a pet who needs to paw at the back door to be let inside. I hear voices coming from the TV room. I want to go that way, but I'm afraid if I do, I'll be one of them, one of the ghosts. I don't want to be a ghost. I look back the other way towards my doorless room. It's quiet. The sunlight isn't rivering across the floor anymore from the tiny window. I still want a shower, but I don't want to knock on that glass capsule again. I crawl back into bed, pull the scratchy covers over me again, and sleep.

V. I WAS RIGHT HERE, AND YOU DIDN'T SEE ME

The thing about many ghosts is that the horror is in their lack of awareness. All they know is the trauma of their own passing, to be lived over and over. Their sense of self shifts to a moment, a sliver of time, and in that time, they fade, wandering the hallways between the land of the living and the place of the afterwards. They find themselves invisible, and that invisibility is terrifying. Being left behind while the world continues on—while loved ones continue on—without them is a horror unto itself.

I remember the first night I tried to make myself permanently invisible. I remember feeling alone, and facing that aloneness was like staring down a stone well with only darkness looking back up at me. I couldn't trust my past and who it was making me into. I couldn't rely on a future that I knew didn't exist. I only had the now and, during those days and those long, long nights, the now extended forever. An endless, sleepless midnight of wandering, alone and invisible. The only way through, I thought, was to take my own life.

I wonder if that is a feeling common among folks who have tried or succeeded in taking their own lives. For those people who are facing whatever mental unwellness or life circumstance that has driven them so far down into that well, is it only darkness they feel, an unrelenting darkness that is coming up to collect them? Maybe this is why I love a good ghost story so much. Perhaps it's why I want to like the ghosts the most. I know the feeling, and even decades later, I still remember what it was like to be invisible.

There's a loneliness to mental illness. To being different. And yet, so many of us *are* different. Why then are we so lonely?

The night before Nell's funeral, together with Hugh, the family argues over her coffin and eventually the conflict becomes about her death and how such a tragedy could possibly happen. As a storm rages outside, they ask, *Didn't Nell know the consequences of taking her own life? Why did she not reach out? Who among us is guilty of neglecting her? Who is to blame? Why did she feel like she couldn't talk to us?*

The story then returns to six-year-old Nell, during a similar storm at Hill House, while the family gathers in the foyer. The Crain children are afraid, but Steven, ever the big brother, tries to console his scared younger siblings. Busy trying to remain calm and fix the power outage, the Crain family doesn't notice that Nell has disappeared. Olivia and Hugh search the house for her, but Olivia's own haunting—her mental illness—is beginning to consume her as well, and it seems the family forgets what they are trying to do in the first place: find Nell.

Near the end of the episode and as the storm passes by, the family returns to the foyer to find Nell standing there, sobbing. "I was right here, I was screaming for you, but you didn't see me," she tearfully says. "You didn't see me, and I was right here."[10]

The scene returns to the funeral home, Nell's coffin, and her siblings still not understanding how Nell could disappear yet again. As her twin walks away from her coffin, Nell's ghost—the Bent-Neck Lady—watches, crying, as six-year-old Nell's voice can be heard— *You didn't see me. I was right here, and you didn't see me.*

You didn't see me.

Nell has always been a ghost. But was it the house that took her or was it the invisibility of mental unwellness? Maybe it was both. Maybe to be consumed by Hill House is to be made invisible, fated to walk alone, begging to be seen. I can't deny that's what it's like to live with mental illness, to navigate one's way through a mental health crisis.

Shirley Jackson's novel concludes where it began:

---

10   *The Haunting of Hill House*, episode 6, "Two Storms," directed by Mike Flanagan, featuring Victoria Pedretti, Kate Siegel, and Henry Thomas, aired October 12, 2018, on Netflix, https://www.netflix.com/ca/title/80189221.

> Within, walls continued upright, bricks met neatly,
> floors were firm, and doors were sensibly shut; silence
> lay steadily against the wood and stone of Hill House,
> and whatever walked there, walked alone.[11]

Tragedy is to walk alone, a ghost of the empty halls. Tragedy is in the unavoidable. Tragedy is a word we use for not knowing what we could have done in the first place. It's helplessness.

In Flanagan's iteration, however, there is a fundamental difference: he makes a final connection between the haunting of Hill House and the Crains, how the perception of mental illness has changed for both the Crain family members and (hopefully) the viewers. Oldest sibling and previously staunch denier of the paranormal, Steven, voices over a pan shot of the house, now empty, wreathed in mist and foreboding. In his voice, there is the acknowledgement of the Crain family trauma, the loss and grief, but also a deeper understanding of the complexities and that a haunting can be literal or metaphorical. And sometimes it's both—

> Within, walls continued upright, bricks met neatly,
> floors were firm, and doors were sensibly shut; silence
> lay steadily against the wood and stone of Hill House,
> and whatever walked there, walked *together*.[12]

Steven's acknowledgement of his sister's and mother's fates, unfortunately, comes too late. It's this latter, delayed part of tragedy that is so frustratingly elusive—the perpetual *what if, should have, if only I could go back.*

---

11 Jackson, *The Haunting of Hill House*, 182.
12 Flanagan, "Silence Lay Steadily."

As someone who lives with mental illness and has experienced stigma deeply rooted in my own family, as well as confusion and a lack of understanding, Steven's acknowledgement is hard to watch. It hits close to home simply because that's what I needed but never received. When my mother couldn't see me because of her own mental illness, I needed my father. I understand Nell begging to be seen and heard. But still, can I blame my family for not understanding? Can I blame my father for feeling at his wits' end, for being confounded about why his daughter was behaving so erratically? No, probably not. But it still affects me. I still feel resentment. And I'm still not sure I have room for forgiveness.

A while ago, my friend sent me a letter published in *The Atlantic* in 2019 called "Dear Therapist: My Son Is Angry about the Way He Was Treated Last Christmas." In the letter, a father laments his son's inability to get over his anger for being basically gaslit by his family— his brothers and father particularly—during what seems to be a severe episode of depression. The father compares him to his other sons and their success, while also emphasizing that the son with depression seems to be doing okay now, so why is he still harbouring resentment?

The father also writes, "I find myself annoyed that my son appears to be so self-absorbed that he can't see how he affected those around him (and continues to). We all walked on eggshells over the holidays. . ."[13]

I read this article just as a feature I'd written for a local newspaper, the *West End Phoenix*,[14] was published—a piece that investigates the effects of psychiatric hospitalizations on youth. The parallels made me laugh mirthlessly. The article I'd worked on focused on a

---

13   Lori Gottlieb, "Dear Therapist: My Son Is Angry about the Way He Was Treated Last Christmas," *The Atlantic*, December 9, 2022, https://www.theatlantic.com/family/archive/2019/12/my-sons-mental-health-is-affecting-our-whole-family/603223/.

14   K.J. Aiello, "'Then There Was Me,'" *West End Phoenix*, November 9, 2022, https://www.westendphoenix.com/stories/then-there-was-me.

Toronto woman, Becca Lemire, and the loneliness, isolation, and misunderstanding she felt around her mental health challenges, and how hospitalizations contributed to that. Basically, stigma derailed her for years. My story, Becca's story, and the story of this father's son, all seem to have a similar thread.

The therapist's answer to the father in *The Atlantic* letter is poignant:

> Let me share with you what patients with depression have told me they wished their families knew . . . First, depression isn't an attitude. It's an illness . . . I want you to consider that your son isn't "self-absorbed"— he's in pain. And what he's telling you is that he felt his brothers were ignoring this pain, and nothing is lonelier than being utterly alone in one's pain.[15]

I know my father didn't understand the pain and fear I felt. And I say *my father* only because my mother, struggling with her own illness, didn't have the capacity to understand my challenges, reasonably so. But I'd always seen my father as my protector, the one person I'd follow deep into the forest. The person I looked up to, the one I wanted to be just like. His lack of understanding wasn't his fault, but what I can blame him for is not trying. And that's hard to live with.

The therapist writing in *The Atlantic* finishes by describing what the father *can* say: "I'm here for you. I know it's really hard sometimes. I love you."

Sometimes that's all we need. That, and maybe a ride to therapy.

---

15   Gottlieb, "Dear Therapist: My Son Is Angry about the Way He Was Treated Last Christmas."

I am brought to my parents' house, skinny and limp. My days are melting together. I sleep, I wake, I eat, I breathe. I put on some weight, but not enough. I take my pills as instructed. I watch the moonlight. I fade during the day. My cat, Loki, keeps me company. He presses his paws to my belly as I lie on my bed. I hear him purring, and it anchors me. I don't feel quite so alone. I know my Shadow isn't really a shadow, but I also don't know what it is. And it won't go away.

Winter deepens, and the snow creates waves of white up along the hill behind my parents' house. I see it blowing at the crest, the sun breaking the colours apart. I tell my parents I want to return to school, but I can't afford it. I try to extend my student loan, but the bank rejects me. I watch the days slide by, knowing that my peers are registering for classes, marching towards graduation and a future that I no longer see. I am left behind. My mother tells me that a university degree isn't all it's cracked up to be anyways. That it's just not in the cards for me. That it would be better if I got a regular job and just lived a normal life and why can't I just be happy living a normal life? *She* lives a normal life and is just fine, is perfectly happy. Her chin lifts, her eyes are hooded, and she looks into the distance when she says that.

My mother doesn't call me her girl all bathed in sunshine anymore. I'm not my father's little helper. I don't know who I am. I thought feeling nothing would be easy. That numbness would be a relief. But the nothingness, the numbness, the deep dark emptiness hurts so much I can't breathe. And I want to breathe. I want to feel something, anything, other than that pain. It's not long until I swallow all my pills again. Maybe I do have a VIP pass. I wonder if I'll get a punch card.

When I'm in the ER, I wait for my parents to come. But they don't. I'm taken to the psychiatric hospital by a police officer. When I'm released, I wait again, but my parents don't pick me up. I ask the nurse to call me a taxi. I try not to look at her face when she says,

"Sure, honey." The taxi driver looks at my socked feet as I stand outside the hospital, and we both know that I don't have any money to pay him. He takes me home anyways.

I sleep. I wake. I eat. I breathe.

One day, in an endless afternoon that is miles away from the relief of night, I tell my mother I don't want to feel like this anymore. She looks at me, blinks, and says, "Happiness is a choice. All you have to do is choose."

I wonder why I keep making the wrong choices. I want to choose right, but I don't know how. Maybe I'm all wrong. Maybe I'm just bad. Maybe I'm selfish and stupid and a failure. My mother says, "Your grandmother said we should have kicked you out for your behaviour. But I shut her down. I'd never do that to you."

Loki watches as I slowly unbox my few things. There is a small bookshelf and my old paperback novels are still there from before I tried to make a life for myself. Their spines are colourful, and I pull one off the shelf. I see the dragons, the wizards, the magic. In my mind, I see an image of a tower in a swamp. I shiver, unable to quite recall where that tower is anymore. I toss the book into a now-empty box. The rest of the books follow. When the box is full and the shelf is empty, I take the box out to the garbage.

My student loans come due, and I don't have a job or any money. Soon, the phone starts ringing, and I know that sound. I know what that sound means and what it does and how it hurts and ruins and chews people up and spits them out. The people on the phone tell me I'll be arrested if I don't pay my bills. They tell me I'm worthless. They tell me they'll ruin my life.

I tell my mom I'm scared. "That's what they do," she says. "They say horrible things and they scare you." And then she walks away.

I sleep. I wake. I eat. I breathe.

One day, I ask my mom if I can use some of her paints and brushes. The pink of her cheeks glows just a little brighter, and she says, "Sure, but make sure you clean up." I don't know what to paint, but I mix dark colours, smear them on the canvass and watch as the white disappears beneath deep purple and indigo. I try to move the brush in a way that will create something meaningful, but it just makes sludge.

My dad puts his arm around me and tells me to look out the window. "See all that snow? Look at the colours and how nice that is." He smiles down at me. "Why don't you paint something nice and normal like a landscape?"

I smile and say okay.

I paint a lighthouse in a purple twilit desert.

I'm starting to feel anger again, the Shadow sliding closer to me with each passing day. I feel like there are ants crawling under my skin, and I can't sleep anymore. My thoughts are gaining momentum, and my body is twitching. The phone keeps ringing, collection agents on the other end, until one day I scream into the receiver. Then I rip the phone off the wall and hurl it across the room.

My mother gets angry with me. "Stop that right now. What has gotten into you?"

I turn to her and bellow. Her mouth opens, her eyes widen, and she backs away. I step closer, I pull my body up, I grow large enough to rip the roof off the house. My voice explodes, and I yell, and my mother sinks into the chair. I stand over her and she shrinks, and I eat her up and spit her out and scream like I've always wanted to, and I tell her that I hate her and I hate me and I hate this life and I want to die why can't you let me die let me die I fucking hate you.

My mother's back rounds, her shoulders curl inward, her thumb slides into her mouth. When she speaks, her voice is that little broken bell of so long ago. "Don't hurt me. Please don't hurt me."

I stop. I shrink. I am a shuddering girl again. And she's moaning and crying and begging me not to hurt her. She tells me she's scared of me. I tell her I'm sorry, and I try to gently touch her shoulder, but she cries louder and looks at me like I'm going to sink my teeth into her and tear her apart.

I back away, afraid. I call my dad, and he comes home from work. He murmurs to my mother and gently collects her up and eases her into their bedroom. I hear the quiet click of the door as it closes. Her cries are muffled. I'm cold. My body is trembling, and I sit on my bed and try to remain as still as possible. I don't want to move. If I move, things will crash down around me. If I move, my body will break. If I move, I will hurt my mother.

The sun slides through the sky. Loki is pawing at me for food, and I wonder if he knows how ghostly I am. My mother's cries have faded. I hear the clock ticking downstairs. It tells me time is moving on with or without me, and I hate it for that.

My room falls dim. I hear the door open at the end of the hall and footsteps move closer to my room. My father's form is framed in the doorway, and I look at his feet.

"I'm sorry," I mumble. He walks in and turns on the lamp. I squint in the light. He sits beside me, slouches, hands dangling between his knees. "I'm sorry," I say again. He takes a deep breath, raises his arm, and wraps it around me. I lean into him, and I'm crying. I keep muttering I'm sorry.

When he speaks, his voice is so soft and gentle, and I feel it rumble in his chest. "Whatever this is, kid, you have to stop. It's too hard on your mom."

I raise my head and look at him, and his smile is so soft and gentle even though his face is pale, the skin around his eyes tight. He hasn't smiled at me like that in a long, long time. It's a smile that reminds me of green forests and sepia stags and burrowing into the snow waiting for the beaver to come out of her dam.

And I want to say, *Can't you see me? I'm right here. I've been right here all this time. But you didn't see me. You didn't see me. I'm right here and I'm screaming, and you can't see me.*

I nod. "Okay, Dad," I say instead. "I'll try harder."

Chapter 5

Magical Rings, Rain, and Fireflies

I'm driving to my parents' house. It's the deep of winter, dark and cold. So cold that the snow squeaks and the sun turns the frozen air into crystals. The wind hurts to breathe.

It's late and the road is long: a straight stretch through farmers' fields that ripple gently over the land, blanketed in crisp, unbroken snow. There is no moon. The stars have arrived, multitudinous to the point that they look like spray paint across a velvet canvas. I've turned off the radio and am listening to the muffled engine as my foot presses harder on the gas, rocketing me through the centre-bare road. I'm thinking. Listing things in my mind that I want to do, that I've failed to do, that I know will never happen. I've already attempted to live on my own twice now, both dismal failures. Both late-night departures, broken leases, and each time, what few belongings I have shrink. I hardly have any books anymore. I have a lamp that belongs to me. A bedspread, my clothes. I have a laptop I bought with money I don't have. The idea of school is long behind me. I'm working the regular job that my father told me to get. The steady job that doesn't cover my mounting debt or the oil change my beat-up car desperately needs. I watch the gas gauge, hoping I won't run out of fuel like I've done so many times because I don't have the money to buy gas until payday. I'm too far from home. It's too cold. It's too late at night. My days are long, my drive even longer. I can't afford to live closer to work, and I can't afford not to work. I'm trapped.

I see something far in the inky distance. A blur of light, like a column rising. I continue to drive the snowy road, watching it rise higher into the sky. The colour is greenish, a brilliant streak stretching upward.

I realize it's the Northern Lights. I let out a sigh, a small smile creeping across my mouth. I pull my car onto the shoulder and cut the engine. I step out into the frigid night, my jacket wrapped closely around me. I stuff a toque on my head, lean against my car, and watch as the streaks smear up into the dark sky, waving gently with green watercolour light. I think maybe my mom would love to see this. She's never seen the Northern Lights.

When I arrive home, the house is dark, its windows are black eyes. To the north, the spires of pale green light still striate the sky. I quietly enter my parents' bedroom and hear my father snoring gently. When I press my hand on my mother's shoulder, she lets out a little gasp. "Mom," I say. "Come look." She's irritated, but I press. "It's the Northern Lights, Mom. Get your coat."

I remember the fireflies of once upon a time.

My mother meets me out on the front porch. Across the road, an empty field spans into the horizon to our north, the snow set aglow by the columns of light rising into the sky. As we watch, they begin to pull, moving across the expanse. I hear my mother let out a sigh. "Oh, ducky," she says. "It's incredible." We look at each other, and her cheeks are ruddy from the cold. Her smile reaches her eyes, and for a moment I feel worthy of being her daughter. I feel like maybe there is magic, but it's slumbering, waiting to be woken. Maybe it knows I'm not ready yet.

"It really is," I echo her. I try to keep my failures, my evil corruption, my Shadow, from lacing my voice. Because right now, she's looking at me like I looked at her all those years ago. That summer night when the air was moist and smelled green and my mother wrapped her warm arm around me, leaning in. My brother was beside us, sitting on the step, nestled between my father's pyjama-clad legs. We'd watched the little lights winking in the trees, and my mother told us about their magic. That fireflies lie dormant waiting for the right conditions to blossom into a perfect twilit night like that one had been. And when they do wake, they bring with them magic from other worlds. They are fairies dancing among the ferns and silver birches and mossy ground.

Do you know, my mother had said to us, *that there's a special sort of magic rain? It's the first rain of the spring. It's warm and turns the whole world green. You can see the buds bursting and the flowers taking their first breaths.*

My brother and I had looked at her, and I'm sure the light of the fireflies reflected in our eyes. *It's called the Magic Rain*, she'd said. *It's what helps the world grow. And if you're quiet enough, you can see the fairies.*

I want my mom to tell me those stories now. No one will hear us, no one will see us. "Do you remember the fireflies, Mom, and the Magic Rain?"

She looks at me, a wistful look on her face. "You kids were so small."

I want to ask her if she still believes in magic. I want to ask her if she remembers the cocoon we created together when she read to me from that beautiful book with the Evenstar on the cover. I want to ask her if she made up those stories about magical rain and fairies and if, once upon a time, she was sure that there was something special in this world. Something to hold on to. That the dark nights don't have to be so dark. That maybe every night can be streaked with green spires of light and twinkling fireflies and soft rain.

The questions press behind my lips. *Do you still believe in me?* I want to ask. *Did you ever believe in me in the first place? Do you wish that I was that little kid again, not the broken woman I have become?*

I want to ask her if sometimes, in the quiet afternoons when no one is around, when no one can hear or see her, she wishes I were no longer here.

I. THERE'S NAUGHT LEFT IN HIM BUT LIES AND DECEIT.

I have to remember the beautiful moments. I have to gather up all of those tender memories, teasing them apart from the bad ones, and hold them tightly to my chest. When I do this, I picture a box made of lovingly polished sandalwood, mother-of-pearl inlay on the lid, where I carefully place all of those memories for safekeeping. They belong to me, those memories. No one can take them—or how they made me feel or what they helped me believe—away from me. They belong to the parts of me that want to keep going. Parts of me that maybe I can be proud of, that remind me there is something out there I need to continue for, even if it's only for just one more day. Those memories are laced with glittering summer afternoons, sunlight through green foliage. Watching my father dance to CSNY or sway to Dan Fogelberg. The look on my mother's face when I showed her the dragon that I'd sketched—the one I was, and still am, most proud of. The feeling I had when my mother's hand fluttered to her chest when the psychologist told her just how smart I am.

I have to believe in the self I used to be.

The memory of the safe haven my mother and I created all those years ago, lying on her bed, *The Lord of the Rings* resting between us, is one of my favourites. The sound of the onion paper as she turned the pages, how the light broke on her gold wedding ring. The way the soft skin of her finger puffed up around it. The moment when she first told me about dragons and magic and elves.

I carefully close the lid and tuck the box away, the sandalwood scent still lingering on my fingertips.

Sometimes I struggle to read Tolkien's trilogy for the memories it brings back. And sometimes I relish in it, how two little hobbits can be so loyal and loving to one another. How they can believe in one another so unquestioningly that they'd walk into a fiery mountain not just for each other, but for the whole world.

I also adore how unrelenting that loyalty and love is. How, in Peter Jackson's film version, Frodo Baggins's best friend, Samwise Gamgee, carries Frodo the last steps of the long journey, shouldering them both, burden and body. We can all learn just a little bit from hobbits. Maybe that was the point of Tolkien's Middle Earth—not an epic story about a dragon named Smaug, or a wizard named Gandalf, or a lost King of Gondor, or the almost all-powerful Sauron come back to cloak the world in shadow.

Maybe Tolkien's point was simply the love of two friends and how that love can save the world.

While *The Lord of the Rings* is packed full of characters and steeped in seemingly endless mythology and worldbuilding, in Peter Jackson's film version, there is one character in particular that deserves attention: the One Ring. It has a consciousness, carrying a certain amount of independence from its maker, Sauron. It plans its manoeuvres, it speaks when it wants to, influences at will. All with the sole purpose of getting back to Sauron, who now exists in Mordor as the Eye, an entity similar to Voldemort and his Horcruxes in that he is not a physical being, but a being of only consciousness and power. But once Sauron is reunited with the Ring, he will become corporeal again, filled with the entirety of his true power . . . and a *massive* threat to all of Middle Earth.

The journey that the One Ring has taken is thousands of years old. Created in the fires of Mount Doom, Sauron imbued his power—and part of himself—into this ring. During the Great Battle of Middle Earth, the One Ring was cut from Sauron's finger, vanquishing him.

Almost.

The tiny shard that was Sauron still lived on in the One Ring, which took control over its own destiny. It corrupted people, drove them to kill or be killed, and, eventually, slipped out of time until "history became legend. Legend became myth. And for two and a half thousand years, the Ring passed out of all knowledge. Until, when chance came, the ring ensnared a new bearer."[1]

This "new bearer" is a hobbit named Sméagol, whose own cousin and best friend finds the ring in a riverbed. Carrying it to shore, Déagol wonders over it, enraptured. Sméagol looks to see what has captivated his cousin and when he lays his eyes on the Ring, Sméagol knows it must be his. The cousins, who were once close, embark on a fight that ends with Déagol's death at Sméagol's hands.

Sméagol is cast out of his community for this murder, and he takes to the Misty Mountains where he burrows deep into the darkness, holding and loving his Precious, his One Ring. He lives there for centuries, the Ring's power over him strengthening, twisting him into a creature only of possession, of insatiable want. Over hundreds of years, Sméagol's physical appearance changes: his skin greys, his eyes become large and perfectly adapted for living in the deep belly of the mountains. His body withers away, all bone and sinew and corded

---

1   *The Lord of the Rings: The Fellowship of the Ring*, directed by Peter Jackson, featuring Elijah Wood, Viggo Mortensen, and Sean Astin (2001; United States: New Line Home Entertainment), Netflix, https://www.netflix.com/title/60004480.

muscle. The slow transformation continues until Sméagol is no longer and Gollum is born.

When Bilbo Baggins comes along during the events of *The Hobbit*, he wins the One Ring from Gollum in a game of riddles. In terror and fury, Gollum tries to kill Bilbo to get the Ring back, but Bilbo escapes.

Years later, Bilbo (mostly unwillingly) bequeaths the ring to Frodo who then becomes the Ring-bearer. Part of me wonders if this is an allegory for intergenerational trauma, although Bilbo is fully aware of the harm that he is passing to his nephew.

Gandalf instructs Frodo to take it far away, "keep it hidden, keep it safe."[2] Ultimately, this means taking the ring into Mordor and casting it into Mount Doom, where it came from.

While Frodo may be the hero of this story, it's Samwise who saves his life because he believes in Frodo and refuses to leave his side, no matter how far-gone Frodo becomes. It's an unrelenting love and confidence that Samwise holds for his friend that keeps Frodo from (literally and figuratively) tipping over the edge. This is probably why everyone loves Samwise so much, as I do too.

In the end, after thousands of miles, fraught nightmares and being hunted by Sauron's undead riders—nine ancient kings of men who fell to the power of the Ring—Frodo and Sam make it to the mountain. By this time, the Ring has almost consumed Frodo, and he can't continue. He is exhausted. The Ring has become so heavy on his mind and body, and he can no longer see the light. He can't smell the spring air. He can't remember the feel of the sun, or the taste of fresh strawberries and cream. It is only darkness he sees with his waking eyes.

I know that feeling. It's a weight so heavy that you're sure it will break your bones. It's perpetual night and smokey air and food that turns to ashes. It's depression at its worst. And Sauron's Eye is

---

2   *Fellowship of the Ring*, dir. Jackson.

relentlessly watching, searching, hunting—the mental illness that simply won't go away. It feels so similar to my own mental illness before I was properly diagnosed and started treatment. That was my thought as I watched Peter Jackson's *The Return of the King*, as Sam holds his best friend, watching Frodo fade away into the magic that is pulling him under. The devouring nature of the One Ring.

This story is about a quest to save the world. But when I really look at the journey Frodo and Sam take, the story is about the love of two friends. It's about loyalty and trust and sacrifice. Frodo wouldn't have survived if Sam hadn't been there.

But underneath that, too, lingers a question I keep asking: Who is worthy of that friendship? Following that, I wonder, was I?

Some nights I don't sleep at all. Some, just a few hours. Some mornings I can't wake up, no matter how close I am to losing my job. I'm terrified of losing my job as much as I hate it. But getting up at four thirty every morning to drive the two hours into the city to work for nine dollars an hour makes my dad smile at me just a little bit. It keeps my parents happy, even though it doesn't pay my bills or keep the collections agents at bay. Some nights I come home after midnight. I'll pull up and the house will be dark. When I enter, Loki, my fat tabby, will greet me with a small meow, which makes me smile. I'll pour myself a bowl of cereal soaked with too much milk and struggle to ascend the stairs to my bedroom, Loki following behind. My mother wanted the cat to love her, but he loves me instead, and she doesn't like him for it. She says he's a pain in the ass and fat, and she gets annoyed when he meows. She was excited when she first brought him home, but he never really seemed to take to her. Not like she wanted. I try to tell her how much I love him, but she always scoffs and reiterates how much of an asshole she thinks he is. I love his warm heaviness when he sleeps on me. Or the way his paw curls over my bowl of cereal as he tries to pull it towards him. I love his meow when he is looking for me. He will spend the night with me. I will fall asleep to his purrs. There is something unconditionally reassuring about him, despite him being just a cat.

Sometimes, my Shadow and I will scour the internet, on these new websites that connect singles, and I'll find whoever will make me feel better about myself. Who will tell me I'm pretty and look at me as though I'm not broken, even if just for a night. We'll drink until the sun comes up, our blood singing with cocaine or ecstasy or blurred and glittering from a thick cup of mushroom tea. I replace meals with gin.

One Saturday morning, my dad flings open my bedroom door and tells me to get out of bed. There's strain in his voice, and I can almost hear him thinking: *Why is my kid lazy? Why is she aimless? I don't understand her. This isn't what I expected of her.*

"Get your ass up. You have twenty minutes."

I pull the covers over me again. I hope he won't come back, but I know he will. He's relentless when he's annoyed, and right now, all I ever do is annoy him. All I ever do is disappoint him.

The minutes pass, and I'm almost asleep when the door opens again, banging against the wall. He places a mug of coffee on my bedside table, not gently. "Up," he says. "Don't make me tell you again."

I make my way outside, my body creaking with the effort, and see a pile of rough timber resting across the brown yard that's still soaked from the melted snow. Last fall, my father had planted a willow tree, but it's too small to look like a willow yet.

My father is pounding a post into the thawed soil, each swing powerful and sure. My mother said once that my father spent his life picking up a hobby, perfecting it, then, growing bored with the perfection, moving on. I wonder if this is his latest hobby. I also wonder when he'll become bored of me and move on.

He sees me, wipes his brow, and says, "You're going to help me build an arbour." His voice doesn't carry the harshness and disappointment from earlier. I watch his face break into a grin, and I'm sucked into the possibility that maybe I can be his little helper again.

I walk over, my boots sinking into the soft ground. He starts to tell me how we'll construct it and how long it will take the clematis to consume it. He shows me where we'll build a small bench so we can sit out here in the summertime with our martinis and watch the sun and birds and lovely things grow. It sounds delicious, and I think maybe he's trying to build his own forest.

"It'll be like stepping into another world. Like *The Secret Garden*," I say quietly. I don't often speak around my dad because I don't want him to tell me to lower my voice when I get excited or to speak clearly when I mumble. When I get really excited, he tells me to sit on my hands while talking to him.

He's inspecting the posts, taking measurements of the ground. He says, "Won't it be nice?"

I smile. *Sure, it'll be great. Just perfect. I want it to be perfect. Please let it be perfect.*

We work all day, and he shows me how to use the drill and how to set the posts and pickets just right. We build the frame, and he points to the top. "You need to climb up there and secure the wood across." He brings his hand over his head, sweeping it down in an arc. "That's how the vines will grow. But you need to make sure it's sturdy."

I look up and shake my head. "I can't get up there. It's too high, Dad. I don't want to fall."

He makes a *pft* sound and pushes me up the ladder. "You're small enough. There's nothing to be scared of." I look down at him, and he smiles. "I'll catch you."

I think maybe I should fall anyways.

My mom brings out coffee and tea and juice and snacks throughout the day, and as the hours pass, I forget that I'm a soiled and sullied girl. I forget about all the times I drove through the night to get home, about the failure that I am and the drugs I've consumed and how recklessly and relentlessly I'm trying to destroy my body. I forget about a life I once thought I'd live and the classes that I left behind years ago and how my peers have moved on, my presence disappearing behind them. I forget about my Shadow, lingering in the periphery, waiting . . . just waiting.

For these hours, I'm my dad's daughter again, and we're having fun. I realize that in some ways I might be like him: relentless. I remember the time our roof leaked and it was me, not my brother, my dad pushed up onto the roof, heavy shingles slung over my narrow shoulders, legs shaking under the weight. I was so pissed off with him. "Why do I have to do this?" I'd said.

"Because no daughter of mine won't know how to do these things for herself."

It's not lost on me that I am, once again, creating a roof to keep those inside safe and comfortable.

That night, we celebrate with mint juleps and then a bottle of Merlot at dinner and a martini on the couch, Gordon Lightfoot playing in the background. He looks at me like I'm special, and my mom likes that we're bonding. I do too.

We continue the next day, a grey and heavy day. I'm tired and my muscles are sore and the shimmery excitement of yesterday has dulled to harsh edges. My father's steely look is back, and he regards me with ice eyes and no room for mistakes. "Get it right. Pay attention. What did I tell you? You're doing it sloppy." I'm frustrated, but I can't tell him, and it starts to occur to me that if I don't do this, he will be disappointed in me. But if I do this—if I do this *right*—there's the possibility that I'll make him happy.

I look at my dad, hands braced on his hips as he inspects my work from yesterday. I wonder if he looked at his dad like I'm looking at him now. I'm only four years younger than he was when his dad died. I can't imagine not having my dad in four years. I can't imagine my father's voice falling silent in four years. His heart not beating in four years. I also can't imagine my father knowing who his daughter really is.

We finish the arbour before dinner, and, as we stand back and look at it, I am proud.

"Why don't you ever do this with my brother?" I ask him quietly.

My dad just shrugs and says, "I like spending time with you."

I try not to expand with happiness. I don't want to reveal that my dad telling me he likes spending time with me is a gift I didn't know I needed so badly. I take a step back, hoping he won't see my face screw up, trying not to cry. I breathe, swallow down the tears. This is good, I think. I can do this.

My dad says, "Listen, kid. About Loki." I wonder why my dad wants to talk about my cat, here under this arbour we've created. I remain quiet. "Your mom and I think you need to find him a new home."

Ice curls through me. I look at him. I don't believe the words I just heard. "But why?" I ask. "What did he do?"

My dad doesn't look at me. He shrugs. "He didn't do anything. It's just . . . it's too much work. You need to find him a new home."

"That makes no sense. He has a home. *I* am his home." I shake my head, panic bubbling. "Mom just doesn't like him." I wonder how far my mother would go to get rid of something she doesn't like. *He's a pain,* she always says. *He's a bad cat. He shits outside the box.* I know he does this sometimes, but I hate it when she grabs him and rubs his face in it, yelling at him. I want to tell her to stop, but I don't want to feel her ire. I wonder how easy it would be for my father to do the same. I decide that he's not really serious.

"A month is enough time to find him a new home," he says.

I look at the arbour, bare wood waiting for green foliage and summer evenings and afternoons filled with fragrant lilacs, and I gather the ropes of electric nerves that coil through me and tie them tight. I hold on to the searing vulnerability of their exposed ends and remain motionless. I show no emotion. I say nothing. My face is impassive. I don't bother trying to rationalize what seems so irrational. What did Loki do wrong? What did *I* do wrong?

He's my only friend. Please don't take him from me.

I'm so helpless. I'm so scared. I want to plead with him: *I'll do better. I'll look after him better. I'll keep him in my room; you'll never have to see him.*

It'll be like he doesn't exist.

I want to keep my cat. My dad isn't serious. He can't be serious.

I won't do it. In my mind, I've already brushed away his words. I feel like Loki is all I have. He is okay with all my bad sides. He doesn't see my Shadow.

My father puts his hand on my shoulder and squeezes. "That's a good kid," he says, then he turns and walks into the house.

Some stories are too hard to tell, the truth of them far too raw. This is reasonable. It's also reasonable that some stories are too hard to hear. But does that mean they can't—shouldn't—be told? How does one tell a story that is both too hard to tell and too hard to hear? How does one exact change without the truth? How does one even just get the words out there when a tough story is just *too* tough?

It burns if it doesn't get out.

As small as it seems, I feel this way about my cat, long gone, nearly forgotten. Remembering Loki and how much I loved him and needed him is like scooping out my guts. So I shoved those memories down for years. The feel of his soft fur, his warm head when he pressed it against my cheek. His eyes so green and kind. When he was gone, a part of me was gone, too, and it was like the last loss that pushed me over the edge. I let myself dissolve into substance use and self-harm, rejecting anyone who tried to get close to me.

Friends leave anyways. Friends aren't loyal. Friends are duplicitous and malevolent. That's all I believed, even if I never admitted it. So, a story about friends who would sacrifice so much for each other has always amazed me. And made me envious for years.

The power the One Ring holds over the characters makes it seem like the choice to take it up is hardly even a choice. This is parallel to a conversation that comes up again and again around mental health and so-called mental health awareness: addiction.

Looking at Gollum, Bilbo, and Frodo, all the elements of addiction are there: the introduction of something all-consuming, the subsequent possession of the user or Ring-bearer, and finally, the bearer's near inability to let this external element go, despite it meaning their own downfall. Maybe this is also why Frodo understands Gollum so much. He sees himself in the mercurial trickster. If one hasn't experienced the hardship of being a Ring-bearer, it's nearly impossible to truly understand, as Frodo emphasizes to his faithful friend Sam.

But why does Frodo not succumb where Sméagol does? Again, in Jackson's version, it's not about being a hobbit; both Frodo and Sméagol are hobbits. It's not about their different personalities, although Frodo is demonstrably more thoughtful and wiser than Sméagol ever was.

As I watch wretched Gollum crawl across Middle Earth, guiding the hobbits to Mount Doom, I wonder why Gollum is less worthy of the kind of love Sam embodies. In the end, there really is no difference between Frodo and Gollum, as the two Ring-bearers fight each other to keep the Ring. It's only chance that it's Gollum who slips and falls into the fire, while Frodo is caught and saved by Sam.

I have a hard time wrapping my head around that clear delineation. There has to be more to it than that, right? It can't be as simple as the love of a friend. Isn't that . . . well . . . naive?

That can be true, but there's also another truth, one that, as much as it feels crummy to say, makes me question the kindness and compassion that seems to be embedded in Sam's very nature.

Gollum is a villain. He's a trickster. Throughout the journey, he has deceived and will continue to deceive for his Precious. He has been this way for centuries, living alone under the influence of the One Ring with no one to help him. But then when he is guiding Frodo and Sam into Mordor, there's a glimmer of hope in Gollum. Frodo reverts to using Gollum's real name, Sméagol, which seems to reach into Gollum and pull out something that was once good, humanizing him (or hobbitizing in this case). By being kind and compassionate, Frodo earns Sméagol's loyalty and kindness and gains his trust. It seems like Frodo just *gets* him, and I wonder: If the friendship between Frodo and Sméagol—however that looks—were to have continued, what would have become of Sméagol? Would he have a redemptive arc? Would he be able to overcome Gollum and stay true to Sméagol? Would there be a shadow of a hobbit there, after all these centuries? Would he—*could* he—be a good person?

We'll never know what Sméagol's fate could have been, and what bothers me is that Sam makes the decision to reject him, saying, "There's naught left in him but lies and deceit."[3] I wonder if that's entirely true.

(Again, I love Sam, but it still irks me.)

What I do know is that this is how people with substance use disorder can often be perceived. It's doubtful that this was Tolkien's objective, but some interpretations suggest an insidious and deeply embedded belief system around addiction and those who live with substance use disorder and mental illness. What do we believe an addict looks like? Is there a widely accepted playbook for addiction

---

3   *The Lord of the Rings: The Two Towers*, directed by Peter Jackson, featuring Elijah Wood, Viggo Mortensen, and Andy Serkis (2002; United States: New Line Home Entertainment), Netflix, https://www.netflix.com/title/60004483.

and mental illness, a list of criteria in order to meet a threshold beyond which you have a problem (or *are* the problem)?

It turns out, there is.

The *DSM-5* sets out eleven criteria for alcohol-related disorders, including alcohol use disorder, alcohol intoxication, withdrawal, and other or unspecified alcohol-related disorders. The list of criteria begins with: "A problematic pattern of alcohol use leading to clinically significant impairment or distress. . ."[4] Frequently, the term *abuse* is used, and, of course, subjectivity is always underlying a diagnosis (as in, what is "problematic"? I don't doubt there are problems with substance over-use, but the threshold is subjective). But even to be diagnosed with alcohol-related disorder indicates a delineation between those who are disordered and those who are not disordered. Or, as used in Alcoholics Anonymous text, *The Big Book* (which is still mostly the same since its first iteration in 1938 and has heavy Christian underpinnings), the "normal" versus the "abnormal."[5]

Them and us. The Other.

I'm not saying these substances aren't addictive. They absolutely are. They can ruin and sometimes even take lives. I'm also not saying that people in the midst of substance use disorder aren't difficult to be around, or sometimes even love. I know the reality. What I'm saying is that the language we use in the stories told of addiction are of responsibility versus irresponsibility, moderation versus immoderation, and this can be an isolating binary. Good versus bad. Worthy versus unworthy. Who is responsible and how can one gauge this threshold of "a problematic pattern"? Labels that are used to indicate someone who lives with these disorders can, for some, end up

---

4   *DSM-5*, 490.

5   Alcoholics Anonymous, "There Is a Solution," in *The Big Book*, 4th edition (New York: Alcoholics Anonymous World Services, Inc., 2001), 23. https://www.aa.org/sites/default/files/2021-11/en_bigbook_chapt2.pdf.

becoming a removal of personhood while the addiction moves to the forefront. Alcoholics, junkies, crack heads, booze hounds, winos. Gollum versus Sméagol. Where is the line drawn between addiction and normalcy? If someone is past that line, do we give up on them, withdrawing our friendship and support? Do we say there's not much left in them but lies and deceit? I know this is a tough question for friends and family living with someone who has a substance use disorder, and I'm sure many folks simply don't have any more patience or trust for the one they are watching become consumed. It's a nearly impossible situation.

In my twenties and early thirties, I used substances a *lot*—mostly alcohol. I never sought treatment, I never went to my doctor saying I thought maybe it was a problem. I "quit" alcohol for many years, but does that mean I had a substance use problem? Would I have been diagnosed? It's highly likely. But I know if I had been diagnosed, I would have had that diagnosis—and thus, identity—for the rest of my life. That, I think, would have made me even more different, more *abnormal*, than I already felt.

AA's *The Big Book* has some interesting language around alcoholism:

> In a vague way their families and friends sense that these drinkers are *abnormal* but everybody hopefully awaits the day when the sufferer will *rouse himself from his lethargy and assert his power of will.*[6]

As though quitting substances is a matter of self-control and will, and not at all related to life circumstance, mental illness, trauma, and even neurophysiology (the latter of which addiction mostly is).

---

6   Alcoholics Anonymous, "There Is a Solution," 23–24. Italics added.

The language—the same language that is used in AA meetings today—doesn't stop at the individual. It slips into our collective consciousness and influences medical care and public policy. In an essay in *Stat*, physician Sean Fogler, who lives with substance use disorder, writes about his first-hand accounts of the effects of institutional, cultural, and social stigma on people living with addiction. "This duality," he writes, "showed me how people with mental illness and substance use disorders are treated by my colleagues in the health care system. I saw their judgements and their scorn, and I saw how U.S. grid policy was harming people right before my eyes."[7] He continues to argue that this social stigma—equivalent to a scarlet letter—comes from the beliefs that addicts' "poor personal choices, 'moral failing,' and defects of character are to blame for the disease." When looking at our primary go-to legal and social treatment for "alcoholism," Alcoholics Anonymous, it's clear there's a deep-rooted belief that those living with addiction "are dangerous and employers should be allowed to deny them employment."

I hear Sam's voice in those words: "there's naught left in him but lies and deceit." It is, like mental illness, isolating. I imagine it's very lonely.

A friend of mine has had their own experiences with both Alcoholics Anonymous and the labelling of addiction. Bryen Fulcher found AA to be disempowering to the point of rendering them submissive, filled with gaslighting and blame. "I'm labelled this *thing*,"[8] Fulcher said to me, explaining how they are perceived not just by AA but in general. They say that because one might choose *not* to drink or consider whether they should drink at all, one's own self-control is called into

---

7   Sean Fogler, "As a Physician and a Patient, I've Seen the Damage Caused by the Stigma of Addiction. It Must End," *Stat*, December 8, 2020, https://www.statnews.com /2020/12/08/stigma-weaponized-helps-fuel-addiction-crisis/.

8   Bryen Fulcher, Zoom call with the author, January 16, 2022.

question. "I'm considered to be in recovery for the rest of my life," they said. Fulcher's frustration goes farther back than that. "Even terms like 'abuse' . . . that implies it's the individual's responsibility. So as an individual you can choose to take [alcohol], but if you get hooked . . . it's your fault."

Fulcher says this problem stems from how we collectively and socially perceive alcohol. There's a culture built around "big alcohol," as Fulcher explains, with alcohol companies and Western society complicit. Advertisements highlighting a bottle of vodka covered with a veneer of youthfulness and sex panders to the self-perceived disenfranchised who crave some semblance of friendship, acceptance, and maybe a little excitement (I can relate to that). Lagers are paired with warm gatherings of friends. Alcohol is equated with being socially accepted, sexy, and *fun*. And really, we all want to be loved and accepted. We want to be seen and included. These companies know that. Gollum, I'm sure, wanted to be loved and included.

But if one were to become addicted? Is that person any less worthy of love, respect, care, and, of course, friendship?

Tolkien's One Ring can represent addiction, and that addiction can hold tremendous power. But the difference between the One Ring and our culture of alcohol is that there is a very clear understanding that *anyone* can be taken by the Ring, whereas the way we popularly understand addiction is to largely attribute weakness to the people who are struggling or blame them for it.

But what happens to those who already live with mental illness or trauma or both and also struggle with addictions? What if alcohol is, for them, a way to take control, a way to give self-permission, and a way to numb? A way to grant power to the self? It's not really much of a surprise that folks who live with mental illness, trauma, or both are far more likely to develop substance use disorders than those who don't. Like many, I struggled with mental illness and trauma (and still do) and self-medicated with alcohol and other substances. Some folks self-medicate with cannabis or mushrooms in microdoses. For some, this substance use can be helpful, as recent studies have shown, particularly with mental illness (although doing so without the supervision of a physician isn't generally recommended, but access to this type of health care can be riddled with barriers).[9]

But then if one seeks treatment and is labelled an alcoholic or an addict, judgment is often passed. People with substance use disorder are more likely to be treated unfavourably by healthcare professionals and receive inferior healthcare treatment.[10] They are far more likely to either not secure employment or to lose their jobs if their employer finds out about their addiction—regardless of sobriety. Structural stigma exists across "various institutional systems and social contexts, including employment and income, housing, and education."[11]

Substance use can significantly change behaviour, and users can become single-minded about the substances they crave—much like Gollum and his Precious. Everything else, including friends, family, and jobs, can disappear into the background. But this is where folks need empathy the most. I acknowledge that providing help can be really difficult on friends and family, and it can be incredibly hard to empathize with someone who is facing addiction. Those friends and family can disappear, enacting boundaries because they simply can't

9   University Hospitals, "'Magic Mushrooms,' Psilocybin and Mental Health," *The Science of Health* (blog), May 15, 2022, https://www.uhhospitals.org/blog/articles/2022/05/magic-mushrooms-psilocybin-and-mental-health.

10 James D. Livingston, *Structural Stigma in Health-Care Contexts for People with Mental Health, A Literature Review* (Ottawa: Mental Health Commission of Canada, 2020). https://www.mentalhealthcommission.ca/wp-content/uploads/drupal/2020-07/structural_stigma_in_healthcare_eng.pdf.

11 Livingston, *Structural Stigma in Health-Care Contexts*, 4.

allow the destruction that can happen with single-minded addiction into their lives. I do understand this. My father's father lived with substance use disorder and, from what my mother told me, was virtually impossible to live with. In the two years following my father's immigration to Canada when he was sixteen years old, his family moved to nearly thirty different locations as my granddad chased job after job.

But this also means that for the one living with substance use disorder, isolation can come crashing in as people start to disappear from their lives as a result of frustration, anger, and burnout. And then what happens? The individual, who is now without their community, is at far greater risk of relapse or heavier usage. With no one to advocate for them, their addiction is subject to an even deeper moral judgment of character and worthiness as they try to navigate health care, work, and other systems. They are marked as someone with a lack of control, a deep-seated personality flaw.

The One Ring can take anyone, even a benevolent hobbit like Frodo. The implication, however, is that if the Ring does take you entirely, as it does Gollum, then it's your fault, your flaw. *There's naught left in him but lies and deceit.*

In the end, the Ring doesn't claim Frodo, so does that mean he's a better person (hobbit)? Does that mean that Frodo has more control? Does that mean Gollum is flawed and Frodo is not? Are those who live with substance use disorder similarly inherently defective? Weaker? Less deserving of love and care?

Perhaps this is why Frodo understood Gollum so deeply. He knows exactly what it's like to be under the influence of the Ring—the fear and exhaustion, the desire to just give in. Sméagol was taken by the addiction of the One Ring and was entirely unable to shake that addiction, even as it integrated itself into his physical form and identity. This was exactly what Frodo understood and had empathy for, even if Sam believed it to be vile.

In Jackson's film version of the novels, Frodo questions Sam's treatment of Gollum. He asks why Sam treats Gollum the way he does.

"Why do you do that?" Frodo says.

Sam replies, "What?"

"Call him names? Run him down all the time."

"Because that's what he is, Mister Frodo. There's naught left in him but lies and deceit. It's the Ring he wants. It's all he cares about."

Frodo blinks, red-eyed and pale. "You have no idea what it did to him. What it's still doing to him." Then, softly, watching as Sméagol blissfully catches salmon in a stream. "I want to help him, Sam."

Sam is confused. "Why?"

"Because I have to believe he can come back."[12]

My dad wakes me early. He has an aunt—a woman he hasn't seen in ages—who is coming from the UK to visit, and my mother keeps mumbling things like "we simply can't afford this" and "she's going to have to find her own entertainment" and "she's a bit clueless about how much it costs." I hear the resentment lacing her voice. Although I don't know what it is my mom thinks she can't afford, time or otherwise. I realize the truth is that my mom just doesn't want to host her. She feels put out. Maybe she's a bit envious. My aunt has what my mother thinks she never can.

I remember this aunt from a long time ago. Her husband—my father's blood uncle—had Parkinson's and trembled and never spoke, and that confused me. He passed away, and now my aunt wants to travel and is excited to see me again. My mom says it's because my uncle was a burden on her. "Or maybe you're annoyed because she's travelling and you're not," I shoot back for the first time. My father tells me to shut up, that I'm being bitchy. I probably am.

---

12   *The Two Towers*, dir. Jackson.

My father is tasked with driving all the way into the city to pick up my aunt from the airport and bring her all the way back here so she can spend three weeks in our house with nothing to do because my mom says she can't afford the time to keep her occupied. I can't really figure out what "time" my mom is referring to. She never leaves the house anyways.

I'm secretly excited though. I want to travel and fly on an airplane and land in a country I don't recognize that smells like nothing I know. I want my aunt to tell me what that's like. I want to bathe in those dreams. I know my mom wants that, too, and she's angry that she can't have it. She tells me, "You can't travel right now so just be happy."

"Remember," she says, "happiness is a choice."

"And what choice did you make?" I snap again. I don't know where this voice is coming from. I remember her saying my old friend, the one in the engineering program with the curly chestnut hair, was a bit trashy. I remember her saying my golden boyfriend of long ago wasn't good enough for me. Now, I realize that my mother was wrong. One evening, before my aunt arrives, my mom tells me this aunt wrote a letter to my mom, asking if I could travel with her next summer. She wanted to take me to see any country I would like. Images of the hot Sahara Desert and pyramids bloom in my mind. I would just have to pay for my plane ticket. I don't know how much a plane ticket costs, so I start to add up numbers in my head, trying to find a solution. But before I say anything, my mother shakes her head and says, "You can't afford it. I already told her no for you."

I'm starting to realize that my mother can't let go of the idea that nothing will work out, that she'll never see any of her dreams come true. Maybe, even if not now, someday I could finish my degree, travel, move out on my own, afford my own rent, pay my own bills, be independent, make friends, form bonds and relationships that help me feel better about myself and help me find a way to be good to other people. That help me ignore my Shadow and all it has made me do. Maybe someday I won't be quite so fucked-up. My mom can't envision this for herself, and so she won't envision it for me. And for the first time, I wonder if my mother has her own Shadow. I think about that little girl she became and wonder where my mother has hidden her.

My mother never says *what if?* She never even dips a toe into the possibility that things could be better, for fear of it being chopped off. But I don't think she realizes how important those two words are or how much I need them right now. I tell only Loki these things as he looks at me, gives me a small meow, and purrs his agreement. I've decided to keep him, no matter what my father asked of me. I will try my hardest to pay my bills and get an apartment for me and my cat. Loki doesn't need another home; I am his home. I don't care if my mother doesn't like him.

And now, something in me is starting to say *what if*, and I can't get that question out of my head, and I need someone to believe in *what if* with me.

What if things won't always be like this? What if the days continue to march on and slowly change until, eventually, they will have changed so much that I will look out the window of my own apartment that I pay for myself and say to Loki, "Hey, yeah, things sure did change"?

What if?

It's a charged question, full of buzzing electricity, and it fills me with both hope and fear.

The morning my aunt arrives, my dad and I drink our coffee. I dress and meet him at the car. It's an early morning, a dusky August dawn covered in a sheet of dew soon to be burned off by the rising sun.

As my dad drives, I watch the sky lighten across the fields bursting with corn. We stop at a coffee shop where he buys us another coffee and donuts, and we continue driving, CBC Radio filling the silence we always seem to fall into. I wonder why we are always silent when we are together. I wonder which one of us is the one who doesn't want to break that silence and which of us is the one who does. I wonder how deep the silence goes between us and if there will ever be enough words for us to be close.

Fields give way to small towns. We stop for lunch at a roadside diner, and I listen to how my dad talks to the older man who takes our orders. They chat about the weather and the crops and drivers these days, and "this is my daughter," my dad says, and I smile when the man says how nice it is that we have such a good relationship. We eat our all-day breakfast and, for a small thing, I'm good at packing back three eggs, Texas toast, hash browns, sausages, and more coffee. My dad pays, and we are back on the road.

As we approach the city outskirts, the roads become wider, more populated. We aren't far now, and I'm nervous about seeing my aunt who is worldly and independent.

My dad turns off the radio. I watch as his hand grips the steering wheel, then releases to the gear shift, then to the steering wheel.

"Listen, kid." His tone is *that* tone, and I wonder if he wants to ask me a favour or tell me something terrible or gently break it to me that my behaviour needs to change because my mom just can't take it. "You might have noticed I wasn't at home this morning."

"No. Should I have?"

"Or Loki."

Breath leaves me. My skin is grave-cold. "No," I whisper, and I'm already filled with regret over my inability to care for my cat. "Where is he?" I ask.

He glances at me. "We told you to find him a new home. You didn't do that."

No no no no no.

"But he has a home. I am his home." My father doesn't respond. "Where's Loki?"

I hear him say words I already know, and something in me cracks. There's a crevasse that slices through our seats and he is flung so far away from me and my hatred and rage.

"We had him put down."

We killed your cat.

We stole him while you were sleeping, and now he's buried up on the hill under a pile of rocks in a black garbage bag.

"Kid? Did you hear me?"

I look out the window. Nod once.

"Okay, now just make sure you put on a brave face for your aunt. No nonsense, okay?"

My throat is closing, my chest is punched in. I no longer have a heart. My fingers have become claws. I squeeze my jaw shut, purse my lips, and watch the cars in the other lanes as we merge onto the highway, and I *fucking hate him.*

I never hated him before. I always wanted to be his little helper, to make him proud, to do the best I possibly could just for three little words—*I love you.*

I hate him.

I feel a pressure on my knee and see my dad's hand there. I look at the hair on his knuckles and the long fingers and I remember those hands guiding me as we scaled rocks and shimmied under bushes and climbed trees. He gives my knee a squeeze and releases.

"Brave face, okay?" His voice is soft and gentle, and I wonder if it's possible to loathe someone so intensely but still love them so much.

We are only minutes from the airport, so I don't bother letting any tears come. I know I won't be allowed to cry or be angry or scream the way I want to. I become numb. I slip out of myself and shelve those violent emotions that aren't permitted in my life and give my aunt a trembling smile and remember that I'm really good at being a quiet girl, so I do what I'm really good at doing.

My Shadow looms large—bigger than it's ever been.

My aunt and my dad talk the whole way home, and I slouch in the back of the car, chewing my fingernails, watching as the buildings dissolve into the distance, swallowed up by the fields of corn and trees and tractors and, eventually, forests. I don't cry, and my eyes are burning. There is a physical ache in my chest, and now I realize why people say they die of a broken heart because I think my heart is shattered. I try not to think about it. I remember exactly how to shut it all off.

We arrive home, and I slip past my mom. I hear her telling me we're going to be having a late lunch together so make sure I wash up and come right back down. I try to count the hours until I can be alone because when I'm alone—only when I'm alone—will I allow myself to fall apart.

I ascend the stairs. My legs are blocks attached to my body, and it hurts to move. There's so much deep pain in my belly, and I look down the hall and expect my cat to be sitting there, looking at me, waiting for me. All I see are flecks of dust in the pale light that pools across the floor.

I enter my bedroom and shut the door behind me as quietly as possible. I hear the faint click, and I'm alone.

I look at my unmade bed and I'm sure there's a cat-shaped imprint. I think I shouldn't be so upset for just a cat. He was just a cat. Cats come and go, right? It's not normal to love something that much, right? But I feel so alone. I realize I have no friends because I don't even know how to be a friend, and the hole that Loki has left is too big for me to bear. I start to tell myself all sorts of terrible things. I say I'm worthless. I say I'm garbage. I say I should die. And my voice slips into the deep hissing voice of my Shadow, hovering over me, pressing on me. I slide into an emptiness that is familiar, and suddenly the words that kept me hopeful and anchored for so long, *what if*, no longer exist.

Chapter 6

A World to Fall Into

I have found an apartment all for myself, and I'm driving along the highway, pushing the gas pedal, and singing as loudly as I can. I see the city in the distance. My car carries me and my few possessions towards Lakeshore Road, in Toronto, where my new home is. I'm renting from a nice guy named Raven who looks like he should be in a biker gang but talks like he could be a therapist. Before I'd signed the lease, I asked him if there was a possibility that I could have a pet, something small. I think about Loki and feel a bit traitorous for wanting another cat. When I told my mom I was thinking about getting one, she'd paused, sighed, and said, "Why don't you start with a plant first. If you can keep that alive, maybe you could look after a pet."

Raven had laughed when I asked him, and said, "You can have a Great Dane, but good luck in that small space."

Small doesn't quite describe my new home. It's a 330-square-foot gerbil cage with a stacked washer and dryer and an oven that could fit a fifteen-pound turkey, and if I sit on the edge of my futon, I can reach and eat right out of the fridge. It's perfect, and I don't think it's real. How did I get so lucky? I'm sure it will all fall apart. I've never been able to do something so grown-up as making my own way in the world before. Every time I've tried, I've ended up in the back of a police car, in an ambulance, or just broken in the middle of the night begging my father to come get me. I can't ever seem to fly.

For now, though, I'll just pretend I have at least a little bit of control. I'll pretend this life belongs to me and that I have a clear story and that I matter. I decide to make this small space my home. I ask Raven if it's okay if I paint the walls. He says he'd be happy to do it for me, all I have to do is pick the colour. I pick a shade of yellow that looks like whipped butter.

My first night here I can't sleep. I'm worried about my shitty car sitting in the construction zone at night because I can't afford to pay for a parking spot. I'm worried that someone will smash it up. I'm worried that I can't pay my bills. I'm worried that I can't manage on my own. I'm worried that it will all fall apart, and I'll have to move back to my parents' place, and I remember the ache I felt living there. I want to make a story of my own, but I can't stop hearing my mother's voice telling me what is and isn't possible, how the world is a cruel place and things just aren't in the cards for me. I can't stop thinking about how I couldn't even make friends if anyone ever found out that I'd been in a psychiatric hospital. There are entire parts of me that I try so hard to slice off, but they simply won't leave me, and I don't want anyone to know. Meanwhile, the Shadow still lurks in the corner and I'm sure its presence is my fault, a flaw in me, and I just need to try harder. I need to take control. I need to smarten up. *Brave face, okay?*

I want to make my own story.

I'm working retail in a mall just north of my place, and I hate it. The people crowd around me, and I'm angry all the time. Everything spins. I'm clutching at time, trying to hold still so I can get everything done that I'm supposed to. A few weeks in, I watch the police take away two of the staff for theft. I'm told to do something to keep spirits up. I wonder where my spirit has gone to.

One day, one of the staff tells me she hates me, saying it's because I'm so thin, and I don't even really know what she means by that. She asks me how I manage it, and I tell her it's because the rest of my life is a mess. She laughs. I laugh. I don't eat lunch.

I'm old enough now—my late twenties—to have regrets in my life, but I don't feel so old that I don't want to do anything about them, and I know if I *can* do something about those regrets, if I can make some change in my life, I will be different than my mother. I wonder if I can try going back to school. I wonder if I might be able to finish my degree. I send some emails and make some calls and discover that I can re-register at my old university, and I'm excited. I can actually do it right this time. Maybe I can finish my classes between my full-time job and the sleep I'm not getting.

It's been seven years; classes are more expensive than I remember, so I can only take one at a time. I have no way of getting a loan, so I decide to try and save the money myself. I'm not eating much anyways. I will have to apply for a transfer to the University of Toronto because I simply can't afford to keep my car and pay for the gas to get to my old university. I sell my car and start the process of going back to school. I pretend I'm excited, but the deepest part of me knows I've already failed.

I tell my mother I'm going to return to school. "Don't hang your hat on this idea," she says. "Even idiots have degrees, so don't be disappointed if this doesn't work out."

"But you're not one of the idiots," she adds. "You know I think you're so bright." She's quiet a moment, then says, "I spoke to a friend, and he said your degree won't be worthwhile because if you wanted to do more, everyone would see you as a non-starter." My mouth opens, the retort brewing like dragonfire, then she says, "You know I think that's bullshit, though, right?"

I laugh. If I don't, I'll get angry. My dad isn't happy with me going back to school because, he says, I just can't seem to ever be happy with what I've got.

I say the words *I'm fine* more than I can count. *I'm fine. It'll be fine. Just be happy for me.*

Don't remind me that this, too, will become a disaster that will carve another hole out of me.

While I'm at it, I decide I don't want to work retail anymore, and that bewilders my father even more. I think he's a bit ashamed of me. I call my mom crying a lot because I'm just too scared to breathe. My mother gets irritated. I feel desperate when she gets irritated, and then I get angry.

"You're on your own now," she says. "We've warned you. If you screw this up, we can't come and save you." I lash out. My father calls me a bitch. I disconnect the call. We all know where this is headed. I quit my job anyways.

My old friend from long ago, the one who was in the engineering program—has moved to the city, and I feel less alone. She has bought a condo just east of me. She's divorced and is beautiful and successful and has lots of beautiful and successful friends. We see each other more than we ever did when we were younger, and it's like we've picked up where we left off. We will gather at her condo or my apartment, drink, prep ourselves for a night out, go to a nightclub, and dance and drink until the dawn arrives. People love her, and I feel ugly. She speaks with an easy grace, and I feel very shouty and irritable. But I love having her around. She brings a light and familiarity. She doesn't know how fucked-up I am. Even when I tell her in a rapid staccato-like voice that I'm going to work full-time, go to school full-time, and travel the world and do whatever it is my brain is telling me I can do, all while drinking right from a bottle of gin. I watch her delicate eyebrows rise when I tell her all these things, and my voice tumbles out at breakneck speeds and she just says, "That's great."

It's not long until I'm spinning out of control. It's not long until I fall again. I spend the night talking to a nice young woman on a crisis hotline while I continue to drink. We watch the sun come up together, and I realize it's another day. Another day where my story hasn't ended, and I don't know if that thought makes me relieved or just exhausted.

I continue on because I don't know what else to do. I try my hardest at my new office job, but I'm not doing very well at that because I keep calling in sick. I know I'm not sick because I don't have a cold or a fever or tummy ache, but when I wake up, my heart is fluttering, and I can't seem to make my limbs carry me to the shower. I can't seem to get dressed, and the very idea of opening my door and walking to the streetcar and making my way downtown is so terrifying that I'd rather face the shame and anxiety of calling in sick when I'm not really, truly sick. I'm not really, truly sick . . . am I? The Shadow is growing larger. It has its own gravity and now I can hear its whispering, hissing voice.

My old friend is my relief. I don't feel so alone because it's like she likes me for who I am. We both know I'm more than a little odd but, for some reason, she still sticks around and gives me nicknames, and when she's feeling crummy, she'll spend the night at my apartment. A night sometimes turns into two, maybe three. It's nice to not feel alone, and we're goofy in a way that only old friends can be goofy. When we're together, she makes me feel smart, she makes me feel needed. When it's just us, she makes me feel loved and important and not quite such a mess and the Shadow isn't quite so close.

I keep entire parts of me secret from her though. I know we will never truly be the friends she thinks we are because how can I be completely honest with her? How could she possibly still want to be around me, care for me, or respect me if she knew what a horrible person I really am?

I say none of this. I hardly whisper it to myself in the long nights that I can't sleep through. I want to find a doorway through which there is a world that is carved just for me. A place where I can be okay. A place where I can be my own hero. A place where I won't hate myself.

But there's no doorway. I have no story.

I used to walk a lot. I'd put my earbuds in, turn on my music, and walk for hours. I'd pass coffee shops and bookstores and buildings towering so high they reminded me why they're called skyscrapers. I'd watch the lines form outside nightclubs, pass by groups of people smoking outside a record store. As I walked, I'd imagine what it would be like if the never-ending hum of the city were broken by the sound of massive wings pulsing on the wind. A shadow would pass over, and I'd picture silver scales reflecting off the mirrored buildings of the Financial District. In my imagination, that silver beast would be my wish. *Being* that silver beast would be my wish.

Or I'd imagine seeing a shimmer in the air as I approached the corner of an alley. A hum of something not mundane, and I'd look between the dirty buildings—a dim sum restaurant on the left, a variety store on the right—and down the narrow lane I'd see a glittering doorway. I wonder what would happen if I made the choice, right there in the darkness of night between two obscure shops, to step through.

I love the fantasy of portal worlds and fantastical worlds that could layer onto ours, like tracing paper over the original. I love the idea that a doorway or an experience can pop up anywhere, and if you look closely enough, or are worthy enough, you can turn a handle to open a portal, and anything is possible on the other side. Afterwards, if you squint your eyes just so, you can see the leftover shimmering film layered over our mundane world. I love thinking about the magical glitter left behind as the door closes or the film dissipates, newspapers shifting in the breeze along the asphalt. Nothing is left to mark the place where that magical world collided with ours but a hint of smoke, a shimmer in the air.

I also love these fantastical stories because they can be about anyone; someone who doesn't quite fit in or who is so desperately mediocre that it makes sense that they would be invited into fantasy. They might be someone who is uncomfortable in crowds, maybe someone who doesn't ever feel like they fit in anywhere or who is bullied or living in adverse circumstances. Or maybe they're looked upon with suspicion because they make a habit of believing in six impossible things before breakfast.

To me, these stories of portal worlds and fantastical intrusion are wishes. They tell us that our reality isn't all there is and that someone who is just as average and inconsequential as we are, or someone who is odd and maybe a little off, is worthy of experiencing magic. We can hope that there is something else that is different, beautiful, terrifying, fascinating, and entirely *not normal*.

There's a reason why these stories have become so entrenched in our libraries. The possibility of being worthy enough to experience a fantastic portal world that dovetails with ours prompts the questions: Who is allowed into the world? Who is the one who gets to make the story?

As mentally ill folks, who is the author of *our* stories? Or are we allowed to be our own authors, despite our mental illness and otherness? Do we have agency over our own lives, or are we, in some way, perceived as incapable of making our own logical decisions? These are the questions that have haunted me my entire life, and I have looked for answers in stories.

Leah Lakshmi Piepzna-Samarasinha is a queer disabled femme writer, organizer, performance artist, and educator, and is the author of *Care Work: Dreaming Disability Justice*. In her book, she seeks to open conversations and change hegemonic beliefs both around and within the disability community.

> What does it mean to shift our ideas of access and care
> (whether it's disability, childcare, economic access, or
> many more) from an individual choice, an unfortunate

cost of having an unfortunate body to a collective responsibility that's maybe even deeply joyful?[1]

While Piepzna-Samarasinha talks about physical bodies, she also explores the concept of different minds as well, which is where I find her work dovetailing with my own ideas. Shifting our ideas means shifting narratives. Allowing someone with mental illness their own agency is a radical concept for a group of people who have been labelled "idiots" and "lunatics" for centuries. Maybe that radicalism can also take the form of storytelling, using fantasy, magic, dragons, and the unlikeliest of heroes. Maybe those stories can also be about agency.

I know that my social anxiety, agoraphobia, and bipolar disorder have played a large part in shaping me. There are parts of me I've hidden for so long that I don't have the energy anymore to keep them secret. I think of all those parts, and they remind me of stories nesting into one another, doorways that connect those worlds, bringing them all together. Maybe even a land where the stories live, protected and unadulterated, waiting for the protagonist to come and claim theirs. This might also mean that while all those parts—the mental illnesses, the traumas, the quirks of personality—have historically been viewed as disparate, and, in the medical community, something to be fixed, they might in fact be pieces in the mosaic of a whole, *unbroken*, person. While this doesn't align with our current medical and psychiatric pedagogy, the possibility that all the parts of the self—the so-called ugly included—are, in fact, pieces of a whole. And maybe, just maybe, those of us with *different* pieces are more than capable of authoring our own story, because who knows our narratives better than we do?

1   Leah Lakshmi Piepzna-Samarasinha, *Care Work: Dreaming Disability Justice* (Vancouver: Arsenal Pulp Press, 2020), 33.

I remember the long nights I spent alone in my shoebox apartment, dust slowly collecting from the Gardiner Expressway and perpetual construction. How I wanted a portal, how hard I *tried to make* a portal for myself, maybe just a place to let go. Let go of everything that I was desperately trying to hold or stitch together: my crumbling mental health, the dark hole of a future I envisioned, the confusion and anger and trauma.

It wasn't long after I moved to Toronto that I started to truly become afraid. I started seeing doorways everywhere—but they weren't portals to a magical world where my story was intricately entwined with other magical stories, a place where I could truly flourish and breathe. This wasn't what I saw.

The doorway I saw coming closer and closer each day was a doorway of my own ending. The final ending of a story that had been assigned to me but that I had never authored in the first place.

Through this doorway, I saw a story that was ended by myself. My own suicide. I knew this, I saw this, I believed this. But I felt powerless to change it.

I. THE CHOICE OF DEATH

In 2016, I was asked by my school newspaper, *The Varsity*, to attend a lecture and write an article for their upcoming edition. The keynote speaker was a Canadian-Colombian physician with a specialty in palliative care. The lecture was entitled "What Is a Good Death?"

In the bowels of one of University of Toronto's old buildings, around corners and in between close hallways, a classroom was nestled. I walked in a little tentatively, my gaze scanning the press of students all squeezing into the classroom and spilling out into the hallway. I don't do well in crowds.

In the middle of the room was a stainless steel surgical table that an autopsy might have been performed on. Lying on the table was a body draped in a white sheet. A foot—a very lifelike foot—stuck out with a tag on the toe. On the pull-down projector screen was the title of the lecture and the name of the keynote speaker: Dr. Alex Jadad.

The crowd settled. As time protracted, an expectant and somewhat uncomfortable hush fell. Then the form moved. The drape was gently pulled away from the face, and a slight middle-aged man sat up. He looked around the collection of students, his face calm, his smile reassuring and relaxed. He then asked us what we would like our deaths to be like. What do we want at the time of our death? Do we want to be alone? With our loved ones? Do we want it to be painless? Do we want reminders of the beauty that our lives were? Or do we want to be in a medical setting, surrounded with tubes and charts and sterility? Basically, do we have any control or choice over the end of our lives?

I thought about my partner and the nights he had held me as I fell apart. The more I cracked, the tighter he held me, as though he could press me back into a whole person. I thought about the other nights I was alone and wanted suicide to *not* be my only choice. And I realized that what my partner gave me was exactly what I wanted in both my life and at the moment of my own death: peace, reassurance, love.

What, indeed, is a good death? Who is the arbiter of what a good death is? "We have plenty of evidence to show that we die badly," Dr. Jadad said at a 2017 speech given to Palliative Care Australia.[2] I wonder if suicide is included in that criteria. For as long as people have lived, suicide has also existed. Until the term *suicide* cropped up in the mid-seventeenth century, terms like *self-murder*, *self-destruction*, *self-killer*, and (my particular favourite) *self-slaughter* set the tone for popular perceptions of the act.[3] Suicide itself wasn't decriminalized

---

2   Canadian Medical Association, "Dr. Alex Jadad: What Do We Mean by Health?"
      YouTube, August 16, 2019, https://www.youtube.com/watch?v=Y3uDNi1LaCw.

3   *Merriam-Webster Dictionary*, s.v. "self-slaughtered," https://www.merriam-webster.com
      /dictionary/self-slaughtered.

in the UK until 1961,[4] and in Canada, suicide wasn't decriminalized until 1972.[5]

Imagine that—wanting to end your own life but being unsuccessful at it, and then, as if you're not feeling crummy enough, you're charged with a crime. This has been the prevalent view of suicide for . . . well, since the time of Aristotle and Plato and Socrates.

(Although ironically, as he was on trial for heresy, Socrates took his own life in the end, wanting the choice of his death to be his alone. Fair enough.)

Suicide has been a philosophical debate for millennia—to die or not to die? Albert Camus said suicide is the only real philosophical problem we have[6] (I can think of a few others—climate change being top of mind—but I'm not Camus).

Suicide has historically been viewed as the ultimate violation, a monstrous act that throws shade in the face of all that is good. A rejection of life is the paramount of sins, or so we're told.

The problem (if there's only one problem, which I fully admit there are many more) is that suicide is addressed as a single act and the committer of the act is often defined by it and not by all the other factors orbiting suicide. Those factors are multitudinous: racism, oppression, poverty, intergenerational trauma, mental illness, disability, dementia, hopelessness, climate change, abuse, financial uncertainty . . . the list is endless.

What would happen, I wonder, if we addressed suicide with softness, love, and compassion? With empathetic understanding and a desire to learn. Rather than viewing it as a monstrous act where the individual

4   J. Neeleman, "Suicide as a Crime in the UK: Legal History, International Comparisons and Present Implications," *Acta Psychiatrica Scandinavica* 94, no. 4 (October 1996): 252–257. https://doi.org/10.1111/j.1600-0447.1996.tb09857.x.

5   Florence Kellner, "Suicide in Canada," *The Canadian Encyclopedia*, February 7, 2006 (last updated May 1, 2022), https://www.thecanadianencyclopedia.ca/en/article/suicide.

6   Ronald Aronson, "Albert Camus," *The Stanford Encyclopedia of Philosophy*, October 27, 2011 (last updated December 13, 2021), https://plato.stanford.edu/entries/camus/.

who dies by suicide is both the "committer" and the "victim." Which, paradoxically enough, I still hear in conversations today, although this is also shifting as awareness of mental illness and suicide has become more commonplace.

I'm not *for* suicide, particularly. I'd rather the pain one faces to be relieved in *this* world, in this life. But let's be real, for mentally ill folks, sometimes that pain is just too excruciating and the circumstances around that pain are nearly inescapable for them. Being mentally ill can be isolating enough, and, because suicide is such a difficult topic, that isolation only grows more acute. Knowing that one needs to hide all their tumbling, fiery thoughts is isolating and painful and just *so damn impossible*.

In 2020, the Centre for Addictions and Mental Health (CAMH), Toronto's psychiatric hospital, ran a campaign in an earnest attempt to open conversations around suicide. The campaign was called *Not Suicide. Not Today.* As in, today is the day I will choose not to kill myself. Today is the day I will decide to continue living. Today is the day I will overcome the urge to fling myself off a bridge because the entire world and the circumstances in which I move and breathe and exist are just too much for me, and I can't see a way out other than the aforementioned bridge and flinging. Except once I decide not to fling myself off a bridge, all those same circumstances probably will still exist, and I will still be unable to manage them.

Not today, sure. But tomorrow? What will tomorrow bring?

When I first saw the CAMH campaign poster, it didn't sit right. My immediate reaction was to cringe and then to feel anger. (I know, I feel angry about a lot. There's a lot to feel angry about, let's be honest.) I can appreciate wanting to eliminate suicide. Death by choice is one of the most impossible things for us to wrap our minds around. Death itself is . . . well, it's hard to talk about despite it being an inevitability for *every single person ever*.

But when someone actually chooses to die? That's even more unacceptable, we say. How can we prevent this from happening? But should the prevention of suicide be placed on the potential suicide victim, or is it something that is quite possibly out of their control? *Not suicide, not today* implies a choice made by the individual seeking relief, and says nothing of the responsibility of the world in which we live that is inflicting the pain.

It's a big question, and one I can't answer for everyone. What I *can* say is that suicide for mentally ill people isn't always about the choice to die, but rather it's about the impossibility of living in a world that caters to self-love and self-care and toxic positivity without taking into consideration all the circumstances that cut across mental illness, from gender to race to income. Of course, the act of suicide is a choice, but if external circumstances were changed that might alleviate some of that pain, a living wage being just one? Then would suicide for mentally ill folks be as common?

How this campaign approaches suicide is the same narrative we use when we talk about mental illness: individual responsibility.

Yes, the world is falling apart, and some pretty shitty things have happened to you, but here's some self-care, make sure you take action. Your mental health is your responsibility. Ignore the fact that there is a lot to feel mentally unwell about.

There is no reason why we can't step away from these types of campaigns and how suicide makes us feel and instead step into a world where we consider everything else around the person facing suicide. Without this, an integral part of the story is missing.

In Canada, the conversation around suicide has expanded in the last few years with the passing of medical assistance in dying (MAiD) legislation. MAiD is one of those controversial laws that allows licensed medical practitioners to assist individuals in dying, so long as the individual meets certain criteria. One of the criteria that has received a lot of contentious debate is that the individual must be suffering from a "grievous and irremediable physical health condition" and death has to be foreseeable. Previous iterations of the legislation explicitly excluded folks with only mental illness. Plainly put, folks living with mental illness and who were suffering could not legally seek medical assistance in dying.[7]

Of course there were (and still are) a lot of very heated conversations around this legislation, ranging from anyone who wants to die should be allowed to do so with dignity regardless of circumstances, to life is paramount despite suffering.

It's a tough call, naturally. Green-lighting the ability for someone to legally receive medical assistance in a peaceful, pain-free death is a hard decision to make. But the question that has lingered is *whose decision is it?*

This is where mentally ill folks enter the picture. It's difficult for medical practitioners to confirm if death is reasonably foreseeable, or that their mentally ill patient won't ever be free of suffering caused by their mental illness. It's hard to gauge exactly how much suffering is happening or to determine future quality of life for mentally ill folks. And as someone who is mentally ill and has had my own mental health crises, it's also a challenge trying to convey just how *excruciating* that pain is. But isn't my life my own choice? Or perhaps if I wait long enough, things will get better?

The answer from my own experience is that, yes, things got better, but that's also because other factors in my life got a lot easier—a stable home, a loving partner, and friends who truly understand me. I'm also

---

7   "Medical Assistance in Dying (Maid) and Mental Illness—FAQs," CAMH, February 2023, https://www.camh.ca/en/camh-news-and-stories/maid-and-mental-illness-faqs.

lucky enough to not have to work a regular job, but instead, I can look after my mental health, first and foremost.

This doesn't mean that some days aren't still excruciating though. Ironically, I first learned about MAiD when I was googling *suicide* in the middle of the night during a severe bout of depression. If it had been available to me—the choice to die with dignity—I'm not sure I'd be here. I don't know what would have happened, and while I think everyone should have the choice to die on their own terms, the idea that I may have chosen assisted dying terrifies me.

As I write this, MAiD will be expanded to include mentally ill folks by March 17, 2024[8] (although that narrative is constantly shifting, and I have doubts if it will actually be enacted then, or ever). The proposed criteria for an amendment to the MAiD legislation includes a ninety-day assessment period, after which two mental healthcare professionals will decide if the individual is a candidate for MAiD. A wait period is a good, deliberate idea, and it's reasonable to have two mental healthcare professionals weigh in on the complexity of suffering, outcomes, and prognosis for the individual. But the problem isn't with MAiD itself. The problem is the system in which it works.

In Ontario, where I live, it can take anywhere from one to eighteen months to get a psychiatric assessment. That is only after someone has gone to their family doctor or a walk-in clinic to receive a referral. The only way for someone needing a psychiatric assessment to get one faster is to present to a hospital emergency room in a mental health crisis.

So, here's my question: Why should it take longer—up to eighteen months—to receive mental health care for someone who *does* want treatment than it takes—ninety days—for a group of healthcare

---

8   Health Canada, "Medical Assistance in Dying: Overview," Government of Canada, https://www.canada.ca/en/health-canada/services/medical-assistance-dying.html.

professionals to decide that an individual should be allowed to die with dignity?

That's just one factor. The other, which I feel like I will never stop talking about, is a much wider systemic issue: the accessibility of ongoing mental health care, disability assistance, and a living wage. Disability assistance in the province of Ontario is woefully below a living wage, and many folks living with insufferable mental illness simply can't work, as I struggle to. While I manage my mental illness fairly well, the pressure of full-time regular employment has caused a relapse for me in the past, and a few years ago, I came to the realization that I simply can't work a full-time job, no matter how much I may want to. Those are difficult terms to accept. And if individuals living with mental illness can't work and are struggling to feed themselves, how can they pay for therapy or medications or even find some semblance of hope, let alone treatment?

I'm not the first person to point out these issues when it comes to MAiD, but I'm also not sure MAiD for mentally ill folks should be rejected outright. I simply don't have an answer, nor is it my responsibility to have one. But what I do know is that everyone should have the choice to live or die with dignity, and right now I wonder, given all the systemic and institutional inequities, if MAiD is even a choice. Because if we measure quality of life solely on how insufferable mental illness is, then we're only looking at one piece of the very large puzzle.

That to me, doesn't seem like a choice at all.

II. WHAT, THEN, IS A GOOD DEATH?

In recent years, there have been a number of works that tackle suicide in speculative fiction that address it without the stigma and voyeurism. Works like Shaun David Hutchinson's *We Are the Ants* and Laura E. Weymouth's *The Light Between Worlds* give us new stories about suicide and, by extension, mental illness, that aren't just about the act itself (or lack thereof; again, choice) but about everything surrounding it.

The Light Between Worlds, published in 2018, is about three siblings, a magical woodland, war-torn London, and transformation. The novel is quite obviously telling the story of mental illness, but what Weymouth has done is particularly compelling: one of the interpretations a reader can take is that she's given mental illness, suicidal ideation, and suicide a soft, magical touch.

The Light Between Worlds is an exploration of what life might have been like for Lucy, Edmond, Peter, and Susan after their return from Narnia. It's a retelling—or rather, an expansion—of C.S. Lewis's *The Lion, the Witch and the Wardrobe*. It's a "well, what now?" story.

The three siblings, Evelyn, Philippa, and Jamie Hapwell (our stand-ins for Lucy, Edmond, Peter, and Susan in *The Light Between Worlds*), are survivors of the bombing of London during WWII. While Jamie—the eldest—is a character in the story, he is purposefully not integral. The story, Weymouth explains on her website,[9] is about the invisibility of women during and after WWII. The trauma faced by those who were on the sidelines, the waiting and the not knowing, is the space where Evelyn and Philippa's story lies. And in the aftermath of the war, one's inability to return to life as it was before. Because nothing is as it was before. How could it be?

When we meet Evelyn—Ev—she's a sixteen-year-old girl who has been sixteen years old before, many years ago in another world. In flashbacks, Ev, along with her siblings, was taking shelter in a bomb bunker during the blitz on London, when Ev psychically called out for help. Her call was received in another world—the Woodlands—and

---

9   Laura E. Weymouth, "The Light Between Worlds Discussion Guide," Laura E. Weymouth, April 24, 2021, https://lauraeweymouth.com/the-light-between-worlds-discussion-guide.

the Hapwell siblings found themselves taken out of the bunker and into a magical green wood.

Weymouth doesn't do much by way of worldbuilding of the Woodlands, just enough to make Ev's grief over her eventual loss of the woods to be immense and believable. In the Woodlands, Ev comes to life. She feels secure in herself, authoritative, and grows into an adult with confidence and a sense of place. The Woodlands becomes her true home where she flourishes. But the older siblings yearn for home.

Just like the Pevensie siblings of *The Lion, the Witch and the Wardrobe*, the Hapwell siblings continue to age while in the Woodlands. Time runs differently there, meaning these siblings live nearly a lifetime—grow up, learn, love—all within the magical world Ev has pulled them into. Their personalities and identities become entangled with the Woodlands. Until they are unceremoniously dropped back in the bomb shelter with no Earth-time lost.

This is the place where Weymouth begins—the aftermath. Ev is heading back to her all-girls boarding school. Philippa and Ev have a strained relationship, and Philippa has left for America. Jamie just sort of seems to do his own thing.

Of the three siblings, Ev struggles the most. Weymouth has written a character who is both self-aware and absent. She lives with the ghosts of the Woodlands and the memories contained there. To add to that loss, Ev never chooses to leave the Woodlands, just as she never chooses to enter—not specifically. When she needs it the most, the Woodlands hears her call. But being thrust out of the Woodlands isn't her choice either, and for the few years after the war ends, Ev tries to find her way back.

Weymouth has written a character who doesn't know a state of living that *isn't* pain. These emotions are a staple in Ev's life, and her world is built around a sort of nihilistic acceptance bordering on shattering emptiness. When she returns to her boarding school, Ev already has the mind of a grown woman who has lived and experienced a life that isn't of or in this world. Her sense of loneliness is palpable despite her school peers being kind and welcoming. For the most part, Ev tries to live in this life, but those memories never leave her. At one point, she tries to cover the pain she feels with physical pain—she self-harms in subtle ways, such as purposefully digging her hands into poison ivy and letting them fester simply to feel the discomfort.

About halfway through the novel, Weymouth takes us on a different route, one that focuses on Philippa. Philippa's story is both intertwined with Ev's and also completely different. Where Ev is brought into the Woodlands and flourishes, Philippa struggles. She misses her home, worries about her parents, and can't find a place that is truly meant for her.

On a very fundamental level, where one sister finds happiness, the other finds struggle. There is no world in which both sisters can exist and be happy and, yet, their love for one another is deep. No matter what the sisters do, there will always be loss.

When Philippa discovers that Ev is missing from her school, she struggles to unpack the events of her sister's life, the part of her that was separate from being a Hapwell sibling. Philippa learns second-hand the loneliness and depression her little sister has felt, how she tried to make a life for herself, and how something was always missing.

As Philippa searches for Ev, a possibility starts to bleed into her mind and her worry is compounded—*Did my sister take her own life?* Or did Ev find a way back to the Woodlands and leave their world forever?

Either answer could be true, depending on what we the readers want to take away from this novel. And just as we have the choice of believing one ending over another, so does Ev have the choice to stay in or leave this world. Even if the Woodlands isn't a metaphor, Ev still decides to leave behind the world where her siblings live. She is essentially killing the Ev of Earth and stepping into the life of Ev of the Woodlands.

Her choice to leave, while heartbreaking, is not just accepted by her sister and brother, but sorrowfully blessed. Ev is able to move into a new existence softly, with love and knowledge that her passing won't rip a hole in the lives of the siblings she leaves behind. There will be pain and grief and loss, but it won't be a brutal pain. It will mercifully be free of the questions, anger, and guilt that accompanies a loved one's suicide.

I return to Dr. Jadad's question—*What is a good death?*

A good death is a wish, a story, a woodland through a magical portal. A good death is the choice we all want—the choice that *I* want, the ability to write our own stories surrounded by love and support, wherever they may take us, right until the end.

III. WHAT, THEN, IS A GOOD LIFE?

I remember the night I saw an alien. Not a real alien, but it was terrifying, nonetheless. I'd been trying new medications. My mental health was slipping, and the medications that had worked previously were no longer as effective.

My doctor and I were shuffling through the trials of medications and one of the anti-psychotics has a side effect of extreme irritability, twitching, and restlessness. Less common is paranoia. Even less common is a "departure from reality."

The restlessness started like twitching in my legs. My muscles were contracting in small ripples. I couldn't sit still. It felt like ants were crawling under my skin. The irritability hit shortly after, whether from a side effect of the medication or simply because the sensation of ants crawling under one's skin is, well . . . irritating.

Then things changed. Irritability turned into an overwhelming sensation, rocking, shaking, confusion. I pressed my palms against my thighs to make them stop moving. I clutched my hair to put out the fire in my brain. I started to experience a derealization, an inability to discern if I was alive, if I existed. Nothing seemed *right*.

I was sitting in the dim of the bedroom, the window behind me, the mirror in front of me, when I saw it. A distorted shape in the mirror, watching me through the window. I screamed.

Light bloomed as my partner came into the room. "Close the drapes," I yelled. "There's someone there. There's something there."

"What's there?" he asked.

I lowered my voice to a whisper. "An alien. I can see an alien."

Of course, there was no alien. My partner tried to reassure me, but I couldn't shake the feeling. It wasn't until the medications were fully out of my system that I started to slide back into the reality in which I lived—which was still a distorted reality, minus the alien.

I know—and knew then—that what I saw wasn't real. It was a product of paranoia and irritability and a vulnerability to the fantastical that lived in my mind. It was intrusive, as many experiences of mental illness are. Sort of like a film layered over one's reality that no one else can see. But that doesn't make the film any less impactful to the one experiencing it. It isolates and causes havoc.

It's also, in my writerly opinion, a great place to start a story.

While probably the least popular of fantasy literary devices, intrusion fantasy, because of its very nature, can also be used as a storytelling method to describe suicide and suicidal ideation, which is what Shaun David Hutchinson has done with his 2016 novel.

We Are the Ants tells the story of a teenage boy, Henry Denton. Henry's life is pretty shitty. His father left when Henry was thirteen. Henry's brother, Charlie, is abusive, his mother is rough around the edges and seemingly unloving, and he is watching his nana slowly fade away because of dementia. Henry is beaten and ridiculed in school and is in an unhealthy and abusive relationship with a boy who continually degrades him and even assaults him.

These circumstances alone would be too much for anyone, but a year prior to the events of the novel, Henry's boyfriend Jesse died by suicide. On top of that, Henry is regularly abducted by aliens.

It's a lot. It's *purposefully* a lot.

Hutchinson sets the tone for the novel with Henry reflecting, "Life is bullshit."[10] His life truly is bullshit, and it's hard to see a way through for Henry, and it's impossible for him to see that for himself. This is where the aliens come in.

Often, when Henry is abducted, he will be absent for days, but it's curious that no one—not even his mother, nana, or brother—notices. When the aliens dump him back in his small town in Florida, he's usually naked and a few miles from home. Because why not?

The intrusion here is the aliens, or what they represent. We can either assume that Hutchinson really does want us to believe they're aliens, or we can assume that Hutchinson is using aliens as a stand-in for something else, something a lot harder to talk about.

Henry's shitty life doesn't necessarily make for a captivating story. It's hard for storytellers to craft an engaging narrative about abuse, assault, trauma, depression, and suicide in a way that doesn't feel like it's simply too much for the reader. It's through the aliens that Henry is given choice and agency—something he hasn't had in his life on Earth, particularly after the death of his boyfriend.

When the aliens abduct him, they perform a series of Pavlovian-esque experiments on Henry—guess correctly, and he gets rewarded. Guess wrong, and he's zapped with electrodes attached to his body. The aliens show him an image of the Earth blowing up and then a red

---

10   Shaun David Hutchinson, *We Are the Ants* (New York: Simon Pulse, 2017), 1.

button. After a few tries, Henry understands what the choice is that they are offering him: push the button and you save the world. Do nothing, and the world will end in 144 days.

Your choice, kid.

They couldn't have picked a worse person for the job. Or so Hutchinson would have us think.

"I don't know why I didn't press the button for real when I had the chance," Henry says, "other than that I don't think the aliens would have given me such a long lead time if they hadn't wanted me to consider my choice carefully. Most people probably believe they would have pressed the button in my situation—nobody *wants* the world to end, right?—but the truth is that nothing is as simple as it seems."[11]

And this is the point of the novel.

Over the course of the 144 days, Henry is assaulted, violated, overlooked, and generally beaten down. His nana continues to deteriorate, and his brother announces that he and his girlfriend are expecting. On top of that, Henry blames himself for Jesse's suicide and often oscillates between rage and grief and feels entirely guilty for both.

But slowly, tiny drops of hope come into Henry's life. Some of them—like a science teacher who truly believes in him—are so innocuous that Henry overlooks them. Some of them are much bigger, like the arrival of a new kid in the school, Diego Vega. And even bigger still, the idea of becoming an uncle starts to bloom in Henry's mind.

As the timer counts down, relationships begin to form around him—a bond between him and his soon-to-be sister-in-law, Zooey, and a mending of his friendship with a classmate, Audrey. Henry starts to gain deeper understanding of his mother and what she's been through and continues to go through as a solo parent while her own mother is dying. And truly seeing his nana as a person, not as someone who

---

11   Hutchinson, *We Are the Ants*, 19.

is slowly succumbing to dementia, helps Henry gain some clarity. Eventually, he mends the toxic relationship with his brother, Charlie. Henry also learns to cut out harmful people and let in those who love him for exactly who he is.

Eventually, Henry learns to love again and realizes that although that love may not last forever, it's still worth trying for.

What I feel like Hutchinson is trying to get at is that the aliens represent mental illness, and the abductions and choice Henry is given to save the world or let it end is a suicide metaphor. Henry's aliens—or as he calls them, "sluggers"—are that representation, his psyche in a way. They're the embodiment of his intrusive thoughts.

To return to the start, Henry was first abducted by the aliens when he was barely a teenager. This developmental shift into puberty can often bring on feelings of depression, anxiety, body insecurity, and, for Henry particularly, his confusing sexuality. It was also at this time that his father started excluding Henry from the "father-son" activities they used to do when Henry was younger. It was right after Henry's first abduction that his father left and never came back. This first abduction was Henry's first episode of derealization, depersonalization, and severe depression.

Between the years of Henry's first abduction and the events of the novel, Henry is often "abducted," and although no one believes he's actually being taken by aliens, he still earns the nickname Space Boy in school. But when he meets Jesse Franklin, the abductions stop. Maybe Jesse gives Henry a reprieve from his mental illness. Maybe with Jesse Henry feels a sense of solidity and home. It sort of reminds me of Nell Crain and her husband, Arthur Vance, and how, for the brief time she had him in her life, Nell's haunting ceased.

When Jesse dies by suicide, Henry starts experiencing abductions again, which makes sense. Living through the suicide of a loved one— particularly for someone who is already as developmentally malleable as a young teenager—is an incredibly traumatic event. Henry continually blames himself for not loving Jesse enough. He lives with both rage and overwhelming grief. He's perpetually confused as he tries to figure out why Jesse killed himself.

While this is happening, Henry does what a lot of people would do—treats himself like garbage. He berates himself, blames himself, hurts himself by continually seeing another boy at school in secret—a boy who also abuses him to the extent that the boy and his friends attack Henry in the school showers and, eventually, that boy tries to rape Henry.

But here's the choice: the aliens have given Henry the opportunity to save the world. But why the hell would he press the button and save everyone if life is shit anyways? Why should he let *his* existence continue? Why should he save *his* experience?

The choice to press the button and save the world or to do nothing and let it implode is, of course, Henry's choice to end his own life.

These abductions are moments when Henry is so mentally unwell that he loses reality. He experiences the time slippage that comes with dissociation that many of us who have been in the darkest trenches of mental illness can experience, where things don't make sense and the body's ability to function becomes a sort of elusive feeling relegated to the periphery.

> It happened like always: the shadows, the urge to pee, the helpless paralysis. The dark room. I love and loathe that room. It's there that they deconstruct me, study me, and rebuild me . . . As they perform their experiments, which make little sense to my primitive intellect, my mind wanders. It wonders. Why me?[12]

---

12   Hutchinson, *We Are the Ants*, 291.

This time slippage and dissociation is something I'm very famil-iar with. During the worst of my depression, as I'd lay in bed, nothing seemed to be real. Time was condensed and felt similar in texture to peanut butter, if time can have a texture, which during a depressive epi-sode, it does for me. My body wasn't really mine, and the sensations that Henry describes—needing to pee, particularly—had this murky quality.

The only time Henry's family finally notices he is missing is when Henry is starting to see reasons why he *should* press that button and save the world. Maybe Henry is starting to take inventory of what he might lose if he continues with the status quo. The rebuilding of his friendship with Audrey, mending the tattered threads with his brother, and finally understanding his mother and all she faces. The relation-ship with Diego Vega, a boy who challenges Henry's beliefs about Jesse and the feeling of responsibility he's held over Jesse's death for months, give him a deeper understanding of human nature. Slowly, Henry is starting to see the world as it might truly be: filled with flawed people who love him, a place that will never be perfect but maybe there's a bit of hope. And that even though the boy he loved most in this world ended his life, Henry does very much deserve love.

This is the choice—the freedom—that the aliens represent.

The second way of reading *We Are the Ants* is that Hutchinson is giving us a story about real alien abductions. It's still an intrusion fan-tasy because . . . well, alien abductions are pretty intrusive. But just because the aliens are real, that doesn't mean that Henry closing in on suicide isn't. Because he is and there's a countdown. It's just with real aliens this time. And if every abduction is a real one, they still work to both isolate Henry and help him with a deeper understanding of the messy imperfection of his own life.

Everything would be easier if someone told me what
to do: push the button, stop seeing Marcus, get over

Jesse. The problem with choices is that I usually make the wrong ones.[13]

But what is the right choice when it comes to ending one's reality? To ending one's life?

The fact is, Henry will never *not* have that choice to end his life. He *should* have that choice. Hutchinson also reasons that having that choice is important: having choice gives more purpose to the decisions we make. If Henry knows that on any given day he might die, then the days he does live might be more purposeful, and he might be more thoughtful, more present. And while he's contemplating that, life will continue, and, slowly, he might see that he's not actually alone.

But suicide doesn't often look like what we think it does because, on the other hand, feeling as though one has *no choice but to die* by suicide isn't freedom either. The freedom is in choice—the same choice both Henry and Ev had—but without the burden of stigma.

I won't tell you if Henry presses the button or not. But what I will say is that *We Are the Ants* is a beautiful and fluid story about suicide and choice. Or as Henry says, "The [aliens] didn't give me a choice, they gave me freedom."[14]

I try to keep a wall up, but I still want softness. I am too filled with harsh edges, so I think maybe I'd like some company in my life. My apartment, while small, feels so overwhelmingly empty. Nights are dark and waking in the morning is nearly pointless.

I meet someone. He's a doctor, and I try not to be impressed with how smart he is, but I can't help feeling as though there is a spotlight on me when he gives me attention. He's nothing like my

13 Hutchinson, *We Are the Ants*, 65.
14 Hutchinson, *We Are the Ants*, 56.

golden boyfriend from so long ago. When I look at him, I see an emptiness, a simmering rage, and confidence that is intoxicating. I feel unworthy, and I think, in the back of my mind, that he likes it that way.

"What's your uni program again?" he asks me as though I haven't told him before. I try to assume he's just forgetful. We are in my shoebox apartment. It's dark out. When he arrived, he started making himself coffee. I hope I have enough milk. He makes a comment about picking up better coffee beans.

"Political science," I tell him. He rolls his eyes. "What's wrong with poli-sci?"

He looks at me like he would look at a little kid. "That's what everyone who doesn't know what they want takes." He, again, reminds me he went to medical school at the University of Toronto. A *top* school, he emphasizes. "I know what I'm talking about."

I mumble: "But I do know what I want."

"No, you don't."

He reminds me of how far I am from any *real* life accomplishments when he takes me for a late dinner and gets angry when I try to pay. He flings my money back at me and says, "You're broke. Don't be stupid." I try to remember I didn't really want to go to this restaurant anyways. He tells me he could buy me a condo if he wanted to, and he cuts a look at me that I know means there's more behind that potential purchase and most of it has got nothing to do with me. But still, I feel wanted. Even if he only wants me after the sun has set and before it's risen, only at night when no one can see us. No exceptions.

Each day, my sense of self chips away. I want to think of myself as strong, but every time he comes over I am reminded I'm not. I hardly wonder if he might not be good for me or that I might deserve better. I know someone better will never want me anyways.

"I'm going to travel," I tell him one night.

He says, "Drunk vacations aren't travelling."

"No, Egypt. I want to go to Egypt." I lower my voice. "I've always wanted to see Cairo. Ever since I was a kid." I think about the atlas I used to read under my mother's writing desk. I whisper the words *what if* to myself.

He shakes his head. "You'd do better with a drunk vacation. Start there."

I turn over and ignore his hands pawing at me.

I try to keep up with my studies and work. I try to keep up with the breakneck speed at which I have to run. At lunch, I sneak out of the office and race to the subway. I always arrive to class late, breathless and sweating. I never understand everything the professor says, but I can't stay after class because I have to sneak out right before he finishes lecturing so I can slip back into the office without anyone knowing I was gone. I study when no one is looking. I make mistakes at work. I'm not good at my job and not a great student either. I just want to accomplish something, but my mind is crumbling again.

I'm not swimming. I'm drowning. There's no edge, no lifeboat, no light. The Shadow is growing, feeding on every sleepless night, every dehumanizing thought I have about myself. I am not okay.

I'm starting to become uninterested in this doctor who flings my money back at me and how he makes me feel, because how he makes me feel is angry. I tell him I don't want to do anything with him, but he tells me to shut the hell up and let him fuck me and he pins me down and I realize I have no choice so what I do doesn't even matter anyways. I am glad to know I haven't forgotten how to slip out of my body. I make patterns in the stucco ceiling. I look at the blinking smoke alarm. I feel nothing. I don't cry. I stop wearing makeup.

I circle. Night comes and I am not sure if I can—if I want—to make it until morning. I call a crisis helpline again. I tell no one. I go to work the next day; I race to class. At night, I don't stop him from doing what he wants to me. His fingers grip my wrists, and it hurts, but I don't care. I am blank and empty.

"I'm dating this chick," he tells me one night. I open my mouth to respond, but nothing comes out. "Don't get all upset, but she's more my type."

"And what exactly is your type?" I think I should have said I never wanted to be his type in the first place. He just shrugs. "Does she know about me?"

He laughs, feigning shock at how stupid I am.

I become fatigued and pale, and I chalk it up to my breakneck speed. It's not until I feel nausea that I realize all my choices are wrong. Two lines on a little take-home test confirm my terror. In the back of my mind, a little voice is saying *but you had no choice*, and that voice makes me even angrier because not having a choice is terrifying and the powerlessness is terrifying. I had no choice, he took that from me. Hate burrows into me and whether it's for him or myself, I can't quite tell.

But I know there is one choice I can make, and I do it.

"I never asked for this," I say.

I arrive at my appointment and I'm crying and I'm angry that I'm crying. The intake nurse thinks I'm crying because of loss and in a way she's right, but it's not the loss of the violation inside me, it's the loss of who I could have been and the grief over how damaged I am.

After, I feel nothing but empty and that feeling is a relief. I am free. I return home and stand in the middle of my tiny apartment and stare out the window and wonder if there is possibility. I wonder if I can make a different choice. But then I wonder if I had much control over any of my choices in the first place. I slip into bed and sleep until tomorrow.

I see him one last time. We walk to Kensington Market, and he says I should know about this Very Important Place in Toronto. "I'm going to show you what a real city is like," he says. I don't tell him that I already know about his favourite coffee shop and that I've already been here many times. I don't know what difference my telling him would make.

We sit outside the coffee shop, and I don't really like how the coffee tastes. I set it on the bench beside me. He starts to tell me about this girl he really likes. "She's petite," he says, looking me up and down. "She looks after herself. She has style."

I look down at my periwinkle blue and white skirt and ballet flats and ask what's wrong with my style.

"I know I can be an asshole," he says. I wonder if he's admitting it to me particularly or just in general. "She makes me want to be a better person."

"And what do I make you want to be?"

"Don't be petulant."

What the fuck am I doing?

"You're a bit chubby for me anyways. You should look after your health more."

I hear myself calling him a dick.

"You just don't like the truth." He looks down at the coffee he bought me. "Drink it before it gets cold."

"I don't like this coffee."

"Of course, you don't." He rises and tells me he is going to go into the shop across the small lane and to wait for him here. I nod and watch him disappear into the store.

I look up the lane. I look down the lane. I hear the streetcar rumble by. I watch people pass me. No one glances my way. I am in the shade. I am all shadow.

I have a choice. If I want to be okay ever again, I have one single choice. So, I make it.

I rise and walk away.

It's not until I am on the streetcar making my way home that my phone buzzes. I don't answer it. There are text messages *pinging*, and I delete them. He calls me again and leaves a message that I don't listen to. I erase him from my phone.

When I get home, my apartment is bare and quiet. I am alone, lonely. I slowly lower to my bed and slide my half-broken laptop closer and open it. I search cat rescue websites. I see one and scroll through all the photos of feline companions looking for a home. I'm looking for a home, too, and they all look like they deserve one.

I stop on one photograph of a small grey and white Manx kitten. Her eyes are wide, and the description tells me she's playful and loving, and that's just what I want. I fill out an application even before I convince myself that this is just another Bad Idea. Later, I receive an email saying that an interview will be scheduled between me and this critter's foster parent.

The picture says this kitten's name is Bunny, but that doesn't really fit her. She's chaotic, I already know this, and beautiful and unapologetic. I think about stories that I'd like to layer into my life. Places I love. Cities I adore. I remember the atlas I used to browse when I was a little kid, and the country I always landed on. I remember the life I always dreamed of, filled with love and travel and wonder, the one still glimmering in the deepest parts of my mind. Hope.

I have decided that this is a Good Idea. I will bring this tiny creature home, and I will look after her. We will have a story together, and I will step into this life.

I name her before she gets home—Cairo.

CHAPTER 7

Am I Brave Enough?

Years have passed, and I am not alone again. He knows I like listening to music, so one day he brings me a pair of speakers that are beyond what I'd ever expect, and I tell him it's not my birthday and I can't accept these, and he says, "But you like music, right? Music should be listened to on good speakers." When I'm alone, I love my new speakers. I think about my childhood Beethoven cassette, and I look up Sonata No. 7, 2nd Movement, and play it on my new speakers and sit on the edge of my bed and I listen.

He says he just wants to get to know me, but I know as soon as he does, he will be horrified. I can't let him know about me, the real me. He can't find out about my hospitalizations or suicide attempts or abortion or how unhinged I am or that I dropped out of school again or that I can hardly pay my bills. He can't find out about the Shadow still clinging to me or how angry I always am or the days I can't move from my bed because I can't seem to get my limbs to work. The world is darkness, and I want to fall down the rabbit hole of No Longer Living.

He can't know about the story of the Sorcerer in his tower that lingers in the periphery of my memories. He can't know about any of that. But I can't keep it in any longer.

I tell him I hate him more than I tell him he's a good person. Sometimes, I see tears in his eyes, and I want to cut myself for cutting him.

He suggests I move into his house, and he says it might be a good thing if I didn't have to pay rent. I think maybe if I don't have to pay rent, I could pay for tuition and finish my degree. He works in the house as a personal trainer and has a gym and he says we can exercise together. I laugh. I don't even run for the subway let alone for my health. But I look around, think about all those rooms and that maybe I can spread out a little bit.

"See?" he says. "This could be good."

Before I think twice, I say okay, I'll bring my things and my cat over and tell my landlord I won't be renewing my lease. I don't say the words *move in* because I'm not moving in. I'm just relocating my life. He corrects me when he says, "Merging things. My things are your things too."

I say, "Those speakers are *mine*." I smile. He does too. "But I want a room of my own," I tell him.

"Done," he says.

We merge things.

I don't tell him how much I used to love fantasy and that, when I'm alone, I think about stories with dragons and magic and under-dogs who save the day and are just the coolest. I don't tell him that I wish heroes really existed and I wish I was one of those heroes. I don't tell him about the stories I tore up all those years ago and that those stories are starting to percolate to the forefront of my thoughts, even all these years later, and that I'm grieving.

We argue. We argue a lot. I eviscerate him because I can't eviscerate myself and give oxygen to the words *I live with trauma* and

I'm fucked-up that are pressing against my lips, clawing to come out. I'm terrified and I'm ashamed. I don't know how long I can keep any of it inside me anymore. Every day that goes by and we live in the same home is a day closer to the truth coming out. I'm scared.

We are invited to my old friend's birthday party, and we go together, and I'm ready to drink my face off because otherwise I'll be too terrified to be around people.

The party is loud and hot and there's so much booze. There's food strewn all over the kitchen island. Music is playing and it's pressing into me, and I just want to drink into oblivion. My old friend hands me a shot glass filled with crystal liquid, matching hers, and we down them together. I throw my head back and laugh. The liquor zings through me, sets me on fire. We have another and she loops her arm around my shoulders and hollers, just because she can. I holler, too, and the room erupts with laughter. This feels good and freeing, and no one knows anything about me. I catch my partner's eye, and I know what is going through his mind, his brow tight, lips a thin line. He's seen this before. I don't care though. I drink again. He comes closer, and I flatten him with a look.

Each drink loosens the chains on my rage, and I'm inching towards explosion, a grenade that just needs one tug of the pin. I've never felt powerful, and I desperately want to feel powerful now.

My old friend asks if I can help her encourage some people to go home, and she glances at a very large, very intimidating-looking guy, and I hear the words "sweetheart" and "I'll do what I like." His voice is a deep, laughing baritone, and I don't know how it happens but I'm standing in front of this guy who is almost twice my size, and I think he's an asshole so I tell him. He looks me up and down and grins, repeating that he'll leave when he wants. I tell him I'll cut him down. I tell him I will fucking end him. He looks down at me, calls me "little girl."

The pin has been pulled. I snap. I pull my arm back, my fingers curled, my body tense. But an arm laces around me, yanking me away. I am shoved into my jacket. I can hear the guy yelling at me, and I hear my own voice telling him to go fuck himself. And all I can see is white-hot, searing rage. All I can feel is injustice. All I want to do is rip everything down, and I can't stop. I don't want to stop. It feels too good.

My partner pushes me into a taxi and I'm yelling at him. I'm telling him that he can't see what an asshole that guy is. That that guy probably does whatever he wants to anyone he wants, and he thinks he owns the world because he has a dick. Because he *is* a dick. And my partner just keeps saying, "I know he is, but you can't hit him."

"Why not? Why not hit him? He deserves it. Why does everyone think it's okay for assholes like him to get away with whatever they want?"

My partner shakes his head, and he is blurry in my liquor-filled vision. "I don't know. They just do. But you can't hit him."

"Why not?"

"Because he's the kind of guy who would hit you back."

This makes me angrier. The taxi stops. My partner pulls me out and I am near-immobile with rage. We enter the house, and my partner closes the door behind us. I lean against it, looking down at the floor. My shoes hurt my feet. My party clothes reek of booze. My palms are raw from digging my nails into them. A bead of sweat trickles down my spine. He turns and looks at me. "Why are you still standing there?" he says.

I hear him draw a deep breath. He walks into the other room, and, for a moment, I think he's too angry with me. I think that this is it, the moment I've finally succeeded, he'll chuck me out of this dream, and this beautiful home—and it could be beautiful, what we are building—will come crashing down, and I deserve it because I am a shitty person and a whore and a fucking mental case.

He comes back to the front door where I am still standing with my sneakers in his hand. Tosses them on the floor in front of me. "Put them on," he says.

I'm pulled out of my frozen rage. I look at the clock. "But it's three in the morning."

"Don't care. Put them on." He flips on the light in his gym. I watch as he hoists up the punching bag and clips it to the bar. He turns back. "Put them on."

I put on the sneakers and take a step into the gym and see myself in the mirror—makeup smeared down my face, my clothes a rumpled ruin. I watch as he pulls out boxing gloves, and, lifting my arms, he stuffs them on my hands. He points to the bag. "I'll hold. You punch."

All I say is, "He's a dick. You know he is."

He nods as he grips the bag. "Punch."

I feel silly, but he taps the bag and nods again. "This is stupid," I mumble.

"So is trying to fight a two-hundred-and-fifty-pound guy. *Punch*." I slump. I can't do it. I'm ridiculous. I'm a failure. "I know you're angry," he says. "Please, just work with me."

I give the bag the weakest, limpest punch it's ever received. He tells me to do it again, harder, to curl my fingers, don't keep my thumb straight. I inhale, focus on my hand, feeling each finger. I punch again, harder, and a loud smack echoes. My lungs expand with a deep tremulous breath.

"Again."

I punch again, harder, louder. Pain lances up my wrist and into my forearm. "Keep your wrist straight. Line it up with your arm." He shows me how. "Again."

Slam. Inhale, exhale, my body starts trembling.

Again. *Slam!*

I switch hands, and he tells me to keep my feet apart, to pivot my foot, knees bent. I slam my fist again. And again, and again. I'm grunting, my vision blurs, and I blink. Tears join the mess that is my makeup.

"Get loud," he says.

I get loud. I scream, and I cry, and I slam my fists into the punching bag that holds my memories and hatred and fury and how powerless I am. I hit it again and again and again, and my arms are on fire, and I keep crying and hitting and crying. I do this until I can't lift my arms anymore. Until all the booze is out of me, and I can see just a bit clearer, and I'm panting. I tumble to the floor and sob, grinding my forehead into the boxing gloves.

"I'm so angry," I whisper.

"I know," he says.

I tell him everything. I tell him how angry I am about my family and the Sorcerer of long ago who still lives in my ugliest, aching memories, and I tell him that I was in a psychiatric hospital and that I'll never finish university and I'm just a fucking failure. I tell him about the assault and the abortion, and I'm sure he's going be disgusted with me.

I tell him everything because it's four in the morning and I'm exhausted and I have no strength left to hold back anymore.

I look up at him, sweating and crying and a complete mess and say, "I can't live like this."

He doesn't say anything. Slowly, he slides the gloves off my reddened and raw hands, sinks to the floor, and holds me while I cry.

I. CONTROLLING THE DANGER

One of my favourite superheroes is Marvel's Jean Grey, aka Phoenix. Jean was born a mutant—a species of humans who have mutated genetics that result in particular powers—and she's one of those characters who straddles the line between hero and anti-hero. Some mutants can breathe ice, some have wings. Others can shoot flames out of their eyes (which sounds really inconvenient). Just like any system, there is a hierarchy within the mutant world. Lower-level mutants can do things like morph a limb into a weapon. Higher-level mutants—the most powerful of which are omega mutants—have incredible powers with vast potential of both creation and destruction.

The primary plot driver in the X-Men movies is the public and political fear of mutants and what they are capable of. Power that cannot be controlled by governing bodies or systems is viewed as dangerous. Of course, that philosophy doesn't even consider the idea that systemic power could be dangerous as well, but in this cinematic world, a mutant with unsanctioned, unregulated powers is obviously something to fear.

However, there are mutants who are so powerful that they can rip apart worlds, who trigger so great a fear that the system intends to destroy them at all costs. Jean Grey is one of those mutants. The scope of Jean's abilities is like a grocery list of superhero powers: telekinesis, empathy, telepathy, psychic energy synthesis, mental detection, astral projection, telepathic manipulation, psychic shield, and resurrection (to name just a few). She also has access to the Phoenix Force, which is basically the comics version of the Big Bang, pure power that sort of looks like glowing purple goo and flies around the universe. It's also a force that greatly amplifies Jean's inherent mutant powers, making her a nuclear bomb of magic.

But still, Jean is just a person, and that's an integral part of her story and who she is. It's a mostly unacknowledged burden that she carries, and it's also what makes her, in my mind, a real superhero.

The opening of the 2019 film *Dark Phoenix* starts with an adult Jean Grey asking, "Who are we? Are we simply what others want us to be?" And, as though to answer her own question, the film cuts to the beginning, when she is just eight years old.

She, along with her mother and father, is in the family car, driving along a quiet, peaceful country road. Jean's powers are only starting to emerge, and she might just be dimly aware of them. As they're driving, Jean experiences what seems to be an inexplicable power surge, and she begins to control the radio dial with her mind. When her parents suspect that it's her, she can *hear* their worry. It's like the bottle cap is popped and all the soda comes out at once. She whispers "quiet" and covers her ears, distressed. The command causes her mother, who is driving, to pass out. The car careens into an oncoming pick-up truck.

As the car flips in the air, her parents are tossed, glittering glass showering around them, and it's clear this isn't going to end well. Then Jean, eyes closed, generates a shimmering force shield around her, protecting her alone. It's a superhero version of a child protecting themself and their psyche—during a traumatic event. This is a terrifying situation that she believes is out of her control, and her power will do what it is destined to do: protect her.

This scene could also be viewed as an allegory for how children can protect themselves by creating alter-selves or monsters to externalize the trauma and personify it as a being, a process that distances the child from the hurt and fear. In Dr. Judith Herman's interviews with adults who have experienced adverse childhoods, she finds they have often created selves separate from their main identities, the ones who initially received the hurt.[1] Daenerys Targaryen conjures her monstrous protector, Drogon, who is a manifestation of the protection she wished she had received earlier in her life. It also resembles the power I wish I could have used to protect myself from the Sorcerer and the rotting tower of my own youth—a fantastical motif that is still the only way I can articulate what had happened to me. In my imagined, protective world, like Daenerys, I would have had a dragon too. Or perhaps I would have been the dragon.

The film cuts to Jean sleeping in a hospital bed. There are whispers around her, people marvelling that she is completely unharmed. When

---

1   Judith Herman, *Trauma and Recovery: The Aftermath of Violence—From Domestic Abuse to Political Terror* (New York: Basic Books, 2015).

the scene shifts again, Jean is awake and in a different room, dressed and calm. It's clear she already knows that her parents are dead.

Enter Professor Charles Xavier.

Good-natured Charles explains to her that he is inviting her to his school, which is one for "special" people, like her. To which Jean replies that special is just another word for—

"Weird? Crazy?" Charles finishes for her. But maybe it's another word for kids who are "just really cool," he adds. (On that, I would agree.) Jean says, in a matter-of-fact tone, that she hurts people. Charles explains to her that her power is a gift and what she chooses to do with her gift is up to her: she can help people or become a weapon.

(I wonder if there's really much of a difference, though.)

Then a very wise eight-year-old Jean tells him that he's a fixer and that he thinks he can fix her too. "No," Charles says. "Because you are *not* broken."

But let's remember the opening line of the film, adult Jean's voice layered over a peaceful school setting: "Who are we? Are we simply what others want us to be?"

Charles, ever the saviour, modifies Jean's memories so she doesn't remember the accident or that she was the one who caused it.

I repeat: *he actually messes with her mind*, under the completely misguided assumption that it is best for Jean to not remember until she can control her powers. But how can she control her powers when she doesn't even have all the tools to do so? Those tools are her memories, all of them, and are integral to who she is. They're experiences that help shape the architecture of a personality, that can help Jean, as they help all of us, to learn about herself, her values, beliefs, and capabilities. They are exactly what make her special and a crucial component of what she needs to learn to control.

But in taking those memories without her consent, Charles essentially strips Jean of that entire part of herself. If she had retained those memories, I wonder if she would have become so uncontrollable and destructive in the latter events of the movie. If, with those memories, and the years that she could have had to unpack and understand them, she would have come to embrace all the aspects of herself, instead of fearing them and eventually exploding with emotions she couldn't manage. I wonder, too, if I had had a chance to sit with my own child-hood and process it in safety, what would have happened to me and the rage that marked so much of my life?

Instead, Charles leaves her as a partial-self, always with something missing. He took from her what he had no right to remove.

Jean Grey's story parallels a widely unacknowledged and often unrec-ognized piece of Canada's history—Dr. Donald Ewen Cameron and the experiments he performed on human subjects at the Allan Memorial Institute in Montreal between 1957 and 1964.[2]

Cameron's experiments were funded partly by the Canadian Government and the American Central Intelligence Agency, allegedly as a branch of MKUltra—the soldier brainwashing program. Officially, Cameron was tasked with finding a cure for schizophrenia, but given a blank slate and unsupervised power, the project became far more than that. Cameron's patients were subjected to months-long insu-lin comas, hypothermic "treatments," electroconvulsive therapies far above recommended levels and duration, isolation, sensory depriva-tion, prolonged and forced LSD use with hallucinogenic suggestions, and isolation from friends, family, and supports. These patients were trapped, held prisoner, put in comas, their memories eradicated along with their agency and sense of self. All because of Cameron's theory

---

2   *Brainwashed* podcast series, hosted by Michelle Shephard, produced by CBC, aired
    September 2, 2020, through October 28, 2020, https://www.cbc.ca/radio/podcastnews
    /listen-brainwashed-1.5734335.

that if he could erase the problematic memories causing the illness, and restructure new memories, he could cure his patients.

Basically, these people were tortured.

A direct line can be drawn from Nazi camps and the cruel and lethal experiments that were conducted on Jews and also queer and disabled folks to Cameron's experiments in the race to create the first documented method of mind control. After WWII, the concept of mind control became so pervasive that a brainwashing race—similar to the arms race that held the world in thrall—began in earnest.

There is some overlap between the techniques used by Dr. Cameron (and other physicians and psychiatrists, historically), experiments conducted in concentration camps, and how mentally ill patients have been "treated" for centuries. Trephination (the drilling into the patient's skull to release infecting spirits), exorcisms, insulin and hypothermic comas, conversion therapies, psychosurgery (which also included the removal of stomachs and intestines), the use of hallucinogenics, physical therapies (like straightjackets), electroconvulsive therapies, transorbital craniotomies (the founder of which actually received a Nobel Prize for his procedure in 1949, which was later revoked). All in the name of "treatment" and all done mostly involuntarily (or at least with very little information). Who is being treated, though, with these invasive, often violent, traumatizing, and even lethal therapies? Who is being helped? Or protected?

Was Charles Xavier really trying to protect Jean or was he simply afraid of what she was capable of?

Charles's actions seem innocuous enough. He *did* mean well, but that's the problem. Meaning well doesn't always translate to *doing* well. Jean's memories belong to her, as does how she feels about them; her personality and sense of self should have been allowed to grow with them. Instead, Charles forces Jean to push down those feelings, which results in driving Jean away. She's angry with Charles, and when she learns about what happened to her when she was a child, she becomes volatile and directs this rage mostly at him. (I honestly can't blame her.) Soon after, she runs away.

During the movie, Jean's power—now amplified by the Phoenix Force—grows to be nearly uncontrollable. She is terrified, angry, confused—all the emotions Charles never allowed her to experience and unpack in a safe way when she was a child. Jean never learned how to manage these so-called negative emotions, spinning as she was in a void of memory and purpose. Charles always cautioned restraint and control. Of course.

Eventually, Jean does learn that her emotions and powers are intricately threaded; together they make Jean a whole person. She even says, "My emotions make me strong," knowing that this fact will help her harness her full power. Then when she unleashes her power in combination with her anger, she launches into the sky to destroy the (true) villain of the movie, transforming into a bomb made of light and power. Back on the ground, her friends and adopted family watch while the night sky lights up with her magic, as Jean's body evaporates. What's left is pure energy, pure *power*, in the form of a fiery phoenix. She does this, obviously, to save the planet from evil aliens looking to colonize Earth. She is a hero, after all, despite Charles's interference.

In the end, though, the creators of the story don't allow Jean to keep that power as well as her true emotional identity. (Again, this reminds me of Daenerys and what the HBO writers did to her character in the last season.) Jean is stripped of her physical humanity and remains an entity of pure power. She burns up in flames, ultimately destined to orbit the world as a fiery phoenix in the sky. I have always seen this as a punishment, a purgatory into which she is consigned for letting her anger explode and using the full extent of her power, something Charles—who advocated for moderation—would never have endorsed. She can no longer remain simply Jean, a powerful human who also happens to feel emotions.

Jean's earlier question has been answered: superheroes are supposed to be what we need them to be. We no longer need a two-dimensional superhero as fast as a speeding bullet, wearing blue leggings and a red cape, who never crosses the moral grey line. Superman and Wonder Woman filled specific do-gooder gaps when we needed heroes who fought back against real, tangible hardship and tyranny; Superman was created during the Great Depression, and Wonder Woman a few years later during World War II. Then, we needed superheroes and villains who were clearly delineated and did not make mistakes.

But what do we need now?

We need a hero who reflects us back to ourselves. We need a hero who is fundamentally flawed, who lives with sadness and joy, peace and rage, and who knows that together, all of these emotions are what make their powers truly extraordinary. We need to know that fallible people can be heroes, too, that there is heroic possibility in all of us. To deny Jean her grief and rage and confusion would also be denying a pillar of her authentic self, superpowers and all. Maybe we've always needed someone who is messy and chaotic and who makes mistakes but is still a hero, because then maybe that means we can *all* be heroes. Even the messiest of us.

We are often who others need us to be. But what if we all evolved? What if we became something else, someone that *we* need us to be? What if we allow the rage and sadness to hold the reins for just a little while, instead of suppressing and internalizing them, and demand the same self-awareness from a new iteration of superhero, one that involves anger and uncontrollable emotions and the most secret, elusive memories? What if we *unleashed*?

Anger and rage and messy emotions aren't flaws. They can be brave. They can be galvanizing. Maybe if we honestly examined what causes our rage, we would see more clearly the systemic inequities that cause racism or misogyny or transphobia. We'd see even more pink pussy hats spilling into legislatures, more drag story hours, more action for Black Lives Matter. Maybe all of us can work towards what our communities would look like if the police were defunded. Maybe we would see more advocacy for sexual assault survivors. Maybe, despite performative gestures of mental health with #selfcare, we can work towards a model of mental illness justice and health care that doesn't rely on the faulty belief that violence is an inevitable by-product.

Maybe getting properly pissed off is the bravest thing we can do.

II. BECOME YOUR OWN BRILLIANT BOMB

The couch I am sitting on is long and grey, and I wonder if anyone ever lies down like they do in the movies to talk about their lives and their sorrows and anxieties. I'm not lying down. My hands are clenched under my thighs, my arms tight to my sides. I'm perched as though I'm only staying here for a fraction of a moment.

"You seem angry."

I look up at my therapist. My therapist. It's gotten to this, I think. My chin tightens, my nostrils flare. "Do you mind sitting back a little? Maybe take a breath with me," he says.

My therapist is young and doesn't look at all like a therapist. His eyes are icy blue, and he wears a linen shirt and loose, ripped jeans, and I'm pretty sure he burns incense and believes in crystals. "Can you tell me why you're angry?"

I'm angry. I'm angry. I'm always angry. I'm angry because I want to scream, and I can't. I think about words, lots and lots of words that are bombs stacking one on the other. I think about words like, *Does he know how crazy you are?* or *You're disgusting, take a shower* or *It's too much for your mother* and *Brave face, okay?* or *Shut up and let me fuck you* or *Fucked-up fucked-up fucked-up.*

I look out the rain-washed window. Across the street is a grocery store. I focus closer on some plants placed by the window. One of them has droopy leaves, yellowing at the edges. I thrust my chin at them. "You should look after your plants better," I say.

He smiles. "Yeah, I thought they'd warm the space a bit."

"Not if you let them die." I know I'm being rude, but I just don't care. There's a pause filled with silence that I hate. I have no choice but to be here. Yet I have every choice to be here. Just a few weeks ago, I'd been taken to the hospital strapped to a stretcher. I don't remember much. I'd started the night with rum. Lots of rum. Then moved to the bottle of gin. Then moved to the rage that followed me around, that smokey Shadow crushing my shoulders, and its weight had become unbearable, its fingers coiled around my neurons.

I'd screamed in the house. I'd smashed pictures. I'd sliced my skin with the shards like diamonds. I'd laughed at my partner, begging, pleading, goading him to come closer. Come just a bit closer and see what I can do. See what I'm capable of. See the blood on my arms and the hate in my heart. My voice wasn't my own, but my Shadow's, deep and growling.

I'd barfed everywhere and begged for my old friend. I don't know why I wanted her beside me, to witness me like this. But I just wanted to see her face and remember that someone else did love me and that maybe I can be absolved of all that I have done wrong in my life. I want to be washed clean. Aren't people allowed to be washed clean?

The psychiatrist in the hospital peppered me with questions, but I just kept barfing. An IV was pushed into my arm as I sat slumped in a large chair in the psychiatric wing of the hospital. My partner answered a lot of the questions for me. Hearing the answers made me want to sleep. I didn't have to talk. His words were right. It was okay.

The psychiatrist had said he didn't think a psychiatric hold would do me any good, that I would be better off at home. My partner nodded. Memories of concrete walls and VIP passes flickered through my booze- and rage-soaked mind. My numb lips formed the question—What's wrong with me? I don't remember the answer.

My partner brought me home. I had no shoes on. Glass and vomit covered the hallway. He helped me step around it. I slept for days. I ignored messages of love and care and concern from my old friend. She told me that she knew this wasn't the real me and that she loved me no matter what. I just couldn't answer because I knew she was wrong.

I slept as the sun slid through the sky. I slept as Cairo pressed her paws to my chest, her soft purr rumbling through me, small licks on my nose. I tried not to think of my little guy, Loki, his bones still buried under rocks on my parents' property. I slept through meals my partner's mother brought over.

My therapist's voice startles me out of my shame. "Can you tell me why you're angry?"

"Some guy on the subway was too close to me."

He nods.

"I can't stop my mind from spinning."

He leaves the statement hanging within the silence between us, drawn out, waiting to be filled. I realize he wants me to fill it. My jaw aches with tears I am fighting so hard to keep from overwhelming me. "It's jumbled. It's all over the place. I'm all over the place. I can't stop it." I run my gaze over his pathetic plants again. "I'm angry," I whisper. I look down to my clenched thighs.

Ducky, you're so thin. The memory echoes in my mind, from so many years ago, and I wonder when she finally noticed and why she hadn't noticed before. I wonder why they never saw me. I wonder why this is me and my life and why I'm not just some average person living an average life, and I just want an average life.

"It's okay to be angry," he says.

I shake my head. "Not for me. Bad things happen when I get angry." I look up at him, and I'm frustrated because now I'm crying and I don't want to cry. I just want to be numb. "What if I get angry here?"

I remember playing by the riverside, looking for fairies and water nymphs, and I know that once upon a time, I really truly believed in magic. I remember sliding my hands into the mud, finding worms and naming them. I remember believing the trees were magical, and I know I was so small, so fresh and unmarred. Long hair wild and burnt gold in the sunlight. My mother had said my hazel eyes were like the eyes of a wild woodland sprite, peering out at her from the maidenhair ferns. I'd plucked fiddleheads and unfurled them with my small, dirty fingers. I'd giggled with my brother as we watched the geese fly overhead. It feels like I'm watching that little girl, knowing what's to come and how hard she will have to fight for herself. I want to hold her, protect her. I want to be a hero for her.

My therapist tilts his head. "I can handle angry," he says.

"What if I want to hit something?"

I remember how heroes need to have their righteous fury.

He glances to the corner where an inflatable bat is propped against some canvasses of really, really ugly art. I feel my lips pull just a little into a small smile.

Then he says, "Do you want to get started?"

I'm in a bare, ugly room at the mood disorders clinic in Toronto Western Hospital. The room is tucked away in the labyrinthian maze that always seems to be the template for hospitals. I fold my hands in my lap and wait. There is a large window beside me. It opens but has no screen. I wonder if anyone who has sat in this chair has contemplated jumping. I then wonder why there is no screen on a window that opens on the ninth floor of a hospital in the mood disorders clinic. I wonder if they really know their patients, or if those patients are numbers and data and stats and a file folder with charts. There is always a story within those file folders. A why and how and when and how many times. I wonder if, when they think about jumping, it's not jumping they actually think about. It's flying. I wonder how many of my forebears believed they had sprouted wings and fly, fly, fly away.

The door opens, and a stocky man enters. He is about my age, maybe younger, and I feel ashamed of that fact. It's a fact that reminds me that I am behind. It's a fact that he could have been my peer in university all those years ago. It's a fact that he kept his head in the books, razor-focused, and stable. It's a fact that, at the same time, I was swinging through those revolving doors of hospitals. I am reminded of how many times I have failed.

He says, "Hi there" as he looks at my folder. He sits across from me. A desk is to his right, and he slides my file folder on top. I'm sure it contains the details of my last two hospitalizations. How I arrived in the emergency room, my partner pleading with me to stop screaming. I begged them to let me die. Those charts are in there, I'm sure. I wonder how they phrased that—*Crazy person screams crazy shit. Approach with caution.*

The doctor, a psychiatric intern, he tells me, has a soft voice with a gentle Spanish accent. And then I see him give me a small smile. I realize maybe he's interested. In me, in my health, in a medical model that will fix all the broken bits of me. He thinks in prescriptions and quantities, and I realize that's exactly what I want him to think because I want to be fixed. I want to peel away the disease that is infecting me, and I want to see the real person I am. I want to step away from the Shadow I see lingering in the periphery of my vision. I can hardly even remember who I used to be. I don't know who I am, what I might sound like without my Shadow. I wonder if I might be a kind person, a protector. Maybe I'm a little bit smart. Maybe I'm creative. Maybe, just maybe, I could be wise. But I won't know unless this psychiatric intern who is younger than me tells me what is wrong with me and then tells me what he can do to fix me.

He starts by reviewing with me what this assessment will hope-fully achieve. He asks me if it's okay if he asks me questions, and I laugh a little because why would he ask me that? No one ever asks for my permission, not ever. I look at the window. I'm nervous. I blurt out, "I wonder if anyone ever wants to jump."

"I don't know," he says, his voice still soft.

"There should be a screen," I continue, because I'm a train wreck and might as well act the part, right?

He glances at the window. "You're probably right."

He starts to ask me questions. I answer them quickly because, if I think about it too much, I might not tell the truth. He asks me if I struggle to sleep. I ask him, "What's sleep?" He asks me if I take on too much, maybe think I can do anything? I think that's a weird question because aren't little girls always told they can be and do anything they want, don't let The Man get you down? But I know what he's really asking me.

"Do you think maybe you can do something you normally couldn't. Like fly or. . ."

"I'm not *that* crazy," I tell him. Then I realize that's a really shitty thing to say. My own ableism is crushing me. He nods again.

"Do you ever feel like harming yourself?"

"Have you read my file?"

He smiles. "I need to ask anyways."

He asks me if I ever want to harm anyone else, and I know he's trying to see if I'm a danger to others. I think about that. I wanted to tear that guy apart at the party. I wanted to rip him to shreds. But what do I really want, I wonder?

"I don't want to feel powerless anymore," I tell him. I spread my hands in my lap and look at my palms. "I don't want to feel like *this*."

He asks me questions about my daily routine and my life history and my thought patterns. I'm starting to put two and two together, probably at the same rate he is. I feel a word forming in my con-sciousness, coalescing into an answer that might just be the culprit that has been torturing me for so long now. The Shadow in the mirror, the unacknowledged monster, the darkness in the corners. The one clinging to my back. I feel it hovering over me, breathing. I sense it coming out of its own shadows, stepping into faint, feeble light.

The psychiatric intern asks me questions for about forty-five minutes while my partner waits in the hallway. I try to answer as honestly as possible, but I now know what the conclusion will be. I think he does too.

After the intern is done with questions, he smiles and excuses himself. "I'm going to talk to my colleagues. Just wait here a few more minutes."

I wonder if he thinks I'd actually bail after coming this far.

I look out the window again and start to berate myself for mentioning something as stupid as jumping out the window. Why do I say stupid things? Why am I so stupid? Why do I make people uncomfortable? Why am I me?

Why am I broken?

The door opens again, and the psychiatric intern comes back with another doctor behind him. This other doctor is tall, older, huskier. He introduces himself as the director of the mood disorders clinic. I nod. The *director*. I must be either really important or really, really fucked-up. I settle on the latter.

The intern speaks: "Have you heard of bipolar disorder?"

The words collect in my mind, all the pieces pulling together. It's always been there. It was there when I was a teenager. It was there in university. It's been following me for almost two decades. The Shadow.

I nod. He starts to tell me about medications and treatments and outcomes. I nod again. I'll do anything. I'll try anything. I'm desperate. I want to live, but I don't want *this*.

He tells me that's not all though. He says something about PTSD and social anxiety and agoraphobia, and I go through the encyclopedia in my mind of what all of those words mean.

On the way home, I tell my partner about my diagnoses. He just says, "Okay, that's good," like it's no big deal, and I think maybe he's right, maybe it's no big deal. Maybe it's just made a big deal because people are scared of the "crazies" and I'm not a "crazy." But maybe the crazies aren't either. Maybe they've been forced to slide into a role that's carved just for them. Maybe how they are viewed is the only thing they are allowed to be. An ouroboros that must be accepted. A Shadow that remains a Shadow no matter how much it wants—it *needs*—to be seen.

We return home, and the familiar feeling of tipping off-kilter sinks into me. Things are different, changed. I have diagnoses, ones that I truly believe to be accurate. I realize I've known for a while now, but somehow hearing the words from the psychiatrist's mouth feels both terrifying and . . . liberating. I know it's not me anymore. I know this isn't my fault anymore. I can stop apologizing for being a bad person, for being fucked-up, for being exactly who I am.

But then I wonder, if I now know what the Shadow is—my mental illness—then who does that make me?

My partner starts pulling food out of the fridge. He asks me if I'm hungry, and I'm not sure. I just feel tired. I wonder if maybe this might give me some rest, or do I just have another battle ahead of me? I wonder how long it will take the medications to work. I wonder what people will say if I tell them. I wonder what will happen now.

I wonder if I'm brave enough.

I'm so achingly tired. An overwhelming fatigue settles into every part of me, and I think maybe I'll read a book and fall asleep until morning. Because maybe in the morning I will wake up with a path that might be just a little clearer. Maybe I'll feel like a piece of the scattered puzzle has finally been found. Like a memory unlocked or a new power discovered.

But I realize I'm still angry, and my diagnoses haven't taken that away. I'm angry that this is the result of my life. I'm angry for all the years lost. I'm angry that my youth is gone and it's not even like I can reinvent myself because I don't even know who I am.

I slide into bed, pulling the cool sheets over me. I sink into the mattress and feel the years weighing on me. My anger is gathering, no longer scattered and bouncing off every single thought, every single person, event, circumstance. It's gathering into one directable form. Maybe, with a good night's sleep, with just enough rest, and a touch of that well-earned anger, I can be brave enough to spread out into this new self.

I scan the corners of the bedroom, looking for the Shadow, my constant companion, and I see it, small and vaporous. I tighten my lips, take a deep breath. We'll be okay, I think. I hope I'll be okay.

I turn over, turn off the lights, and hope for just one more day.

CHAPTER 8

A Dragon of One's Own

My laptop is open, the screen is bright white. An email draft looks out at me. The compose pane is still empty, but for an address. I need to write this. I don't know how to write this. I don't know how to find the words or what it would mean if I did write them and hit send.

I'd wanted to talk to my parents, to free myself, to find answers to questions that really should have answers but I already know there aren't any. At least none that my parents are willing to admit or even acknowledge to themselves, and it's breaking me. I can't keep quiet anymore and I'm still angry and I now know what to do with that anger. I know where its home resides and I know if I don't do this, I will never change. My life will remain the same and this sameness, this powerlessness, is going to break me.

I'd called my mother a few days ago. I wanted her to know about the Sorcerer—who I also now know was real—all those long years ago. I'd wanted to know why she didn't do anything to help me. I'd wanted to know why she and my father didn't protect me. I'd wanted to know why they never saw me as I became smaller, barely there, curling in on myself, until I lost myself entirely. I know my mom thinks she tried her best, but did she know that her best simply wasn't good enough? Did she know that I needed her to fight for me rather than wrapping herself in her own past, in her own trauma? Did she know that I needed her to be okay for me?

My mother had said, "Why are you still going on about this?" And I wondered when she thought I even opened the conversation. I asked her, "Did you know that while you were sleeping, while you weren't okay, that I still needed you too?"

Did you know that while you were looking out the window, hoping for a better tomorrow, that I was behind you, desperately needing you?

But now I need me, and I know this is the hardest thing I will ever do. I have to say goodbye to them and turn towards building my own life because if I keep them in it, this cycle will go on and I'll continue to be angry, silenced, and never figure out who I truly am. I had already anticipated the answers, but I couldn't not ask the questions. I just wanted to know if they thought so little of me as to think that I could carry this forever and still be okay. Because I'm not okay. I'm just not, and I don't know when I ever will be, but I know if I don't make my fingers move right now and write the words, I won't have a tomorrow or a day after that or a day after that. This will eat me.

I have to be brave. I have to hold on to my anger and let it happen and be braver than I've ever had to be in my life.

My fingers work on their own and the words appear on the screen. I type things like "I can't continue like this," and "I just wanted to be able to talk," and "Why won't you believe me? Why have you never believed me?"

I write, "I can no longer have you in my life," and my chest heaves, my fingers tremble. I write, "This isn't good for me," and a part of me breaks. I write, "I'd only ever wanted you to see me."

A part of me is now gone.

I close my eyes and hit send. I gasp as though I can feel the words flying through the air and crashing down like an asteroid.

I slide off my chair and sink to my knees. I lower my forehead to the floor.

You're gone. You're really gone. I miss you already.

I'm moaning, wishing there were another way. Wishing for just a few words—*we love you, we see you, we believe you.*

I'm shattered because this has been what I've wanted, deep down in the secret part of my soul, for years. I've just wanted to be free. But this freedom is so excruciating, and I can't breathe.

I know my partner must hear me crying because suddenly his footsteps come heavy and quick and his arms are around me, gently pulling me off the floor. I'm gasping, and he has no idea what's just happened. I'm saying, over and over, "I told them goodbye. I told them goodbye. I told them goodbye."

He starts to ask who, then stops. He already knows. I'm sure my limbs will break with the pain, my chest will explode with grief. I'm so angry and sad and broken. But in a way, I also know I've made a choice that will change my life. How it will change, I don't know yet. But the fact that I had to make the choice is what breaks me.

My partner lowers me to the couch, and I cry until I'm numb. He calls my old friend, and she arrives, entering the room and heading right towards me. She sits beside me and wraps me in her arms. I try to tell myself my people are with me, and it's okay. I'm not alone. Here in this room, I'm seen and held and accepted. I'm believed.

Slowly, the weeks slide by, and I ache, but I grow around that ache, though its marks remain like knots in a tree. I'm reaching outwards, trying to find sunlight. I can hardly feel it, but something small is starting to simmer inside me. A spark of power, a little belief.

I tell my partner that I don't really know who I am and I want to know who I am but it's hard without family and belonging. He is washing dishes, his hands covered with soft suds. Spring is slowly arriving, and the backyard is still wet and mucky. I watch our cats, including my little Manx who kept me company during the long nights, as they sleep in what puddles of sunlight they can find.

He rinses his hands and wipes them on a towel. He moves closer and looks at me. His face is screwed up in concentration.

"What?" I say.

"You can have my name, you know," he says.

"I have a name." But I don't want it anymore. I just want to shed it all.

"I mean, you can have family. You can have *my* family. We can be a family. We could get married?"

I roll this new name over my tongue. It sounds good, like someone I could be, someone I could grow into. It's the name of a person I might really like. This person will be brave, they'll have history and have learned and loved and laughed and cried through all the confusion and messiness that is life. They'll have white-hot anger and their moral compass will hopefully be true. They'll have scars, and not all days will be good days. Some days will be hard, some will be brutal.

But they'll be fine. They'll be just fine. They will have magic because in some small way, they're their own hero.

"I mean, only if you want," my partner adds.

I look at him. His brows are hoisted up his forehead, towel still clutched in his damp hands. He's waiting for me to answer, and I wonder if he thinks I'll say no. I wonder if he hopes I'll say yes.

I smile at him. "I would love that."

I. RIGHTING THE ORIGINAL WRONG

A few years ago, I started thinking about my favourite novels again. The ones that took me away to other worlds, the stories around which I crafted my own version of fan fiction—although at the time I didn't even know what fan fiction was. Dragonlance novels are filled with stories, adventures, mythologies, and characters spanning hundreds of years, in different regions of the fictional world of Krynn. Wars create the foundation from which heroes are forged. Legends of dragons are whispered around firesides, magic is mistrusted.

The novels take place during the events of the War of the Lance—a war that is started by the god Takhisis and her legions of evil creatures, including chromatic dragons. Centuries prior to the War of the Lance, Takhisis was driven back into her realm, the Abyss, by the knight Huma Dragonbane and his silver dragon, Heart.

In the years after Huma's death and a cataclysmic event that rips apart the continent, the world of mortals believes the gods have abandoned them. Magic vanishes. The dragons fade into myth. Until even the legend of Huma becomes just that: legend.

Meanwhile, in the land of the immortals, where gods and dragons live, the dragons—both good and evil—swear an oath not to interfere in the world of mortals, just as the gods they serve did before them (it also involves the armies of evil stealing the good dragons' eggs to keep the good dragons in line, but I feel like at least one of the good gods would draw the line at fetal kidnapping). Without that oath, the gods could rip the world apart. And no one wants that.

But in this void, Takhisis has found a way to enter Krynn again, and she's amassing her legions.

Enter our heroes, a scrappy group of elves, humans, a dwarf, and a kender. Upon learning of the return of these evil forces, the companions are thrust out into the night. And so their journey begins.

It's pretty traditional storytelling: characters who really are the most unlikely of heroes, are forced to become . . . well, heroes. But the companions aren't really what most drew me in. It was the shy elf, living among refugee camps of elves fleeing the war and the destruction of their homelands. Even within elven societies, there is a caste hierarchy, and she's pretty much bottom rung. She isn't even a main character—simply one used as a narrative tool to push the main heroes forward. She's had different names throughout the centuries, throughout cultures and races. Among the world of humans, she was known as Silvara. Among the elves, she was Silvart. And among her own dragonkind, her name was D'argent.

Silvara, however, is not what she seems. She is a painfully shy and fearful creature. She avoids conversation and only serves to use her (rather spectacular) healing powers to help the victims of war. The only thing that sets Silvara apart from the rest of the elves, and the one thing she tries to cover, is her long silver hair.

Silvara, you see, is a dragon, one of the only good ones on Krynn. When Silvara first heard whispers of Takhisis's return, she slipped away from the realms of the immortals, shifting into elven form to learn what she could. She wandered among mortals, gathering enough information to take back to the land of the gods where she could plead with them to intervene and stop the killing of thousands of innocents.

This is when our ragtag companions meet her, curing the sick and saving the dying. She realizes that the companions, led by elven warrior Laurana and her brother, Gilthanas, are the ones who will turn the tide of war. But they need the secrets that Silvara keeps in order to do so—they need to know the truth about the gods, the dragons, and how to defeat them. With this plan, Silvara offers to lead them through the mountains and into a magical place called Foghaven Vale where the secrets to defeating Takhisis lie—the legendary dragonlances, which were originally designed to be used by good dragon riders (although they work because they're magic and for pretty much no other reason). She makes this offer knowing that, in order to place this weapon in the hands of the heroes, she must reveal her own secret.

Along the way, Gilthanas begins to fall in love with Silvara, and she with him. Their love story, however, doesn't age very well for many reasons. Silvara knows that Gilthanas will never accept her if he finds out who—or what—she truly is. But Gilthanas, being a man who really doesn't take no for an answer, pursues her anyways and, yeah, Silvara relents and falls in love with him (although I question this love).

Once Silvara has brought the companions into Foghaven Vale, she reveals what she knows: The dragonlances are real, and they will turn the war in their favour. And, of course, that Silvara isn't actually an elf. She's a massive and ancient silver dragon.

Here's where I was always so disappointed, even as a kid: Once Silvara shows her true form, the shadow of her wings flickering against the mountains, Gilthanas is horrified. He actually rejects her. This stunning, powerful, magical creature who sacrifices herself in order to save the world—he is disgusted by what she truly is.

That's not where it ends. Together, Gilthanas and Silvara (in her elven form) travel deep into enemy territory to save the eggs of the "good" dragons that have been stolen and are being mutated into monsters by Takhisis's armies. And then, because Silvara only knows how to be awesome, she convinces the rest of the metallic— aka, good—dragons to forgo their oath and enter the war. So they do. All of them. Legions of gold and silver and bronze and copper dragons fly into the sky and fight back. And it's all because of Silvara, this wondrous creature that a tiny elf could not wrap his head around accepting. After Silvara and Gilthanas achieve what they set out to accomplish, Gilthanas sends Silvara away.

It's not that I wanted them to actually be together. It's that it really doesn't matter what Silvara does—save all of Krynn, convince legions of dragons to fight back—none of it matters to Gilthanas. Once he learns how different she is, he bails. It is after this rejection that Silvara stops using her true dragon name, D'argent, and it's like a part of her, maybe the truest part, has been crushed.

Why did this matter to me so much? Was it that I loved the visceral description of how the sunlight shatters off her silver scales? Or that her dragonfire could light up the night sky? Or that when she finally reveals her true self to the companions, I held my breath at how massive her dragon form must be?

It mattered to me because Silvara's secret—that she was a dragon—was so inspiring. This small elf, someone who was overlooked, shy, and retreating, who sacrificed so much, risked so much, was actually a mythical *gorgeous* creature. But setting her inner beast free cost her the love of a man who truly, obviously, never deserved her in the first place.

This is about the time I decided I didn't want a dragon of my own, but rather I wanted to *be* a dragon. Go big or go home, right?

It's also no surprise that I started writing my own fan fiction around the same time I met Silvara and her undeserving Gilthanas. Even though I didn't know what fan fiction was at the time, I was already finding places where I could insert difference, any sort of difference, into stories so that someone could be as peculiar, or as beastly, as me. When I was a kid, I rewrote Silvara's story so that Gilthanas adored her for everything she was—dragon and all. I wrote her to be the hero and a character who was needed and loved and desired.

But now, what would I write?

I'd write her growing large, her wings bursting from her back, breaking the sunlight into magical rainbows. I'd write her rearing up, her talons so large they could skewer armies of evil creatures. I'd write her lashing her tail, her reptilian lip curling in the pleasure of her own power. I'd breathe her in as I'd write her launching into the sky, ready to fly into battle, dragonfire brewing in her throat.

Now, I'd write her furious.

I would write her choosing her identity on her own terms, when it serves her. I'd write her wielding a sword as silver as her hair, slicing through wave after wave of enemies, driving back tyranny and pain and hurt. She'd become her own brilliant bomb.

Silvara deserves that. The little kid I used to be deserves that. I want her to set herself free.

Silvara was created in a time—the mid-1980s—when she would have been placed in a heteronormative relationship, pining. Her ultimate sacrifice is the shedding of her own identity for the love of a man because difference, *monstrous difference*, is violently pushed to the margins. So maybe these forty-year-old stories get a pass.

Outside of fiction, the stories—medical, psychiatric, social—we are told about ourselves do matter, just as they do for Silvara, but not in the way we might have originally thought. For so long, the prevailing narrative has been that mental health systems or people in power know what's best for us, generating a productive busyness that is designed to treat us and therapize us and medicate us, marching us all towards a goal of wellness and recovery.

But what if wellness doesn't happen, or isn't possible? What if recovery is just smoke and mirrors, an idealized hope that places the mentally ill in a position of constantly trying not to be mentally ill? What if we can't play the protagonist in the way that this role has been written for us? What potentially honest, possibly challenging, but also illuminating stories could we tell about ourselves then?

In the psychiatric community, there's a term, "treatment resistant,"[1] that means despite all psychiatric interventions, a patient's symptoms persist. And the thing is, medical professionals simply don't know why. But I wonder, when we read "treatment resistant" stamped on our medical records, if what our doctors are really trying to say is we are actively resistant and that resistance, in some insidious way, is our *choice*, whether we are conscious of it or not. A suggestion that we are somehow complicit in the failure of this highly accredited,

1   Koen Demyttenaere, "What Is Treatment Resistance in Psychiatry? A 'Difficult to Treat' Concept," *World Psychiatry* 18, no. 3 (October 2019): 354–355, https://doi.org/10.1002/wps.20677.

highly regarded, and empirically sound(ish) treatment plan. And that, whether intentional or not, we are resistant (read: difficult), and that "resistance" means we, the mentally ill, are the problematic ones, not the system in which we are forced to live. In some cases, even vocalizing hesitation or questioning the decisions of psychiatrists and doctors can result in further labelling of the mentally ill patient. In the worst of cases, these questions can lead to further diagnoses, prescriptions, and even involuntary hospitalizations.[2]

What are the stories that are told about us then? My own story consists of lists of medications, diagnoses, hospitalizations, missed appointments, and a subtext of frustration and, for my part, hopelessness. If medical treatments don't work, if we're "treatment resistant," what happens to us then? There isn't really a consistent answer to this because being treatment resistant is mostly perceived as an unacceptable outcome in the psychiatric world. At least, that's been my experience.

But what if we told our own stories?

In 2015, I began the arduous process of obtaining my medical records dating back to 2001—my second psychiatric hospital admission. I was not able to obtain my first psychiatric admission as the records "could not be located."

When the records starting trickling in, I braced myself. Here was a story that had been told about me, in words I don't remember saying, in suggestions and brief examinations resulting in nearly fifteen years of misdiagnosis and, in my opinion, medical mismanagement.

The notes in my records state the following [emphasis mine]:

She was started on Celexa 10 mgs daily 3 or 4 wks. ago.
At this point is quite *willing to stay on it + give it a fair try*,

---

2   Rob Wipond, *Your Consent Is Not Required: The Rise in Psychiatric Detentions, Forced Treatment, and Abusive Guardianships* (Dallas: BenBella Books Inc., 2023).

> including increasing the dose. She has not had any coun-
> selling since returning to school + would like to resume.
> She is especially interested in working through issues
> *related to being sexually abused by* ——.

Given this was my second admission, there was a conclusion made that I hadn't been willing to give medications (Celexa particularly) a "fair try." What is a fair try? Celexa, a common SSRI, can be very effective for people with depression. However, for people with bipolar disorder, SSRIs can cause a dangerous manic episode, which is what happened to me. And yet, a fair try was not given, according to this story told about me.

It's clear to me that at the time of the writing of these records, I was starting to explore the fragmented memories I had of being assaulted, but I don't ever recall receiving counselling for this—or counselling at all. This note is buried among others, a single line, almost illegible. But the smoking gun is there.

My final diagnosis is listed as *Axis I: Possible Major Depression, Axis IV: Academic and financial stressors*, and a note that "adjustment disorder," is present. In the final discharge summary, the years of assault are mentioned again, but not given any weight in my final diagnosis, and therefore not related to any treatment. I did not receive counselling. My "academic and financial stressors" took precedence.

In 2012, when I now believe my mania was at its worst, combined with the bubbling up of trauma I'd long held at bay, I sought out counselling at the University of Toronto Health & Wellness Centre. In a note by my treating psychiatrist, I am misgendered twice, and three times my treatment notes include my mother's body weight. The notes also document me expressing multiple times that I get "crazy, shakey [sic] and crazy thoughts."

Crazy, shakey, and crazy thoughts. Sounds eerily similar to mania, doesn't it?

My diagnosis was reaffirmed to be Major Depressive Disorder and Borderline Personality Disorder (the latter from my first hospitalization, of which the records can't be located). No investigations into bipolar disorder were ever explored. Despite *crazy, shakey, and crazy thoughts.* My excessive drinking—another risk factor intimately correlated with bipolar disorder—was also noted, yet no exploration of a possible misdiagnosis was ever conducted.

The psychiatrist then added to the kaleidoscope of storytelling around who I was and my psychiatric complexities. They listed:

- Sensitivity to abandonment
- Emotional instability
- Relational instability
- Anger
- Emptiness (in the past)

There is a note, again buried deep in my records during those counselling sessions, of a history of trauma. A small note, just a suggestion, buried under *sensitivity to abandonment* and *emotional instability* and *relational instability.* When I told the psychiatrist about the history of assault, he simply asked if I'd enjoyed it.

This is the story that was told about me. A misgendered, fat-shamed, emotionally unstable person who is sensitive to abandonment. Not bipolar disorder, not PTSD, not someone who was trying their hardest to keep the lid on a very large volcano that was ready to erupt.

Weeks into therapy and attempting to give many medications a "fair try," I tried to book another appointment. I was told I was no longer eligible to receive counselling at the student clinic (despite still being a registered student) and that I would be referred to an off-campus psychologist. I received the referral several weeks later, for a psychologist across the city. Her services cost hundreds of dollars an hour. I stopped therapy. I stopped medications. I stopped hoping. I fell apart.

These are my medical records. These are the stories told about me that directly influenced my well-being and quality of life for years. This is a medical narrative that I had no part in authoring. I try not to be angry about this, but I am only human. I try not to feel grief about the years lost, but I am as fallible as the next. I want to move on from these stories, but sometimes it's just too difficult.

II. THE STORIES TOLD BY US

This idea of a medical narrative is something I was introduced to when I worked with a student through her master's thesis, guiding her writing process and generally offering a sounding board for the often-scattered execution of her incredibly insightful thoughts.

Virginia Ford-Roy is a woman in her forties who developed post-operative cognitive changes of "unknown aetiology" following two unrelated surgeries seventeen years apart. Her symptoms "range from difficulty with 'processing detailed complex information' and word-finding to 'executive functioning challenges.'"[3] The symptoms are similar to those who have experienced a stroke or a concussion.

But the reality of Virginia's struggles is far more complex than just those few words. The truth of Virginia is that she is an intelligent, wise, insightful, kind, and motivated person. It's a testament to her fortitude and sheer determination that, for nearly two decades, she, like many others, screamed into the void only to be met with a wall

---

3   Virginia C. Ford-Roy, "Powerless Patient: Reclaiming Agency through Patient Narratives" (master of arts thesis, McMaster University, 2021), 1, http://hdl.handle.net/11375/26483.

of a medical narrative—stories written about her by her medical professionals. Despite how exhausting it is, Virginia will stop at nothing to get answers, to be heard, and to be an advocate for people who live with illnesses and disorders, the people whose assigned stories do not align with their own truths.

During the year Virginia and I worked together, she taught me the difference between medical narrative and patient narrative, which Virginia introduced in her master's thesis. In her thesis, "Powerless Patient: Reclaiming Agency through Patient Narratives," Virginia writes: "I realized the importance of this form of expressive writing as a means to help patients heal and reclaim their agency following any form of illness."[4]

As opposed to their story as told strictly through the lens of a medical professional (the medical narrative), the patient narrative is far more holistic and includes their own account of their illness and their medical experience. It is, essentially, a narrative written by the patient, with or without the assistance of medical professionals. And the primary difference between medical and patient narrative is, as Virginia points out, agency.

"Think of medical narratives like a house with one window," she told me. "When the doctor sees you, they only see through one window. But through *patient* narratives, you poke holes all over the house to allow the light in so people get the full story."[5]

Whether the stories we tell are encased in file folders and written in medical language or are woven with magic and fantasy, they are still fundamentally a picture painted of a protagonist with a problem, a desire, and an inciting event. How the story unfolds is crucial to how we, as readers, view the protagonist.

4   Ford-Roy, "Powerless Patient," 5
5   Virginia Ford-Roy, Zoom call with the author, April 11, 2022.

Author and story coach Lisa Cron writes about the empathy we find in fiction in her book *Story Genius*, and how that empathy connects us to the protagonist, where we can see ourselves as that main character or not.

> We really *are* on the same wavelength, and their experiences quite literally become ours. The exact same thing is true when we're reading a novel. We *become* the protagonist as our brain waves synchronize with hers, allowing us to viscerally experience what she's going through as she tries to solve the story problem and achieve her driving goals.[6]

But then we come to the ending, we close the back cover of the book, and we realize that's not our life—whether we're satisfied or disappointed over that ending depends on how the story is told. Is it a story that dives into the true experience of the protagonist, or is it one that is entirely a unilateral conversation dominated by a medicalized narrative? If it's the latter, perhaps it's time for some fan fiction. Perhaps it's time to, as Virginia states, reclaim our agency and write our own stories. We can take the framework of what's been written before, and tell the truth—the *whole* truth.

In November 2021, two decades after my first hospitalization, I told my partner I was scared. I'd been scrolling the devastating news, the COVID-19 pandemic seemed endless, and all I could see was perpetual night. I struggled to rise from bed, food didn't sit well, and I began

---

6   Lisa Cron, *Story Genius: How to Use Brain Science to Go Beyond Outlining and Write a Riveting Novel* (Berkeley: Ten Speed Press, 2016), 109.

to think, What if I were no longer here? What difference would there be? Would my partner be okay without me?

I started ruminating how many pills it would take to do the job. I contemplated if I had enough bravery to slice a few arteries to ribbons. And I even thought about shutting the garage door, starting my in-laws' old beast of a car, and letting sleep take me away. I started to tell myself all kinds of nasty stories that revolved around my value as a person, or, more precisely, my lack of value. I crafted a story of failure and ridiculousness, one where the protagonist—me—was a shitty person, worthless and empty.

I was *really* depressed. It dawned on me that I'd been looking at my calendar, subconsciously (maybe a little consciously) choosing an appropriate date to do the deed.

After twenty years of living through the cycles of moods, I know when to hit the alarm and set my emergency plan in motion. I recognized the signs of a relapse and tried to remind myself that this wasn't who I was, that I was experiencing a really severe mixed episode—one where the person is both hypomanic and depressed at the same time, a very risky time for people with bipolar disorder because they're depressed enough to kill themselves *and* have the energy and drive to go through with it.

So I told my partner I wasn't okay, that I was scared. We then put our plan into action: he acknowledged how I was feeling (without any judgment or panic), we agreed that I wouldn't be alone for long periods of time, and he took care of food and household chores while I tried to keep my tattering mental health from completely falling apart. I basically kept my therapist (a new one I'd been seeing and who was and still is absolute gold) on speed dial. In the moments it got really bad, my partner and I would lay on our bed and he'd read to me from one of my fantasy novels or he would flip through photographs of all the amazing trips we've taken together—Florence, Rome, Belize, so many wonderful places filled with food and laughter and love. He would remind me that we'll be travelling again many times throughout our long, long life together. I would quietly cry, but he would continue anyways. He's not the person to try to pull me out of my depression, but rather he just sits and waits and helps keep me safe while I ride it through.

For the next few weeks, that was our life as I waited for my psychiatric re-evaluation to discuss medication alterations. A few weeks later, I was sitting on my couch looking at my laptop screen at the face of a young woman with a gentle, slightly tentative voice. She introduced herself to me as Dr. Emily Parkinson and said she was interning with my psychiatrist who, when I was first diagnosed, was also an intern. That fact reminded me of the VIP pass, the punch card of so long ago. But that didn't make me feel sad this time. Instead, I felt a sense of authority. I knew what I was doing. I was an expert at the table of my own health care. I only hoped she'd see that.

This new intern asked me to call her Emily . . . "if that's okay with you," she added.

Sure, that's fine with me, so long as when you're writing your report, weaving the medicalized story that is my broken mind, that you remember my name too.

Of course, I didn't say that.

But what did happen over the next two hours was not something I'd experienced in the medical world before. I heard the words, *I'm sorry that happened to you* and *you've had to be strong for so long* and *have you noticed that you often refer to yourself as broken?*

I asked her what she would refer to me as. She paused, gave a small laugh, and said, "The opposite, I think. But it's not about what *I* think in that regard."

She then asked me what my goals were for treatment, and we spoke about appropriate diagnoses together, and when I disagreed with her about some things, she nodded and said, "Okay, you have a valid point."

This was not the story I had known for the past two decades. This was not *Do you want a tube shoved down your throat?* This was a conversation between two people, both of whom came to the table with their own form of expertise. This was a story that I was co-authoring.

When I finally closed my laptop, I sat quietly for some time, staring out the window into the darkest of winter. I remembered waiting outside the psychiatric hospital with no shoes, a young woman, lost and terrified. I remember my father saying, "You have to try harder, okay?"

Here's the difference between stories of agency and stories authored by other people: real things don't follow a prescriptive path. Having the ability—the agency—to write your own story shouldn't be a privilege only for the able-minded. Not just writing these stories, but reading stories authored by mentally ill folks adds a layer of nuance to a historically skewed narrative. And maybe, with these stories, unlikely heroes can rise, perhaps in the form of a dragon, and launch into the sky. At least, that's how I'd like to write it because it helps me to feel powerful.

III. VIDEO GAMES, SHARED HALLUCINATIONS, AND EMPATHY

After my psychiatric assessment, I informed my partner that I was going to buy an Xbox.

Actually, that was a lie. I'd already hit *purchase*, and my new game system was on the way before I told him. But he smiled and said, "That's cool." I was forty-two years old, and it was the first time I had bought my own video game console.

(Two months later, my partner informed me that I needed a much bigger television for my gaming to which I couldn't reasonably disagree.)

I'd loved video games when I was a kid. I'd steal moments with my brother's Sega Master System, worming my way through the dungeons of *Phantasy Star*, collecting all of the legendary weapons so I could fly into the heavens and kill the Big Bad Guy. I loved that game. Just like with my Dragonlance novels, I loved falling into a new world, this one a pixelated, choppy screen full of magic and dragons and vampires and zombies. And I *loved* kicking ass.

So, as I—like millions (billions?) of others—languished through the pandemic, I started to think back on those moments of delight I had had when I was a kid. I wanted that feeling again.

When my Xbox arrived, I was blown away by the multitude of games available. I was so excited, but in the back of my mind, I felt guilty. Here I was, a grown person buying a stupid gaming console and about to commit *way* too many hours to an entirely unproductive activity (plus, I had a book to write). But when I stumbled across something called *Assassin's Creed Odyssey*, I pushed that voice down and thought, Assassin . . . that's something I can get behind.

So, for almost five hours, packaging still strewn around, I sat on the floor in front of my television like a kid on Christmas morning, and I wandered around Ancient Greece, following my odysseys, uncovering cult secrets, and collecting fragments of armour that would be outdated in about six minutes. I was sneaking into military forts, stabbing soldiers in the back with my magical spear, and then slithering back into the shadows. I was strategizing. I was climbing the Parthenon, imitating the 430 BCE version of a sharpshooter, wiping out entire regiments without ever being seen. I was also slaughtering the legendary Minotaur, Medusa (sorry!), and Cyclops and solving the Sphinx's riddles. And, of course, discovering Atlantis was real after all.

And I was playing a woman. A ridiculously strong, no-bullshit-taking, swearing, badass, blood-covered, horny demigod of a woman. It was *awesome*.

Over the next few weeks, I found myself counting down the hours until I could reasonably numb my brain with some magical-world ass-kicking. But then guilt started to creep in.

I should clean my house. I really should be writing. I should actually move my body instead of making a butt-shaped dip in the couch. I should . . . I should . . . I shouldn't be playing this game. I wasted my money on a stupid toy.

I'm so stupid.

But when I wasn't playing my game, when I wasn't allowing myself to check out of the depression that had been lingering with me for almost two years without reprieve, I found myself not wanting to wake in the morning. I found my ability to be creative nearly absent. My enjoyment came with every stealthy kill I made and breathtaking landscape I explored. My delight came with ancient legends becoming real.

Then I wondered: Why do I love this so much? Why exactly are these games so popular? And why do I find myself having just a little motivation to write, stories starting to coalesce in my mind?

Why do I feel like me when I play?

It's hard not to think of video games—and the sedentary time spent playing them—as not the healthiest option. More insidious, though, is how video games have represented mental illness; when compared to other artistic mediums, video games are up there on harmful depictions—reinforcing "lunatic" stereotypes, portraying mental asylums as nothing short of hellish, using insanity as a punishment, and linking mental illness with violence. In a study of one hundred video games that include some form of mental illness narrative, 97 percent[7] por-

---

7   Manuela Ferrari, et al., "Gaming with Stigma: Analysis of Messages about Mental Illnesses in Video Games," *JMIR Mental Health* 6, no. 5 (May 2019): e12418, https://doi.org/10.2196/12418.

trayed mental illness in a negative way, often using tropes such as violence, the paranormal, mystery, or even mental illness as a consequence of gameplay, as can be seen in *Sanitarium, Far Cry*, and *Call of Duty: Black Ops*. Some video games use insanity as an "overcoming" storyline, relying on characters undergoing experimental and harmful "mad scientist" treatments to move the plot forward. In a 2014 essay for *polygon*, Patrick Lindsey argues that in many video game narratives, the *true* villain is mental illness itself. He iterates a call to action for video game developers to consider mental illness in their inclusivity wheelhouse and work towards more productive and accurate representations of mental illness.[8]

It's clear that so much of our media portrays mental illness in a negative light, but there's also an emphasis on the so-called tragedy of living with mental illness. (The only tragedy that I believe truly exists is misunderstanding.) While living with mental illness isn't exactly the cat's pyjamas, is it something that is simply *that* horrific? Could it be that perpetuating these harmful stereotypes is the thing that makes it horrific? We've come so far to break stigma around mental illness, and yet have we come far enough? In video games, it would seem not.

So, what's the harm? Well, it turns out it's pretty big. Over 1.8 *billion* people play video games worldwide, and the negative, problematic, and harmful ways that mental illness is portrayed in these games can lead to reductions in self-esteem, help-seeking behaviours, medication adherence, and overall well-being and recovery[9] (although I struggle with the term "recovery," as it suggests the only treatment for mental illness is a medical model of fixing, and also negates the possibility of relapse).

---

8   Patrick Lindsey, "Gaming's Favorite Villain Is Mental Illness, and This Needs to Stop," *Polygon*, July 21, 2014, https://www.polygon.com/2014/7/21/5923095/mental-health -gaming-silent-hill.

9   Ferrari, et al., "Gaming with Stigma," e12418.

The portrayal of mental illness in video games hasn't received too much by way of empirical studies, and even less when compared to other forms of media. So, here's my speculation: other forms of media—film, television, literature, and print media and journalism—offer a two-dimensional portrayal of mental illness, a delivery of the message followed by a receipt of the message. Many video games, however, offer a third dimension: one of choice through immersion.

Since the idea and construction of a video game world is pretty stagnant with few genres to choose from, it's hard to move something so robust as the leviathan of the video gaming world. Some game design companies, however, are looking to do just that.

It's important to acknowledge that—just like with film, television, and literature—not all video games are the same. There is one type of video game that does present some beneficial interest to neuroscientists and psychiatrists: open-world role-playing games. Games that are immersive and offer choice with a compelling narrative. Not ones where the player gets to rip around in a Maserati through gang-ridden streets, stealing other cars (although that also is a Friday night well spent, in my humble opinion).

I stumbled across Ninja Theory's *Hellblade: Senua's Sacrifice* through one of my D&D friends when he sent me a message saying, *Not sure if this is what you're looking for, but I thought of you.* I was interested but dubious. It looked like another open-world RPG that dealt in hack-n-slash, gore, and fright. Sort of like a Dark Age Celtic version of *Silent Hill*. I did a little digging and learned that the main character the player has control of lives with mental illness—specifically, psychosis. Of course, my doubt doubled. I thought, here again is another game that uses fear and stereotypes of the "overcoming" narrative versus the "punishment" narrative of mental illness. I was also reminded of Amanda Leduc's fairy tales and how physical disability is often used as a moralistic lesson—*do this, and you'll be punished by physical disfigurement.* Only this time, the punishment is madness.

Turns out, *Hellblade* was much different than I expected.

The primary narrative arc of the game is simple: an eighth-century Celtic woman, Senua, is travelling into Hel (the Celtic underworld) to save the soul of her brutally murdered lover. Easy enough. But it's this simple story that allows for the complexity of Senua's character—and her mental illness—to flourish during gameplay.

Upon starting the game, players are introduced to a woman who is rowing a rough-made boat along a misty river. All that can be seen of her is her back and occasionally a profile of her face as she turns her head, listening to voices, watching the quiet landscape around her. Attached to her hip is the linen-wrapped skull of her dead lover, Dillion. This is Senua.

Immersion in Senua's character is a multifaceted experience. Players immediately hear Senua talking to them, almost as though she's narrating her own story. But this voice refers to Senua in the third person and is soon accompanied by many other whispering voices.

"Oh, how rude of me," the narrator, Senua, says to the player. "I never told you of the others. You hear them, too, right? They've been around ever since the tragedy. Well . . . that's not quite true. Some are old, some are new . . . but they've . . . changed."[10]

As this voice is softly speaking, other voices, the entirety of Senua's consciousness, are whispering "go back," "what is she doing?," "we can't do this, go back, go back!" And, of course, "he's already dead."

Once gameplay starts, the majority of the game isn't about hacking and slashing the enemies (although there is a healthy dose of that). It's about navigating the world through the senses of someone with psychosis.

---

10   theRadBrad, "HELLBLADE SENUA'S SACRIFICE Walkthrough Gameplay Part 1—Prologue," YouTube, August 8, 2017, video, 42:57, https://www.youtube.com/watch?v=H5uj7UKAsho.

As Senua hears voices, so does the player. As Senua experiences visual hallucinations, so does the player. How these hallucinations—auditory and visual—are depicted in the game is unique in that they are almost entirely neutral. They aren't good or bad, the latter of which is often assumed in real life. They can be both or nothing. Sometimes Senua's ability to perceive things that a mentally healthy person wouldn't is actually to her benefit—and saves her life: *"behind you!"* a voice will whisper, and once the player turns, a monster will be looming. Sometimes, however, the hallucinations can be terrifying, as are the voices that constantly try to undermine Senua's confidence and thin sense of self.

The thing that makes Senua's psychosis different from other video game portrayals of mental illness is that we are working within her own sense of the world. Basically, by playing Senua, players enter a mind of psychosis from the perspective of the person experiencing it. It's built right into the gameplay mechanics, and so *Hellblade* takes a stab at engendering empathy in the player as Senua's reality becomes their own.

Naturally, I was completely fascinated not just by the gameplay, but by the idea that a video game could actually achieve an experience of psychosis without catering to stereotypes or making mental illness into something to be overcome. I wanted to learn more.

Ninja Theory, a UK-based game development company, is the creator of *Hellblade*. Creative director Tameem Antoniades says the inspiration behind *Hellblade* was his desire to understand a friend who had recently had a "mental break."[11] He wanted to know *what that felt like.*

Out of that desire, Ninja Theory worked with individuals who have lived experience with psychosis. They also worked with mental health professionals, including Dr. Paul Fletcher, a professor of neuroscience

---

11   "What Is the Insight Project?," The Insight Project, https://theinsightproject.com/.

and psychiatry at Cambridge University, who highlighted the concept of pattern recognition and construction of reality through psychosis, as seen in the video game. Clues to solve problems and move forward in the game are anchored in an experience of psychosis through the common hallucination of patterns and colours (rather than the traditional hallucination of a person or animal). Because of these hallucinations, Senua can unlock codes and move closer to her goal.

I was reminded of how realities can be constructed when we play other RPGs (tabletop and video), like D&D. This is where video games and virtual reality can span the gap between different realities—and *each* of our realities is different from the next. Again, empiricism states that our realities are constructed by what we believe to be true and based on what our senses bring into our brains, and then how our brains process that information. From this information, we construct a worldview, like a blueprint, using that to understand a lot that goes on around us. Our brains do this rather quickly—we take in information through our senses and our brains process it based on what it already knows. Then the output is a reaction. Every new piece of knowledge shifts our schemas just slightly.

Can we say, though, that our schemas are infallible simply because we don't live with traditional hallucinations? If we come to a consensus that a particular reality, one without delusions or hallucinations, is the norm, doesn't that then create a single story? A single narrative into which everyone—no matter who they are—must fit in order to be believed or taken seriously?

"The single story creates stereotypes, and the problem with stereotypes is not that they are untrue, but that they are incomplete. They make one story become the *only* story," Dr. Fletcher says.[12] And that

---

12   Paul Fletcher, "Psychosis: Bending Reality to See Around the Corners | Paul Fletcher | TEDxCambridgeUniversity," TEDx Talks, YouTube, December 2, 2016, video, 12:01, https://www.youtube.com/watch?v=tV2RLLtOgL4.

one story, when it comes to how we define fact as opposed to fiction, is one of a mentally healthy reality. So what happens for those whose realities aren't part of that single story?

Dr. Fletcher makes a compelling argument for the ubiquity of hallucinations. His fundamental point is that reality is considered simply so because that's what we experience. When we say someone who has schizophrenia or bipolar disorder is breaking from reality—to whose reality do we refer? Insisting on one narrative of empirical truth is excluding the possibility of all other realities. It's hard to step into someone else's mind when our own has been so entrenched in the experiences of the world that we have been navigating (and neurophysiologically and neuropsychologically constructing) our entire lives. In short, it's difficult for some people to have empathy for those with mental illness if we haven't experienced the symptoms ourselves. "If someone is building a model that isn't shared by the world, that is a very isolating experience," Dr. Fletcher says.[13]

The questions then become: How can we step into their world? How can we recreate an experience that aligns with what psychosis or mania might be? Can we create empathy by challenging our own perceptions, which, by Dr. Fletcher's argument, could be our own form of hallucinations?

Well, what better playground than virtual reality for engaging other experiences?

Ninja Theory, Tameem Antoniades, and Dr. Paul Fletcher launched the Insight Project in an attempt to do just that. By focusing on personalization, they're trying to understand the individual experience of mental illness—such as psychosis—by fine-tuning one's virtual environment. This seems to be a subversion of the normative codification system of standard expectations, thresholds, and

---

13   Fletcher, "Psychosis."

treatments that our medical models of the *DSM-5* currently use. It's an earnest attempt towards a more multi-dimensional and individualized approach.

I think possibilities in virtual reality and, in particular, open-world RPGs, are exciting; they make me feel a bit hopeful. Imagine a game where the player can tailor the character they are playing to feel and react as they do. Imagine just how empowering that might be for someone who has lived with mental illness or trauma and has been unable to explain the little nuances, the particular feelings and sensations of living in that world. And then imagine someone you love—your partner, your child, your best friend—could play through your senses and understand through gaming what it's like in your world.

When I think of that, I feel a deep, shuddering sigh. There have been so many times I've wanted to explain *exactly* how it feels to live in my own head, but there are simply no words. So those who love me will always understand through a lens.

(Don't get me wrong, they do a great job. It's just still a bit isolating.)

Researchers with the Insight Project ask:

> What if a person is given control of a simulation and is able to fine tune it so that it most accurately captures their inner world? This could be done using a personalised control content by tuning simple sliders, a common mechanic in popular games used for customising levels of characters.[14]

The materials go on to speculate the possible outcomes of this experience: "This in turn could form the basis for individually-tailored

14 "The Insight Project."

game experiences that adapt to the player and their progress in over-coming or reducing their symptoms."[15]

While I'm not a fan of the language of "overcoming," there's something mind-blowing about using technology to step into the reality of someone living with mental illness. I can see the draw the Insight Project could have for someone like me. I also wonder if this project could be used not just by mentally ill people but by their loved ones, caregivers, and healthcare providers. Can it be used by research teams and psychiatrists? Can it be used to restructure the reality we have created around mental illness and what we *think* it might feel like? Because really, how can one be an authority on mental illness and further diagnose severity, treatment, and outcomes without actually understanding individual nuances? From that, could treatment plans for mental illness be individualized, not just scrawl on a prescription pad and hope for the best?

Could we foster empathy—*true* empathy—by stepping into some-one else's reality and understanding what that reality feels like?

I fully acknowledge that my playing *Assassin's Creed* probably does nothing to contribute to understanding, empathizing, and therefore helping to reduce stigma around mental illness. And really, there are a plethora of video games that exist simply for entertainment purposes. But the more complex these video games become, the more layers of choice are given to the player. And I like choice. I like dictating my own experience and where my gameplay will go. I like experimenting. And I still love playing an assassin.

I asked a good friend of mine, writer and gamer Oscar Ceceña, why he plays video games so much and what he thought they did for

15 "The Insight Project."

him. "It's because it allows me to be a part of a magical world and do things I could never do in real life," he told me. His answer, while simple, also got me thinking.

It's interesting that Oscar and, I'm sure, most of those 1.8 billion gamers worldwide would have a similar sentiment. But really, isn't being able to do something you couldn't in *real life* similar to an artificial and intentional hallucination? Maybe sort of like stepping into another reality? Perhaps by entering another world where we can do things we could never do in our real lives—like scale the northern mountains of Ancient Greece, deep dive in the Mediterranean, or fight the Minotaur with the magical Spear of Leonidas and the Breath of Ares—we can also understand the true potential of our imagination and choice. Wouldn't we say that could be therapeutic, expanding into our capabilities with the help of choice and a playground that allows us to do anything and be anyone? For me, maybe it's a place and a character who, like an avatar, gives me control. Would that gift reveal something about our need for a world that might just include a little bit of a hallucination, even someone else's hallucination? Might it help us become a little more empathic towards *difference*?

About a year after I started my gaming, I decided to explore what the online world had to offer. So, like millions of others, I joined Twitch—an online streaming platform where gamers around the world gather to play online (among other uses; but it's mostly gaming). I was nervous—mostly about being female and, let's be honest, close to middle age. I always thought online gaming to be for younger generations, not someone like me. Someone *different*. But it's nice to be wrong.

On Twitch, I met a gamer who goes by the name Nari By Nature. Nari is a music teacher in her mid-thirties and has created a Twitch space that is inclusive, safe, and fun. I knew that was the place I wanted to be. Over the months, as I got to know Nari and some of her over twelve hundred followers, I felt more comfortable being myself and sinking into the online gaming world and what it had to offer. Eventually, I decided to reach out to her. I wanted to know more about her and why gaming—online particularly—is so important to her.

"In fiction," she told me, "You can create a better world. You can be a better you." How you react in situations that you may not be presented with in real life, Nari said, can be incredibly informative. And for Nari, it can be authentic. Stories in gaming can affirm who you truly are.

> There are many situations [in gaming] in which people would sacrifice in such ways: if you die [in the game], your entire squad loses all their stuff and you have to start all over. We [make those sacrifices] in the game [for each other] all the time. It would be interesting to see how that could translate into the real world. Would people learn to be selfless in their real lives?[16]

It was during the 2016 presidential elections in the United States that Nari found herself sinking into gaming as a way to process what was happening to both her and her friends, some of whom were Black, immigrants, identified as LGBTQ, or were otherwise marginalized. Nari herself identifies as pansexual; living in Los Angeles, she and her friends were truly afraid. "To be honest," she said, "I probably dissociated a little bit . . . this was not the world I wanted to live in." In early 2020, when Nari watched the world go into lockdown, she turned to online gaming. That's when, encouraged by one of her

16   Nari By Nature, Zoom call with the author, May 18, 2023.

twelve-year-old music students, she joined Twitch. In that space, Nari knew she wanted to cultivate safety and inclusivity. She wanted the freedom to be vulnerable and to give that freedom to folks who joined her. She wanted to be her true self. I can relate to that.

I asked Nari if she would use the word *empathy* to describe how she felt about online gaming and being her authentic self. She replied:

> [Online gaming] does encourage a great deal of empathy, which I feel is lacking in the world in general today. A lot of people see [empathy] as weakness. But I think it takes a really strong person to go outside themselves and understand where somebody else is coming from. There are so many situations where I see people just protecting themselves. And it's like, what are we protecting ourselves from?[17]

To me, it feels like now is the right time—a mix of uncertainty, rapid change, social and political shifts—for fantasy, *all* fantasy to be used in the ways that Nari describes. Fantasy can help us understand the complexities of our world and ourselves in nuanced and safe ways, and for millions of consumers, fantasy—via literature, films, TV, games, you name it—has become their go-to, an escape in a way. Sales of D&D books and other gameplay tools have skyrocketed over the past few years. Pandemic-related science fiction and dystopian fantasy has topped the charts, and maybe it's just my own cognitive bias, but the fantasy sections in bookstores—including science fiction, horror, and graphic novels—seem to have swelled. Maybe people are reaching for something they simply can't find here in our world. Maybe they need a short, intentional simulation, a *Star Trek* holodeck where they can . . . *breathe.*

---

17   Nari By Nature, Zoom call.

Nari finished her thought with a small laugh. "Why are we more comfortable being ourselves in a simulation than in real life?"

My question exactly.

In a 1999 essay published in *The Globe and Mail* (now available to read on his own website), Canadian fantasy author Guy Gavriel Kay wrote:

> The journeys and motifs of classic fantasy can come closer to mirroring the inner journey of the human spirit than almost anything else. The patterns of myth, folklore, archetype and fairy tale embedded in such works are time-honoured and immensely powerful, and fantasy can tap more directly into these ancient wells than just about anything else: they are the core elements of the genre.[18]

Kay is right in more ways than I think he intended, and his statement goes beyond just classic fantasy. Landscapes in games, digital and role-playing, give us a playground where possibilities can be explored, speaking volumes to and helping us iterate what we still don't understand.

I think back to that little kid I used to be, wild hair and hazel eyes, burnt gold in the sunlight, playing in the forest, at the riverbank, whispering into the trees and wishing fairies were real, that dragons were real, and that magic cupped the world, and I hope kids of next generations can reach for that magic and feel it. Truly feel it. I hope we all can.

Really, it's no surprise that once I started racking up the hours logged on my new Xbox that I began to imagine storylines, characters,

---

18   Guy Gavriel Kay, "Home and Away," *Bright Weavings* (blog), https://brightweavings.com
      /globe/.

stakes, and magic. Maybe this is where my true potential can grow: somewhere I can hallucinate for a little while, pretending I live in a magical place where I have as much choice as I want. A world I control. Where I make the rules. If I can do all of that in a video game, then maybe I can start imagining those endless choices outside the video game too.

Doesn't that seem empowering to you?

IV. A DRAGON OF ONE'S OWN

I have a room. It has four walls, a narrow door, and an even narrower window. The window overlooks a chaotic garden filled with a tangle of tomato and zucchini plants so big they threaten to overpower the stubborn vines. I watch the neighbour's little girl playing with her small dog in their yard, shrieking every time the pup leaps up to nibble her. The sun is thin, but it pushes through the clouds. I breathe. I can feel my breath. I place my hand on my chest, the heaviness and warmth of it a small comfort.

I'm at the tail end of a depressive episode, and I'm exhausted. I'm so overwhelmingly exhausted that my bones ache, my muscles turn to jelly, my mind stumbles. This last episode was a bad one. I lay in bed for days, the curtains drawn. I knew what time it was by the quality of the light that pressed against the fabric, and it made me anxious, reminding me of the moments I was missing.

My mother-in-law came by with a full pot of homemade chicken soup because my partner told her I wasn't feeling well. I can still taste the salty, savoury flavour. There's nothing quite like it. When I struggled to rise, my partner slid his hand behind my back, pulling me up. He brought the spoon of warm soup to my lips. "My piccolina," he'd said.

I know by now that those depressive episodes are like a drop off a cliff before the glide. You have to drop, drop, drop, until you can finally spread your arms, catch the wind, and fly back up to safety. It's exhausting, and each time I feel like small parts of me dissolve in the air. I also know by now that it's just a feeling. That it's just not true. But sometimes I will fall so far that I can't pull myself up alone. It's in those times I wonder what would happen if I were alone. I don't know why, but that thought is comforting—knowing I won't have to experience that aloneness anymore. Almost as comforting as the feeling of flying once again. Not soaring too close to the sun, burning too bright, pushing too hard. Just gliding.

There's a ribbon of sunlight that has opened the clouds. It looks warm. I'd like to go outside, but my head still hurts. Maybe tomorrow. I look around my room. Four walls, hardwood floor. There are cracks in the plaster ceiling. The walls are a gross shade of rose and the room has become an absentminded storage space for things we just really don't need. But in my mind, I can see the refuse cleared away. I can see a small desk with a chair tucked under that narrow window. Across from it, I can see a bookshelf. A deep armchair. Above the armchair, I see my hard-earned degree, the one I fought for sixteen years to achieve. I see a rug on the floor to warm the emptiness. I think I'd like a plant.

There's something I feel simmering just under the surface. It has a soft yet electric quality. It's silver, like Silvara. Like my father's hair as I watched him walking ahead of me in those green, green forests. It's molten silver. It ripples. It's warm. I breathe it in, but it fades again, shrinking back. I turn to see my partner standing in the doorway. He asks me what I'm up to. "Just thinking," I tell him. Thinking about a desk and a plant and a chair right over there and a shelf filled with books of magic and dragons and landscapes that are so eerie and beautiful I want to capture them all.

I look out the window again. A window of my own. A room of my own. He asks me what colour I'd like to paint it. "Lemon," I say. He has no idea what *lemon* means but says we should go to the hardware store anyways and get some cans. Today, maybe. "You're feeling better, right?"

Today I'm feeling better, but I don't know about tomorrow. I think about maybe reading a book or playing a game. I think about stepping into another world for a while where I can be free. Where I can be me.

"Uli?" I say.

He's looking at the light switch, running his hand along the wall, inspecting. Making sure everything will be just right. "Yes, baby."

"I think I'd like to try writing."

He moves down to the baseboards, mumbling something about a can of paint he has in the basement that would work perfectly to touch them up. "I thought you *were* writing," he says.

I press my lips tight. Should I? Maybe I'm just swinging back in the other direction where I spin so fast, so hard, so broken. No, that's not what this is. I feel the molten silver again. I can smell something faint, something warm—smoke? It's in my mind, but still, I know that scent. Far in the distance of my imagination, I hear the great intake of breath, flanks rising.

"No," I say. "I mean writing *seriously*. I don't know if I'm any good, but I'd like to try?" My voice tips upwards, unsure of my own thoughts.

He stops inspecting the baseboards and looks at me. He smiles. His eyes are impossibly green, and I love them. "Okay, piccolina."

"Okay," I echo. We are quiet for a moment. Then I say, "I'll need a desk."

"And a good chair," he adds.

I nod. A chair, a good one. And a plant and a bookshelf and on the walls, framed reminders of my achievements. An armchair for reading and dreaming and scheming stories already gathering under the gravity of my imagination. Four walls the colour of lemons. A small bed for Cairo. In that distant space deep in my mind, I hear an ancient rumble. A silver eye opens. Blinks, triple lids folding forward. The creak of tendons as massive wings unfurl, capturing the morning sun. I wonder if these beasts that have finally woken can survive while I pull the parts of this new self that I have become into a whole person. I wonder if they will fall back to sleep with each medication I take. I wonder if the magic, so new and tenuous, will fade before I can even feel it wrapping around my fingers.

But the thing is, I just don't know. So for today, I'll imagine my four lemon walls and my plant and my desk and a good chair and the stories that are starting to grow in my mind. Stories of dragons and elves and wizards, of myths and folklore and legends. Stories of little kids who save the day and are just the coolest, the ones I'd always wanted to read. Stories I'd destroyed so many years ago.

The dragon's breath is warm. I smile. I should get on with my day, but I stand just a moment longer watching the neighbours' little girl and her pup, imagining glittering tendrils of magic coiling around her.

Finally, I turn, flick off the light, and walk out of the room with a promise to my newly woken beasts—*I'm here. I see you. I hear you.*

And we're going to make some wonderful worlds together.

REFERENCES

CHAPTER I

Cohen, Jeffrey Jerome. *Monster Theory: Reading Culture*. Minneapolis: University of Minnesota Press, 1997.

Cotterell, Arthur. *Classical Mythology: Illustrated Encyclopedia*. Leicester, England: Lorenz Books, 2011.

Diagnostic and Statistical Manual of Mental Disorders: DSM-5. Arlington, Virginia: American Psychiatric Association, 2017.

Duffy, William S. "Medusa as Victim and Tool of Male Aggression." *Verbum Incarnatum: An Academic Journal of Social Justice* 7, no. 1 (2020). https://athenaeum.uiw.edu/verbumincarnatum/vol7/iss1/.

Encyclopædia Britannica, s.v. "Medusa," accessed July 4, 2021, www.britannica.com/topic/Medusa-Greek-mythology.

Fraley, R. Chris. "Adult Attachment Theory and Research: A Brief Overview." Department of Psychology, University of Illinois at Urbana-Champagne, 2018. http://labs.psychology.illinois.edu/~rcfraley/attachment.htm.

Friend, Heather. "Dad Holding Space for His Daughter's Big Feelings."
    YouTube, November 24, 2021. https://www.youtube.com/watch?
    v=fbuvaOsqP-4.

Lepore, Jill. "The Strange and Twisted Life of 'Frankenstein.'" *The New
    Yorker*, February 5, 2018. https://www.newyorker.com/magazine
    /2018/02/12/the-strange-and-twisted-life-of-frankenstein.

Ness, Patrick. *A Monster Calls*. Somerville, Massachusetts: Candlewick
    Press, 2013.

Romm, Cari. "The Enduring Scariness of the Mad Scientist." *The
    Atlantic*, October 29, 2014. https://www.theatlantic.com/health
    /archive/2014/10/the-enduring-scariness-of-the-mad-scientist
    /382064/.

Shelley, Mary Wollstonecraft. *Frankenstein; or, The Modern
    Prometheus*. Durham, NC: Duke Classics, 1818. Libby (Toronto
    Public Library e-book).

Sinclair, Julian. "Abracadabra." *The Jewish Chronicle*. July 5, 2018.
    www.thejc.com/judaism/jewish-words/abracadabra-1.466709.

Tolkien, J.R.R. *The Lord of the Rings*. London: HarperCollins, 2007.

CHAPTER 2

Achilli, Justin, Joseph Carriker, Jess Hartley, Wood Ingham, Matthew
    McFarland, Peter Schaefer, John Snead, Travis Stout, Chuck
    Wendig, and Peter Woodworth. *Changeling the Lost: A Storytelling
    Game of Beautiful Madness*. Stone Mountain, Georgia: White
    Wolf Pub, 2007.

APA Dictionary of Psychology, s.v. "empiricism," accessed March 26,
    2024 https://dictionary.apa.org/empiricism.

Congdon, Olivia. "All Eyes on the Reef." Australian Academy of
    Science. https://www.science.org.au/curious/earth-environment
    /all-eyes-reef.

Cotterell, Arthur. *Classical Mythology: Illustrated Encyclopedia*. Leicester, England: Lorenz Books, 2011.

Leduc, Amanda. *Disfigured: On Fairy Tales, Disability, and Making Space*. Toronto: Coach House Books, 2020.

Martel, Yann. *Life of Pi*. Toronto: Knopf Canada, 2001.

Mendlesohn, Farah. *Rhetorics of Fantasy*. Middletown, Connecticut: Wesleyan University Press, 2013.

Online Etymology Dictionary, s.v. "insane," accessed March 26, 2024 www.etymonline.com/search?q=insane.

Roddenberry, Gene, creator. *Star Trek: The Original Series*. Featuring William Shatner, Leonard Nimoy, and DeForest Kelley. Aired 1966, on NBC.

Rodé, Kitty (@goldenfeatheri). Golden Feather Initiative. X (formerly Twitter). https://twitter.com/goldenfeatheri?lang=en.

Tankard, Miquel. *SINS, Player's Handbook*. Sheffield, UK: First Falling Leaf Limited, 2013.

Weis, Margaret, and Tracy Hickman. *Dragons of Spring Dawning*. Lake Geneva, Wisconsin: TSR, Inc., 1985.

Wizards RPG Team, *Player's Handbook*, 5th Edition. Washington: Wizards of the Coast, 2014.

CHAPTER 3

Campbell, Joseph. *The Hero with a Thousand Faces*. Princeton, New Jersey: Princeton University Press, 2004.

Diagnostic and Statistical Manual of Mental Disorders: DSM-5. Arlington, Virginia: American Psychiatric Association, 2017.

Herman, Judith. *Trauma and Recovery: The Aftermath of Violence— From Domestic Abuse to Political Terror*. New York: Basic Books, 2015.

Herron, Kate, dir. *Loki*. Season 1, episode 1, "Glorious Purpose."

Featuring Tom Hiddleston. Aired June 9, 2021, on Disney Plus. https://www.disneyplus.com/series/loki/6pARMvILBGzF.

Nutter, David, dir. *Game of Thrones*. Season 2, episode 7, "A Man without Honor." Featuring Charles Dance, Kit Harington, and Emilia Clarke. Aired May 13, 2012, on HBO. https://www.crave .ca/en/tv-shows/game-of-thrones.

Nutter, David, dir. *Game of Thrones*. Season 5, episode 9, "The Dance of Dragons." Featuring Kit Harington, Carice van Houten, and Maisie Williams. Aired June 7, 2015, on HBO. https://www.crave .ca/en/tv-shows/game-of-thrones.

Peele, Jordan, dir. *Get Out*. Featuring Daniel Kaluuya, Allison Williams, and Bradley Whitford. 2017; Universal City, California: Universal Pictures.

Rowling, J.K. *Harry Potter and the Goblet of Fire*. Vancouver: Raincoast Books, 2000.

Rowling, J.K. *Harry Potter and the Half-Blood Prince*. Vancouver: Raincoast Books, 2005.

Rowling, J.K. *Harry Potter and the Philosopher's Stone*. Vancouver: Raincoast Books, 1997.

Sapochnik, Miguel, dir. *Game of Thrones*. Season 8, episode 7, "The Bells." Featuring Emilia Clarke, Lena Headey, and Peter Dinklage. Aired May 12, 2019, on HBO. Crave, https://www.crave.ca/en/tv -shows/game-of-thrones.

Shaw, Julia. *Evil: The Science Behind Humanity's Dark Side*. Toronto: Doubleday Canada, 2019.

Shyamalan, M. Knight, dir. *Split*. Featuring James McAvoy, Betty Buckley, and Anya Taylor-Joy. 2017; Universal City, California: Universal Pictures.

Van Patten, Timothy, dir. *Game of Thrones*. Season 1, episode 1, "Winter Is Coming." Featuring Sean Bean. Aired April 17, 2011, on HBO. Crave, https://www.crave.ca/en/tv-shows/game-of-thrones.

CHAPTER 4

Aiello, K.J. "'Then There Was Me.'" *West End Phoenix*, November 9, 2022. https://www.westendphoenix.com/stories/then-there-was-me.

Asma, Stephen T. *On Monsters: An Unnatural History of Our Worst Fears*. Oxford: Oxford University Press, 2009.

Flanagan, Mike, dir. *The Haunting of Hill House*. Episode 1, "Steven Sees a Ghost." Featuring Victoria Pedretti, Kate Siegel, and Henry Thomas. Aired October 12, 2018, on Netflix. https://www.netflix.com/ca/title/80189221.

Flanagan, Mike, dir. *The Haunting of Hill House*. Episode 6, "Two Storms." Featuring Victoria Pedretti, Kate Siegel, and Henry Thomas. Aired October 12, 2018, on Netflix. https://www.netflix.com/ca/title/80189221.

Flanagan, Mike, dir. *The Haunting of Hill House*. Episode 10, "Silence Lay Steadily." Featuring Victoria Pedretti, Kate Siegel, and Henry Thomas. Aired October 12, 2018, on Netflix. https://www.netflix.com/ca/title/80189221.

Fuseli, Henry. *The Nightmare*. 1781. Oil on canvas, 40 1/16 × 50 1/16 × 13/16 inches. Detroit, Detroit Institute of Art. https://www.dia.org/art/collection/object/nightmare-45573.

Gottlieb, Lori. "Dear Therapist: My Son Is Angry about the Way He Was Treated Last Christmas." *The Atlantic*, December 9, 2022. https://www.theatlantic.com/family/archive/2019/12/my-sons-mental-health-is-affecting-our-whole-family/603223/.

Jackson, Shirley. *The Haunting of Hill House*. New York: Penguin Books, 1959.

"Mental Illness and Addiction: Facts and Statistics." CAMH. Accessed 2022. https://www.camh.ca/en/driving-change/the-crisis-is-real/mental-health-statistics.

Muschietti, Andy, dir. *Mama*. Featuring Jessica Chastain, Isabelle Nélisse, and Megan Charpentier. 2013; Universal City, California: Universal Pictures. Netflix, https://www.netflix.com/fr-en/title/70254522.

Pascal, Richard. "Walking Alone Together: Family Monsters in *The Haunting of Hill House*." *Studies in the Novel* 46, no. 4 (Winter 2014): 464–485. https://doi.org/10.1353/sdn.2014.0072.

Pottle, Adam. "How Horror Helps Us Overcome Our Fears." *This Magazine*, February 26, 2020. https://this.org/2020/02/26/how-horror-helps-us-overcome-our-fears/.

Suni, Eric. "What You Should Know about Sleep Paralysis." Sleep Foundation. Accessed March 11, 2022. https://www.sleepfoundation.org/parasomnias/sleep-paralysis.

Watkins, James, dir. *The Woman in Black*. Featuring Daniel Radcliffe, Janet McTeer, and Adrian Rawlins. 2012; Los Angeles: CBS Films. Netflix, https://www.netflix.com/is/title/70206133.

CHAPTER 5

Alcoholics Anonymous. "There Is a Solution." In *The Big Book*, 17–29. New York: Alcoholics Anonymous World Services, Inc., 2001. https://www.aa.org/sites/default/files/2021-11/en_bigbook_chapt2.pdf.

Diagnostic and Statistical Manual of Mental Disorders: DSM-5. Arlington, Virginia: American Psychiatric Association, 2017.

Fogler, Sean. "As a Physician and a Patient, I've Seen the Damage Caused by the Stigma of Addiction. It Must End." *Stat*, December 8, 2020. https://www.statnews.com/2020/12/08/stigma-weaponized-helps-fuel-addiction-crisis/.

Jackson, Peter, dir. *The Lord of the Rings: The Fellowship of the Ring*. Featuring Elijah Wood, Viggo Mortensen, and Sean Astin. 2001;

United States: New Line Home Entertainment. Netflix, https://
www.netflix.com/title/60004480.

Jackson, Peter, dir. *The Lord of the Rings: The Two Towers*. Featuring
Elijah Wood, Viggo Mortensen, and Andy Serkis. 2002; United
States: New Line Home Entertainment. Netflix, https://www
.netflix.com/title/60004483.

Livingston, James D. *Structural Stigma in Health-Care Contexts for
People with Mental Health, A Literature Review*. Ottawa: Mental
Health Commission of Canada, 2020. https://www.mental-
healthcommission.ca/wp-content/uploads/drupal/2020-07/
structural_stigma_in_healthcare_eng.pdf.

Tolkien, J.R.R. *The Hobbit*. London: George Allen & Unwin, 1937.

Tolkien, J.R.R. *The Lord of the Rings*. Toronto: HarperCollins, 2007.

University Hospitals. "'Magic Mushrooms,' Psilocybin and Mental
Health." *The Science of Health* (blog), May 15, 2022. https://
www.uhhospitals.org/blog/articles/2022/05/magic-mushrooms
-psilocybin-and-mental-health.

CHAPTER 6

Aiello, K.J. "What Is a Good Death?" *The Varsity*, November 14,
2016. https://thevarsity.ca/2016/11/14/what-is-a-good-death/.

Aronson, Ronald. "Albert Camus." *The Stanford Encyclopedia of
Philosophy*, October 27, 2011 (last updated December 13, 2021).
https://plato.stanford.edu/entries/camus/.

Canadian Medical Association. "Dr. Alex Jadad: What Do We Mean
by Health?" YouTube, August 16, 2019. https://www.youtube.
com/watch?v=Y3uDNi1LaCw.

The Canadian Press. "CAMH's new campaign tackles discomfort of
talking about suicide." CBC September 10, 2020. https://www.cbc
.ca/news/health/camh-suicide-prevention-campaign-1.5718708.

Health Canada. "Medical Assistance in Dying: Overview." Government
of Canada. https://www.canada.ca/en/health-canada/services
/medical-assistance-dying.html.

Hutchinson, Shaun David. *We Are the Ants*. New York: Simon Pulse,
2017.

Kellner, Florence. "Suicide in Canada." *The Canadian Encyclopedia*,
February 7, 2006 (last updated May 1, 2022). https://www
.thecanadianencyclopedia.ca/en/article/suicide.

Lewis, C.S. *The Lion, the Witch and the Wardrobe*. New York:
HarperCollins, 1994.

"Medical Assistance in Dying (Maid) and Mental Illness—FAQs."
CAMH, February, 2023. https://www.camh.ca/en/camh-news
-and-stories/maid-and-mental-illness-faqs.

Mendlesohn, Farah. *Rhetorics of Fantasy*. Middletown, Connecticut:
Wesleyan University Press, 2013.

Merriam-Webster Dictionary, s.v. "self-slaughtered." https://www.
merriam-webster.com/dictionary/self-slaughtered.

Neeleman, J. "Suicide as a Crime in the UK: Legal History,
International Comparisons and Present Implications." *Acta
Psychiatrica Scandinavica* 94, no. 4 (1996): 252–257. https://doi
.org/10.1111/j.1600-0447.1996.tb09857.x.

Piepzna-Samarasinha, Leah Lakshmi. *Care Work: Dreaming Disability
Justice*. Vancouver: Arsenal Pulp Press, 2020.

Weymouth, Laura E. *The Light Between Worlds*. New York:
HarperTeen, 2018.

Weymouth, Laura E. "The Light Between Worlds Discussion Guide."
Laura E. Weymouth, April 24, 2021. https://lauraeweymouth.com
/the-light-between-worlds-discussion-guide.

CHAPTER 7

Cotterell, Arthur. *Classical Mythology: Illustrated Encyclopedia.*
Leicester, England: Lorenz Books, 2011.

Herman, Judith. *Trauma and Recovery: The Aftermath of Violence—From
Domestic Abuse to Political Terror.* New York: Basic Books, 2015.

"Jean Grey-Summers: Phoenix." Marvel. https://www.marvel.com
/characters/phoenix-jean-grey.

Kinberg, Simon, writer and dir. *Dark Phoenix.* Featuring Sophie
Turner, James McAvoy, Michael Fassbender. 2019; Los Angeles:
20th Century Fox.

Scull, Andrew. *Desperate Remedies: Psychiatry's Turbulent Quest to Cure
Mental Illness.* Cambridge, Massachusetts: Harvard University
Press, 2022.

Shephard, Michelle, host. *Brainwashed* (podcast). Produced by CBC.
Aired September 2, 2020–October 28, 2020. https://www.cbc.ca
/radio/podcastnews/listen-brainwashed-1.5734335.

CHAPTER 8

Cron, Lisa. *Story Genius: How to Use Brain Science to Go Beyond
Outlining and Write a Riveting Novel.* Berkeley: Ten Speed Press,
2016.

Davis, Brian. "'Hellblade: Senua's Sacrifice' Ending Explained: The
Sound and the Furies." *Collider*, August 26, 2021. https://collider
.com/hellblade-senuas-sacrifice-ending-explained/.

Demyttenaere, Koen. "What Is Treatment Resistance in Psychiatry?
A 'Difficult to Treat' Concept." *World Psychiatry* 18, no. 3
(October 2019): 354–355. https://doi.org/10.1002/wps.20677.

Digital Doc Games. "Building Senua's Broken Mind—Hellblade's
Clinical Consultant Dr. Paul Fletcher Interview." YouTube,

November 10, 2020. Video, 35:01. https://www.youtube.com
/watch?v=mRMv1aGYPdA.

Farokhmanesh, Megan. "Hellblade Studio Launches a New Venture to
Explore Mental Health through Games." *The Verge*, October 29,
2019. https://www.theverge.com/2019/10/29/20937907/hellblade
-ninja-theory-insight-project-mental-health-tech-game-design
-neuroscience.

Ferrari, Manuela, Sarah McIlwaine, Gerald Jordan, Jai Shah, Shalini
Lal, and Srividya Iyer. "Gaming with Stigma: Analysis of
Messages about Mental Illness in Video Games." *JMIR Mental
Health* 6, no. 5 (May 2019): e12418. https://doi.org/10.2196
/12418.

Fletcher, Paul. "Psychosis: Bending Reality to See Around the Corners
| Paul Fletcher | TEDxCambridgeUniversity." TEDx Talks,
YouTube, December 2, 2016. Video, 12:01. https://www.youtube
.com/watch?v=tV2RLLtOgL4.

Ford-Roy, Virginia C. "Powerless Patient: Reclaiming Agency through
Patient Narratives." Master of arts thesis. McMaster University,
2021. http://hdl.handle.net/11375/26483.

"Games." Ninja Theory. https://ninjatheory.com/games/.

Kay, Guy Gavriel. "Home and Away." *Bright Weavings* (blog). https://
brightweavings.com/globe/.

Lindsey, Patrick. "Gaming's Favorite Villain Is Mental Illness, and
This Needs to Stop." *Polygon*, July 21, 2014. https://www.poly-
gon.com/2014/7/21/5923095/mental-health-gaming-silent-hill.

theRadBrad. "HELLBLADE SENUA'S SACRIFICE Walkthrough
Gameplay Part 1—Prologue." YouTube, August 8, 2017. Video,
42:57. https://www.youtube.com/watch?v=H5uj7UKAsho.

Ubisoft. *Assassin's Creed: Odyssey*. 2018; San Francisco: Ubisoft. Xbox.

Webster, Andrew. "Hellblade Is a Harrowing, Frustrating Descent into

Madness." *The Verge*, August 9, 2017. https://www.theverge.com
/2017/8/9/16117978/hellblade-senuas-sacrifice-review-ps4-pc.

Weis, Margaret, and Tracy Hickman. *Dragons of Spring Dawning.*
Lake Geneva, Wisconsin: TSR, 1985.

Weis, Margaret, and Tracy Hickman. *Dragons of Winter Night.* New
York: Wizards of the Coast Publishing, 2010.

"What Is the Insight Project?" The Insight Project. https://theinsight
project.com/.

Wipond, Rob. *Your Consent Is Not Required: The Rise in Psychiatric
Detentions, Forced Treatment, and Abusive Guardianships.* Dallas:
BenBella Books Inc., 2023.

ACKNOWLEDGEMENTS

Writing this book has not been a solitary pursuit. There is an entire community of writers, artists, folks with lived experience, editors and coaches, and of course friends who have all supported me in some way during this process. I will try my best to name all of you, but, being gifted with so many people in my life, I will probably forget a few names. Feel free to email me, and I'll buy you an ice cream.

Thank you to my thoughtful and insightful editor, Jen Sookfong Lee. Your excitement and patient guidance through this process has helped me become a better writer and human, in so many ways. You pushed me where I needed a push. Thank you. You're epic. Like, level 20 magic-user epic. You're like a paladin knight with a pen. You define magic with your badassery. Of course, thank you to my publisher, ECW Press. How can I even express gratitude? Am I dreaming? (I'm dreaming, right?)

A massive thank you to the Canada Council for the Arts and the Ontario Arts Council. This book would not exist without your support.

Acknowledgements

A heartfelt and incredibly grateful thank you to everyone who gave me some of their time, entrusted me with their stories or lent me some of their wisdom, who spoke to me about their toughest times, gave me insight, or simply inspired me, whether those conversations made it into the book or not: Christina Myers, Nathan Fréchette, Kitty Rodé, Andrew Pyper, Rachel, Lauren B. Davis, Bryen Fulcher, Dr. Madeline C. Burghardt, Virginia Ford-Roy, Nari By Nature, the Thursday night D&D crew (Jade, Oscar, Manuel, Pascual, and Christian), Dr. Dirk Bernhardt-Walther, Cait Gordon, Rob McCready, and Alheli Picazo. Thank you, every one of you.

Thank you to the ever-expanding Firefly community. I have met so many of you, shared space with so many of you, heard your stories as you have heard mine. Thank you soft writing coaches, Chris, Britt, and Sophia—you never once wavered in your belief in me. Plus, you are always so delighted to see me, and that makes me feel like the bee's knees.

Thank you to my friend, Christine Fischer Guy. Without you, I wouldn't even be writing. You believed in me so long ago. Thank you to my beautiful sister-in-law, Chiharu Tauri. You're always so excited every time I have something published. I love our Phobos nights. I *will* make Nico a writer (a gamer at the very least). Thank you to my mother-in-law, Maria Aiello, whose soup is like a warm hug.

Oscar Ceceña, you're a writer, and I will keep telling you this until you get so frustrated with me that you give in and call yourself a writer. Thank you, Manuel, for saying "hey, I saw this article and thought of you," helping bring Chapter 8 to life. Bet you didn't see that one coming, eh?

Thank you to my therapist, Jeri Reason. The amount of vitriol and tears you've witnessed from me is astounding. I wouldn't be okay without you doing such an epic job of helping me navigate that.

To my boyfriend of so long ago, the golden light who arrived at a time in my life when I needed someone so, so bad. Chris Kant, you are stellar, and I'm so glad we've remained friends all these years. To Jessica Carpentier, thank you for arriving that night I fell apart. I can't imagine what that was like for you, but know that I won't ever forget it. Shaheen Shaikh, thank you for always believing in me and giving me prayers when I needed them. You deserve the world.

My Writerly Shenanigans, Ailsa Bristow and Alli Temple. What can I even say? How much you two have supported me, not just with this massive undertaking, but with so many other challenges, wins, losses, all sorts of life shit—you two have been there. I never thought I'd find best friends like you. Turns out, I was wrong. (One day we will buy our Crones' Cottage and then we'll flounce around and write our epic stories and talk about our middle-aged femme rock band, Misogyny & Migraines.)

A very particular thanks to you, Ailsa. I could not have written this book without you. You're a star. Please tell yourself that every single morning. Your kindness, generosity, and gentleness are so rare and beautiful. Marianne is incredibly lucky to have you. And thank you, Andrew, for being a wicked grant editor!

Thank you, Emily Anglin, for helping me secure the funding to write this damn book. You are a rockstar and I owe you *big*.

To my husband, Uli, our life together has been so up and down, so beautiful and tough. We have so many memories and have grown so much together. I never knew there could be someone as compassionate and patient as you. I think about all the travels we will have together. All the pasta and pizza in Rome. Due cornetti e caffè con latte. Please, please, please teach me more Italian swear words. I love your green eyes and colourful wardrobe, even though I roll my eyes every time you buy another neon pink T-shirt. I love how you love our cats, that you never let me kill bugs when they crawl into the house (even though the hairy ones deserve it), and your compassion for all the critters of the world, mice, squirrels, and trash pandas included. I love that you made sure I had everything I needed to be safe and happy. And I absolutely love that you thought writing was a good idea, even though on a practical level it probably wasn't. But here we are.

Last, to everyone who lives with mental illness. These halls can be so cold and echoing, can't they? It can be lonely and, some days, unbearable. And sometimes we just need a safe, magical place to slip into for a little while. A world where silver dragons exist and *we* are the heroes.

Well, my darling fighters, this magic is for you.

We made it, kiddo.

K.J. AIELLO is a mentally ill award-winning essayist and writer based in Toronto. Their work has appeared in publications such as the *Globe and Mail*, *Toronto Life*, *Chatelaine*, the *Walrus*, and *This Magazine*, among others.

K.J. is still waiting for their very own personal dragon. Sadly, this has not yet happened, so their cats will have to suffice.

Entertainment. Writing. Culture. ————————

ECW is a proudly independent, Canadian-owned book publisher. We know great writing can improve people's lives, and we're passionate about sharing original, exciting, and insightful writing across genres.

———————————————— **Thanks for reading along!**

We want our books not just to sustain our imaginations, but to help construct a healthier, more just world, and so we've become a certified B Corporation, meaning we meet a high standard of social and environmental responsibility — and we're going to keep aiming higher. We believe books can drive change, but the way we make them can too.

Certified

Corporation

Being a B Corp means that the act of publishing this book should be a force for good – for the planet, for our communities, and for the people that worked to make this book. For example, everyone who worked on this book was paid at least a living wage. You can learn more at the Ontario Living Wage Network.

This book is also available as a Global Certified Accessible™ (GCA) ebook. ECW Press's ebooks are screen reader friendly and are built to meet the needs of those who are unable to read standard print due to blindness, low vision, dyslexia, or a physical disability.

This book is printed on Sustana EnviroBook™, a recycled paper, and other controlled sources that are certified by the Forest Stewardship Council®.

FSC
www.fsc.org
MIX
Paper from
responsible sources
FSC® C103567

ECW's office is situated on land that was the traditional territory of many nations including the Wendat, the Anishnaabeg, Haudenosaunee, Chippewa, Métis, and current treaty holders the Mississaugas of the Credit. In the 1880s, the land was developed as part of a growing community around St. Matthew's Anglican and other churches. Starting in the 1950s, our neighbourhood was transformed by immigrants fleeing the Vietnam War and Chinese Canadians dispossessed by the building of Nathan Phillips Square and the subsequent rise in real estate value in other Chinatowns. We are grateful to those who cared for the land before us and are proud to be working amidst this mix of cultures.

ecwpress.com